COUNTER PLAY

WALKER UNIVERSITY STALLIONS

AVA SUTTON

Visit my website at avasuttonbooks.com
Cover Designer: Enchanting Romance Designs, www.enchantingro-
mancedesigns.com
Developmental Editor: Jeannine Colette, www.jeanninecolette.com
Editor: Jovana Shirley, Unforeseen Editing, www.unforeseenediting.com
Proofreader: Tina Otero

This book is a work of fiction. Names, characters, places, and incidents either are
products of the author's imagination or are used fictitiously. Any resemblance to
actual persons, living or dead, events, or locales is entirely coincidental.

ISBN-13: 979-8-9929966-0-9

For my parents, because they let me stay up way too late reading.
P.S. That habit hasn't changed.

PLAYLIST
Beautiful Things, Benson Boone
Lover, Taylor Swift
You Belong With Me, Taylor Swift
With or Without You, U2
The Scientist, Coldplay
Yours, Russell Dickerson
To A T, Ryan Hurd
I Feel Like I'm Drowning, Two Feet
Earned It, The Weeknd
Make Me Feel, Elvis Drew
Teenage Dream, Katy Perry
Slow Down, Chase Atlantic
Sail, Awolnation
Crazy in Love, Beyonce (Fifty Shades version)
Don't You, Simple Minds

PROLOGUE

CHARLIE

"CHARLIE, WAIT!" my twin brother, Casey, yells.

"No chance, sucker! Too bad I'm faster than you. Better catch up, Case!" I shoot back at him.

My twin brother and I are running around the field just outside the playground in front of our school. It's near the end of the school year, so the weather is getting hotter every day. Sweat is running down my back and dripping along the sides of my face. I'm used to it though. I'm pretty much a tomboy. That's why I prefer to go by my nickname, Charlie, instead of my full name, Charlene. My brother is my best friend, along with Beckham, the boy who lives across the street.

Beckham, his dad, and his younger sister moved in a few years ago. He was quiet at first, but Casey and I pulled him into our gang of two, so now it's the three of us, thick as thieves.

To say we like to get into trouble is an understatement. Like playing baseball inside Beck's house and breaking the glass in the front window. And making a homemade Slip 'N Slide to play a football game in the mud in our backyard, which destroyed my mom's flower garden. But Slip 'N Slide Bowl was worth getting grounded for three weeks.

We're together all the time. In the same class all day and running around the neighborhood all afternoon and into the night.

Casey and Beck have started playing tackle football together. I was so mad that I couldn't join the team, too, but my parents thought it was too rough for a girl. Even though they know I'm just as strong as Casey, if not stronger.

I can't play on the football team with them, but they never leave me out. Like today, on the playground. We've been racing our classmates, basically for the right to say who is the fastest in the fourth-grade class. I'm not gonna lie—I win a lot. The only person who can catch me is Beck, who is currently right on my heels.

"I'm coming for you, Charlie," he says with a laugh in his voice.

"No way, Beck. I'm almost to the tree. You won't catch me!"

Our marker for our races is a huge oak tree that sits near the edge of the field, and I'm almost there. Just another six steps, and I've got him.

Just as I'm reaching out to touch the bark, I see Beck's hand out of the corner of my eye. I really want to beat him this time, so I reach out as far as I can, but it makes no difference. He touches it first.

"Dang it, Beck! I almost had you. Can't you let me win just once?"

"Aww, don't be a sore loser, Charlie. I can't help it that I'm faster. When I make it into the NFL someday, I'll get you tickets to my games." He smirks.

Huffing, I start to walk away, but he grabs my hand and pulls me behind the tree. He's got a look on his face I can't read. His grayish-blue eyes are looking from me to the kids who have given up on the race now that they've lost, but his brows are scrunched, and he's moving his mouth from a smile to serious and back.

"What are you doing?" I say as I try to pull my hand free from his.

"Shh … I just want to tell you something. Don't say anything to Casey because I know he probably wouldn't like what I'm about to do."

"What are you about to do?" I ask.

"This." Then he pulls me toward him and places a kiss on my lips.

My eyes are wide, my heart is pounding, and I think I forget to breathe for a second as the sweet sting from Beck's kiss zings on my lips.

I've never been kissed before. If there was a boy who was going to steal my first kiss, I'd want it to be him.

He pulls away, and my eyes are still closed as my heart, which was already thumping wildly from our race, is now about to beat out of my chest.

I open my eyes. My lips part as I try to calm my racing nerves from the surprise that Beckham Linson just kissed me.

Beck swallows and then starts speaking rather quickly. "I've been wanting to kiss you lately, so I thought we could try it. You're one of my best friends, but I like you more than that. I want you to be mine."

Standing here, looking at him, I start to feel embarrassed by the heat that creeps up my cheeks, and it's not from running. "What do you mean? Like, you want me to be your girlfriend or something?"

"I don't know what to call it, but I just know I don't want other boys looking at you. And you feel like mine, so that's what you are," he claims.

I shrug my shoulders, trying to feign indifference even though the butterflies in my stomach are going crazy by the way he's still holding my hand with one of his and playing with one of my braids with the other. The look on his face is fierce, and I can tell he's settled into this decision.

One thing about Beck is that he might only be ten, but I think he's seen a lot more than other kids our age. He had to mature quicker than most—at least that's what my parents told us. They didn't tell us the details, but I heard them talking one day about how hard Beck and his sister had it before they moved here, although I didn't really understand what that meant.

Didn't matter. I've always liked Beck, even if he is a little more closed off than the rest of us. I like him a lot.

"All right then. I guess I'm yours," I declare.

He lets go of my hand and then takes off, running back toward the starting line. "You might be mine, but I'm still not gonna let you beat me!"

I lose the next race, but it doesn't bother me at all because I'm still floating in my thoughts from that kiss.

Later that night, I walk into my room after my shower to see a pink peony from my mom's garden sitting on top of my bed with a little piece of paper folded in half. I pick it up and open it to see a short note.

Charlie,
    Someday, I'm gonna make you mine for real reals.
Then you'll officially be mine to kiss whenever I want.
    Yours always,
    Beck

After that day, things were different between us. We gravitated toward each other even more whenever we were together. I fell in love with Beckham Linson. It stayed that way until the beginning of our senior year of high school, when everything changed.

CHAPTER
ONE

CHARLIE

PRESENT DAY —TEN YEARS LATER

"CHARLIE!" my mother calls from the bottom of the stairs. "Are you about ready to go?"

I zip up my duffel bag and look around my childhood bedroom and sigh.

From the time I was a little girl, my parents always talked about Casey and me attending Walker University. He and I had big ideas about what we wanted to be when we grew up, and we thought we could fulfill those aspirations at Walker. Granted, it *was* where our parents had met and gone to school.

When we were little, I wanted to be a waitress while Casey wanted to be a professional football player. He's had a football in his hands since the day he was born. However, my plan of becoming a waitress quickly died. I tried it in high school, and let's just say, it did *not* live up to my expectations. Casey's dream, well, he's still living it—or he's on his way by playing football at the college level.

Casey went on to become a Walker University legacy. I, however, strayed from the family plan and went to another school.

I followed my friend Britney Stevens to Chandler State University. We had been close since middle school. Once I had gotten boobs and started to get noticed by boys other than Beck, she'd wanted to hang out. So, when we reached our senior year, she literally begged me to go to State with her, saying how great our college years would be together. It took a lot of coaxing, but I eventually caved, especially since my entire life had imploded that year.

Unfortunately, my freshman year of college at Chandler State University didn't turn out exactly the way I had planned.

Britney and I decided to room together, and to say things were tense from the beginning would be an understatement. For someone who was so adamant that I not go to Walker, it was as if once I was at State, she didn't have a use for me anymore. She quickly found a group of friends and often left me behind. I tried to settle in and even joined a sorority and dated a frat guy, Tony Pastorelli, for a while. I made some friends and did okay on my own for the first time in my life. Still, it never felt right.

Britney and I had a falling-out at the end of our freshman year, details of which I try not to think about, and it firmly solidified my decision to transfer. Her manipulation and her mind games were just too much for me to handle—which, looking back, I hadn't recognized in high school, but it'd become blatantly obvious in college. And I resented her for making me choose between her and my brother and my intention to go to Walker.

My family couldn't understand why I'd chosen to go to college with Brit instead of my brother. And even though he didn't say it, I knew Casey was disheartened that I wasn't going to be with him. It was the first time we would be separated for really any period of time. Sure, we'd each gone to sleepovers, and he'd gone off to football camp, but we'd never actually lived apart. I missed him terribly. I did visit him a few times, but it was too hard for me to be around Beck. When it got really bad with Britney and I broke up with Tony, I spent a lot of weekends at home.

So, this year, I'm transferring to Walker, and I can't wait to start this new chapter and be there to support my brother. Casey is a wide receiver and has worked really hard to make the starting lineup this season.

With one last look around my room and one final count of three switches of the light on my desk, I grab my bag and head down the stairs.

"Casey is waiting outside for you," Mom says as I round the landing.

"I still think it's unfair that we have to share the truck," I huff.

"Honey, he's right around the corner from you. I'm sure if you need the truck, you can grab it." She wraps her arm around mine when I reach her at the bottom of the stairs.

Casey lives in a house off campus with some of the other players on the team. She's right; it's not that far from the house I'll be living in. And luckily, the Walker campus is easy to walk around even though it's big. But still, that means I have to go over to his house and potentially run into Beck. Which is really the bigger problem.

My dad is waiting near the door. As we walk up to him, he reaches out to grab my duffel from my hand, and Mom lets go of my arm.

"Thanks, Dad. I'm going to miss you guys, but we'll see you in a few weeks for the opening game."

"Yes, your mom and I will be there early that day, so if you want to ride with us to the game, let us know, and we'll pick you up," he says while putting his other arm around me as we walk out the door.

"You sure you have everything you need?" Mom asks.

"Yeah, I think so. If I forgot anything, I'll have you bring it when you come to campus."

"Okay, that works," she says. "I know you're going to roll your eyes at me when I say this, but I feel much better about you going to Walker with Casey and Beck than I did when you left for State with Britney last year. You know she was never my favorite."

At the mention of Beck, my heart sinks. "I know, and I agree. I feel much better about this year overall. I have a better handle for what I want to specialize in too. I feel like psychology is a good route for me. And I'll admit, it was hard, being away from Casey last year. Twins have to stay together—ya feel me?" I say with a laugh.

Rolling her eyes, she says, "Yes, I feel you. Just please keep an eye on each other and make good choices."

I love to tease my mom, so I can't help but say, "Mother, I promise we will make very good *bad* choices; don't worry."

She shakes her head as we walk up to the truck. "Casey, please keep your sister in line. But seriously, I love you both. Have an amazing year, and we'll see you in just a few weeks. Call us when you get there. Oh, and, Charlie, don't forget to call Aunt Linds when you get closer to campus so she can meet you at the sorority house with your room key."

"Okay. Yeah, I have a reminder set on my phone to call her. I'm just glad they could fit me into the house so I don't have to live in the dorms this year."

My mom was in a sorority in college, which I really didn't think would be my thing, but she made some really great life-long friends, so that's why I rushed last year at Chandler State. And because I was a legacy, it was really just a formality. I'm really glad I did it, given how things ended up with Brit. Now it will also make my transition to Walker easier because I already know a few of the girls in the house. One is Lindsay's daughter, Arbor, and the other is her roommate, Lily. Plus, the house is a freaking mansion.

Lindsay Gibbs—who I refer to as Aunt Linds—and my mom met their freshman year at Walker. They rushed together and have been friends ever since. She's the alumni chair for the sorority, so she basically keeps all the girls in line and helps manage the operations of the house.

"Aunt Linds is practically family. You know she always has your back," Mom says as she gives my hand a squeeze. "Aren't you a little sad you missed the rush festivities? I always had so much fun, making the skits and dances."

I turn to look at her with a *you've got to be kidding me* expression on my face, but when I see her smile is genuine, I just smile and nod. "Maybe next year."

Casey has nothing to load into the truck since he's been at school for over a month now for training. He just decided to come up to get me instead of Mom and Dad taking me.

Dad hands Casey my duffel bag and he loads the last of my things into the back of the truck bed when he says, "Charlie, you need to ride in the back."

"No, sir. Why?" I ask.

"Because I'm sitting in the front," Beckham's deep voice booms as he crosses the street and reaches the truck.

Fuck.

When I turn, I make eye contact with Beckham, and he gives me a snarky look. I just huff and shake my head.

I hear Mom and Dad talking, but I can't really focus on what they're saying. I mean, it's kind of hard to when I have the intense eyes of my ex-boyfriend staring me down.

Literally.

Beckham Linson—the one I once loved fiercely before our relationship shattered into a million pieces. It's been two years since we were a couple, and the pain of the fallout still stings despite the fact that he's remained Casey's best friend and my parents' second son.

I've done everything I could to stay away from him. My heart is still attached to the memories, and my body betrays me when

I look at him. Beck—with his stupid-hot blue eyes that are nearly gray and his brown hair that's almost black—sort of has the whole Clark Kent–looking thing going, minus the glasses. The look he has right before he rips open his shirt and looks all hot and shit. And his height—the only way I can match his six-foot frame is if I'm on stairs or something. He's no longer a teenage boy. He's a man.

A man I will see a lot more of now that we'll both be at Walker. Beckham is the starting running back for the football team. He was recruited heavily by Walker to play football, so he was able to earn a starting spot on the team, even as a freshman.

Between him being Casey's best friend and a star athlete on campus, there's no way I'm going to be able to avoid him.

I hear Mom say one last goodbye, and I head toward the front seat of the truck anyway. Completely ignoring my brother's order. Right as I'm reaching for the handle, Beckham comes up behind me, crowding me against the door.

That imposing frame of his blocks me in, and I can feel the heat of his skin burning through his T-shirt and smell the fresh scent of the cologne he's worn since our freshman year of high school. It was originally a gift from me. I'm actually a little surprised he still wears it, but I can't say it doesn't give me a little bit of satisfaction.

"There's no way I'm sitting in the back. You get back there," he drawls.

Luckily, I've become immune to his good looks and broody charm, which have everyone in this town—other than me—falling at his feet.

"Are you kidding me right now, Beckham? You know I get carsick." *I mean, it's a double-cab truck, and it's a beast, so I probably won't get carsick, but I'm going for it anyway.*

"That's not really my problem, Charlene."

Casey looks over at us and grunts, "Are you two at it already? Can't you call a truce for the two-hour ride? Charlie, you know Beckham can't fit in the back seat. His legs are too long. Just try to deal with it. Put your headphones on and tune out the noise or read your book. Anything to make it a chill ride. I can't deal with you two fighting the whole way."

Beckham still has me crowded up against the door, so I finally turn around to face him. He has a smirk on his face, knowing he's won this round. He's still not backing up, so I have to put my hands on his chest and push him away, which makes him laugh even more.

I reach out to pull the handle of the rear cab when Beck beats me to it. "I've got it. I don't need your help, Beckham."

"Oh, but it's my pleasure, Charlene."

I throw my bag in, step up onto the sideboard, and pull myself up into the massive truck, using the oh-shit handle. I've had to use it many times, so we're well acquainted. Casey and Beckham like to go off-roading in this truck, even though it makes my mom crazy. It's massive and pretty freaking awesome. But it's a pain in the ass to get in and out of. Especially for me. I think my brother took all the tall genes when we were in the womb.

Beckham is still smirking at me as I grab the door handle and pull the door shut.

This is going to be a bitch of a ride.

CHAPTER
TWO

BECKHAM

"I'VE GOT IT. *I don't need your help, Beckham.*"

"*Oh, but it's my pleasure, Charlene.*"

She absolutely hates it when I call her by her full first name, which is exactly why I do it. Especially when she calls me Beckham. It irritates me when she does it. I want her to call me Beck, like she used to. She doesn't like her full name, and I don't like thinking she doesn't care about me anymore. Maybe it's immature of me, but her calling me Beckham … makes me feel like she might truly be over me.

Charlie pushes her hair back, feigning indifference to me with an eye roll and a shoulder shrug. She's got her sarcastic defenses up, and I can't say I blame her. She trusted me once, and I broke it by not speaking up when I should have.

I know I'm the last person she wanted to see, but I really needed to come home to check in on my dad and sister, Brooke, after the latest news we got about my mom. Plus, it'd been almost a month since I'd seen them.

It's just been the three of us for years. We've been through some things together that, without each other, we wouldn't have survived.

I turn back to Mr. and Mrs. King and give her a hug first. Carol always pulls me in and does one solid squeeze before letting me go. I reach out and shake Tim's hand. I've always had a great relationship with Casey and Charlie's parents.

When we moved to Troy, Oklahoma, from Pennsylvania, I was pretty traumatized, although Casey and Charlie don't know the half of it. The Kings took me in and made me feel like part of the family. I'll never forget that.

Carol walks around to the other side to say one last goodbye to Casey.

Tim leans in and quietly says, "You boys will keep my son safe on the field, right?"

"You know we will. I'll keep your girl out of trouble too," I say seriously but with a smirk.

"Yeah, you do that." Tim laughs and pats my shoulder before turning to walk to Casey.

I pull the passenger door open and climb into the front seat. I casually look into the back to see Charlie glaring at me. Or at least trying to. It's kind of cute really.

"Why are you the way you are?" she asks me.

"And how would that be?"

I do love to rile her up. Because if I wind her up, that makes me feel like she still cares about me. And I really want her to care.

"Oh, you know, you act like this perfect gentleman to everyone."

"I am a gentleman."

"Ha. Yeah, right. Sometimes, I think my parents love you more than us," she huffs.

"Nah. You know that's not true. Although I am pretty great." I add a wink just to see what she says next.

"Turn around, Beckham. I'm trying to find my Zen."

Before I can respond, Casey opens his door and climbs into the driver's seat.

"You have everything you need, sis?" he asks Charlie.

"Yep, I'm ready. Let's get going. The faster I can get out of this truck, the better," she mumbles.

As he turns on the car, Taylor Swift starts blaring through the speakers.

"Dude, really?" I say.

"Bro, don't knock Tay. She's the queen." He laughs. "Actually, Noelle and I were listening to it yesterday after we dropped off some new fishing line at her dad's marina."

Noelle is Casey's other best friend. She grew up with us, but she wasn't really into the athlete scene, so we didn't hang out a bunch in high school. She and Casey have some sort of bond that Charlie and I were never really a part of, but we liked having her around.

Noelle went to Walker with us last year too. She's awesome, but she dated this super douche, which was kind of a surprise to Casey because she had never shown any interest in athletes before. She liked the more studious types. Trey Grant, the douche, played baseball at Walker, and we knew him a little before they started dating. Never really had a problem with him until he did Noelle dirty. I still don't know everything that happened. Casey won't betray her trust like that.

"I mean, did you forget that you went to a Taylor Swift concert with us when we were thirteen?" he adds.

Laughing, I say, "All right, all right, I validate that Tay Tay is, in fact, the queen. I'm not really knocking you anyway. Turn it up, brother."

When "You Belong with Me" starts playing, I can't help but look in the side mirror at Charlie, who just so happens to meet my eyes. I see a flash of hurt before she looks down.

"Come on, guys. Don't leave me hangin'. Sing with me. Char, sing!" Casey says.

"Charlie is not available right now. Please leave a message, and she might return your call," she snarks back at Casey.

"Charlene May King, if you don't sing with me, I'll call Mom and tell her you're planning to get trashed tonight at the Lambda Xi house," he threatens.

Wait, what?

"Gasp! Casey, you are a dirty, filthy liar! Blackmail doesn't look good on you, *brother*. Besides, I wouldn't touch those guys with a ten-foot pole. They're nasty," she claims.

"Charlie, no one actually says *gasp*," he says, laughing.

Releasing the breath I didn't realize I had been holding, I laugh along with him and then say, "I got you, bro. Let's turn this up."

If I can keep myself distracted on this ride to campus, I might make it there without cracking a tooth. I can feel Charlie glaring at the back of my head, so I do the next worst thing and move my seat back a little, taking up more space, watching her reaction in the side mirror.

Even though it was my idea to come get her to bring her to campus, the sooner I can get out of this car, the better. Smelling her peony perfume is driving me crazy. And that stretch of freckles on her nose—the ones she thinks no one notices, but I do —yeah, I can't help but stare.

I've always been drawn to her.

I was eight years old when I first laid eyes on Charlene King. I was helping my dad bring boxes off the moving truck. We moved into a new house, and Charlie moved into my heart. Yeah, sounds cheesy, but that's just the truth. She was a little bossy at first, which made me laugh. She was this little thing in baggy overalls with long brown hair braided into two pigtails, golden-brown eyes, and a smile that looked like trouble, especially because she was missing her two front teeth. She gave me a four-leaf clover, and I wanted to be her friend immediately. Then Casey came chasing after her, and from that point on, it was the three of us.

I miss that.

I miss her.

Turning my eyes from the side mirror, I pull my phone out and play Block Puzzle and sing with Casey. I can't say I have a good voice, but neither does Casey. Aside from Casey and me singing along to literally *all* of Taylor's albums, the rest of the ride is pretty quiet.

I'm lost in thought, plotting how I'm going to get my girl back.

Phase one is in motion. She's coming to Walker.

I'm going to make her mine again. She just doesn't know it yet.

CHAPTER
THREE

CHARLIE

"PLEASE TELL me you're joking, Aunt Lindsay. *Please.* This can't be happening. What am I supposed to do?" I cry.

We arrived at the sorority house—and, yes, I'd forgotten to call Aunt Linds on the way. I was too distracted, trying to ignore Beck. Otherwise, I would have known that my room wasn't ready. Or rather that they had overfilled the house and were rapidly trying to come up with a solution for me.

"Charlie, honey, I know. I'm so sorry, and I promise you, I'm working on it. We'll get this shit straightened up," she says while pacing the gigantic foyer. "Maybe you can squeeze into Arbor and Lily's room. We might have to bring in a cot, but I think I can make it work."

I can hear it in her voice that she's already thinking about where she's going to get a cot from. She probably has an extra at her house. She and her husband, Andy, also own a few properties around town that they rent out throughout the school year. I'm sure she's taking inventory of where there might be an extra.

"I'm not going to do that to Arbor and Lily. I wouldn't feel right about it. Plus, I haven't spent a lot of time with Lily yet. I know she and Arbor are tight, and I don't want to feel like I'm intruding."

"Sweetie, no, it's fine. In fact, Casey, why don't you and Beck start taking Charlie's stuff out of the truck and put it in Arbor's room?"

"Oh, no, absolutely not. I'll figure something out. Let me just call Mom and Dad. How long do you think it will take to get the room ready? A week? A month?" I ask.

I feel a little out of my element at the moment. I need to figure out what to do. It's too late for me to get a dorm room, not that I'd want to. Dorm life was not for me.

Looking over at Casey, I can see he's thinking this isn't promising.

"Why don't you just stay with me until this gets fixed? Aunt Linds, we'll take the cot, and I'll just put it in my room at the house," Casey asks. "Char, I think you would be more comfortable staying with me until this gets figured out, yeah?"

I'm listening to what Casey is saying, but my eyes immediately find Beck's. His eyebrows rise, and he clears his throat, kind of like he's choking a little. But in a non-life-threatening way.

"Uh, Case, even though we don't live in university housing, you might want to check with Coach Pettys before you make plans like this," Beck says.

"I mean, yeah, I'm not sure I would want to live with your teammates, even temporarily. You guys stink, and you would have to ask Archie and Pitz if they were okay with it too. You can't just move your sister in. They might think I'll ruin their game or something," I say with a slight panic in my voice, which my brother notices immediately.

Casey and Beckham live with two other football players—Archie Griffith and Liam Pitz. I love both of these guys, but I'm not sure I could live with them for any length of time.

Archie is a total man-whore. I really don't want to share a

bathroom with him, especially with the parade of girls in and out of his room. And Liam is just as bad as Archie.

"Seriously, I think it will be okay. I'm going to step outside and call Coach now and tell him what's going on. You call Mom and Dad," Casey says.

"Already calling your mom, kids. We'll get this worked out. Charlie, you can even stay with us at our house. We would love to have you," Aunt Lindsay says, walking out of the foyer.

Casey looks over at me and reads my face immediately. He knows I don't want to stay there. Not because I would be uncomfortable, but because I just want to get settled into campus life. Plus, Casey's house is only two blocks from the sorority house, so I can still attend the meetings easily and hang out here in between classes. And I wouldn't have to rely on Aunt Linds to bring me to campus every day and pick me up. Urgh, just the thought makes me cringe. I hope she doesn't see it on my face, but she seems too preoccupied with talking to Mom.

"It's all good, Aunt Linds. I have Coach on the phone now. I'll be right back," he says with one last look my way.

Walking toward where Aunt Linds is standing, I say, "I'm just going to use the bathroom real quick while Casey's on the phone. Can you tell my mom I'll call her once we have a plan?"

"Sure, yeah. She's saying you would probably prefer to stay with Casey." Then she tells my mom, "Yeah, Carol, he's on with the coach now, and I think that's what they plan to do if Coach is okay with it."

I nod and walk out of the room toward the common space bathroom. I really do have to go, but I also need a minute to get my shit together before I have a meltdown. Today is not going how I imagined it. First, I got stuck in a car with Beckham for two hours, and now I have no place to live.

I take care of business in the bathroom, wash my hands, and push the door open. Beckham is standing in the hallway across from the bathroom. He's leaning on the wall with his hands in his pockets and his head down. I can tell he's thinking about what he wants to say, but I beat him to it.

"Look, I'm sure you aren't happy about this, and I'm sure as shit not either, but I won't get in your way if you don't get in mine."

"Charlene, Charlene, Charlene. You just don't get it."

"What? What don't I get?" I ask him.

He lifts his head, looks me directly in the eyes, and says, "Casey just got off the phone with Coach. You can stay with us. But here's the thing ... Casey doesn't have the biggest room. I do. Which means you'll have to put the cot in my room."

"I'll sleep on the floor," I deadpan.

"You know Casey will never let you do that. He'll take the floor first."

"There's no way I'll allow him to do that. I'll sleep on the couch then."

"Trust me, you do not want to sleep on that thing."

"Bathroom? Never mind. It sounded gross as soon as it came out of my mouth." I run my hand through my hair. "You mean to tell me, out of a four-bedroom house, there's nowhere for me to sleep other than your room?"

"That's exactly what I'm saying."

It makes sense. Casey's room is the size of a shoebox, and with his dresser and desk, there is no room for a cot. I'm not sure why I didn't think about this sooner or why Casey didn't mention it either. Dammit, this is a mess.

"I'll see if Casey will sleep on the cot in your room and let me have his room while I'm there. Surely, it will only be a week or two," I say hopefully.

I feel like I might cry, and I definitely don't want him to see me tearing up.

He just nods, turns, and walks back to the foyer.

I take a deep breath and place a hand on my stomach, trying to calm my nerves.

It's going to be okay. I will be moved into my room here as soon as possible. I will survive living with Beckham. I will not strangle him or poison his food. I'm trying to manifest this all becoming my reality.

I mean, I won't really harm Beck. *I think.*

But seriously, being around him on a daily basis again isn't going to be easy because I'm not sure I'll ever be completely over him. I'm trying to stay positive, but I can't help but feel like something is going to change, and it might make things worse than they already are. I learned my lesson with Brit. I never felt right about going to Chandler State with her, and I won't ignore my gut this time. So, I guess I need to pull up my boss pantaloons and take care of shit.

When I walk back into the foyer, Aunt Lindsay is standing there with Casey, Beckham, and now Arbor. Per usual, Arbor is salivating over Beck, which irritates me to no end. I know she always thought he was hot. It never bothered me in high school because he was mine. Now, he's … not mine. She's giving off flirty vibes to Casey, too, but she knows he looks at her like a cousin, so she doesn't push that too hard and keeps her attention on Beck.

I walk over to Arbor and give her a hug—sort of to distract her from Beck, but also because I do love her. "Hey, Arbs."

"I know this isn't a great start to the school year, but I'm so happy you're here at Walker." She squeezes me tighter in response.

We have always been pretty close because our families spent a lot of time together. I'm hoping we'll get to hang out a lot once I move in. I could really use some girlfriends.

Arbor and I let go of each other, and I turn to face my brother.

"Hey, Charlie," Casey says. "Coach is totally fine with you staying with us. We'll figure out the sleeping arrangements when we get there. It's all good. Plus, I promised Mom and Dad I'd keep an eye on you. You know, fulfilling my big-brother duties," he says with a laugh.

He's actually three minutes younger than me, but because he's so much taller, he likes to take the big-brother title.

I roll my eyes at Casey, which just makes him laugh harder.

"I texted Arch and Pitz, and they're cool with it," Becks chimes in.

I turn to Aunt Linds and say, "Okay, can you just keep me posted and get me in here as soon as possible? I love my brother, but I'd rather be here so I can actually focus."

"Hey … I take offense to that. Aunt Linds, we're extremely studious at our house. No shenanigans at Casa King," Casey claims.

She just laughs and pulls him in for a hug while Arbor still stands there with doe eyes, looking at Beck.

Time to break that up …

I turn my gaze to Aunt Linds. "Okay, so if you can just bring the cot over to Casey's sometime today, that would be amazing. We'll get out of your hair now so you can get to work on whatever it was you were doing before we got here."

I step in to give Arbor a hug goodbye. She hugs me back.

"See you later, Arbs."

"Totally. And you can sleep over in my room with Lily and me anytime. It'll be so fun to have you here this year, Charlie," she says sincerely. "It'll be just like our family get-togethers when we were kids. Except we won't have to beg to stay at each other's house anymore!" she says with a lift to her toes and a little clap.

"Thanks. I guess I'll see you tomorrow for chapter," I laugh.

Turning, I walk to the door, following Casey and Beck, and turn to say goodbye to Aunt Lindsay, but she is already on another call, so I'm not sure she even hears me.

I shoot my mom a text while walking to the truck.

> Charlie: MOM. MOM. MOM. I cannot believe this is happening to me. Like, OMG! 😶

Mom: *sad face emoji* I'm so sorry. It'll all work out. Just be glad you have somewhere to go instead of turning around and coming home. Not that I wouldn't be happy with you coming home! You know I love you. Aunt Lindsay will take care of it. Just give her a few days. You know she gets shit done.

Charlie: You don't have to write complete sentences in texts. I've told you this 1000x. You could just vm me if ur reply is that long.

Mom: Well, since you're picking on me, I guess you're okay?

Charlie: Urgh, I'll call you later.

Mom: Love you. 😊

Charlie: Love you.

When I pull open the rear cab door, Casey turns to look at me while Beck types on his phone. I don't care who he's texting with. Really, I don't. But, gawd, this means not only do I have to deal with Archie's whoriness, but Beck's too.

He probably has a whole harem of coeds at the house every night.

I think I might be sick.

With a smirk and a bit of sympathy in his eyes, Casey says, "It's going to be okay, Char. And it'll be fun. Like a big sleepover."

"A sleepover? What are we, ten? Case, you do realize she's going to have to stay in my room since I have the most space, right? What the fuck are we going to do about that?" Beck sounds irritated, which makes me defensive.

"Well, fuck you too, Beckham. Do you think I want this? This is my worst nightmare." I grab the handle and pull myself into the truck.

"Okay, okay. I'll just sleep on the cot in Beck's room until you can move into the sorority house. No big deal. I can't have two of my favorite people killing each other. I'd miss you both too much," Casey says with a laugh.

"Case, you can't sleep on a cot. You'll be destroyed, and that will just piss Coach off. You worked so hard last year and in training to earn a starting position. You can't fuck it up. It'll be fine. I'll be nice, I promise," Beck says.

"Charlie, do you promise to play nice with Beck?" Casey asks.

I pinch the bridge of my nose, thinking. "What if I put the cot in the living room? There's plenty of space there."

Casey sways his head. "It's a possibility."

Beckham shifts in his seat and lifts a hand, about to talk, yet he stutters a touch before speaking. "That's a terrible idea."

"Why? Because I came up with it?"

"To start," he says and then looks up, as if trying to find the answer. When one comes to him, he points his finger. "There's always someone in there with the TV blaring. You'll never sleep. Sometimes, the room is packed with random guys who come over to watch a game." He moves his attention to Casey. "Not to mention, she sleeps in those damn boy shorts and T-shirts. You don't want Archie walking in when she's waking up without a bra."

"Absolutely not," my brother says without missing a beat.

"Exactly. At least I know how to be a gentleman and look the other way. And besides, it's nothing I haven't seen already." He grimaces as soon as the words leave his mouth.

Casey turns his head and looks at me in the rearview mirror. "Beckham makes some good points. I know it's not ideal, but do you think you could rough it on the cot in his room for a few days?"

I blow a huge breath out of my mouth, making my lips vibrate.

Can I rough it? Yes.

Will I like it? Not one bit.

"I mean, do I have a choice? I'll stay out of his way if he stays out of mine," I say with a glare at the back of Beck's head since he's looking at his damn phone again.

Seriously, who is he texting anyway?

"Perfect. That's settled. Be nice. Stay out of each other's way. And put a sock on the door if either of you has a visitor."

That makes Beck and me both snap our heads toward Casey.

Beck says, "Like fuck is she bringing some dickhead to my room," while I say, "That's disgusting. There will be no randos while I'm there, Beckham."

Casey doesn't say a word, but there's a smirk on his face and a look in his eye that makes me wonder what he's thinking.

CHAPTER
FOUR

BECKHAM

"CHUCK, baby! What the fuck is up?" Archie hops off the couch he was sitting on, rushes over to Charlie, and picks her up.

It pisses me off immediately. I hate that he calls her Chuck in his Texas drawl, and she thinks it's so fucking funny. All the chicks love his accent, and it's never bothered me—until now. Look, I love the guy. Trust him with my life even. Literally. He's a tackle and a total beast, protecting my ass from getting drilled on the field. He may be one of my closest friends, but he has two seconds to put Charlie down before I lose it.

"Hey, Arch. Good to see you, as always. How's it hangin'?" she asks him after giving him a squeeze, then drops from his hold.

"Well, Chuck, it's hangin' a little to the left today, but with a slight adjustment, we'll be back in center," he says while laughing and adjusting his junk.

And Charlie? She just fucking laughs. For the record, if I said something like that or adjusted my dick in front of her, she would have a meltdown.

"What up, Beck? You need some help or something? Need me to adjust your balls for you? Little slap on the ass?"

Archie's taunting me. Under normal circumstances, I'd play along and laugh it off, but shit's not funny right now.

I need to pull myself together, or this is going to be a long fucking week. Thank God classes start tomorrow. I can't believe I'm saying that. Fuck.

"Where's Baby King?" Pitz says as he strolls into the room with a white T-shirt with the words *Welcome Home, Baby King* written in Sharpie across his chest, his arms stretched out and a big-ass smile on his face.

What the actual fuck? I knew they didn't mind her staying here, but they're just rolling out the red fucking carpet for her.

Liam Pitz is our QB right now, but I have a feeling that's going to change with this new freshman coming in. This kid, Bo Callaway, has an arm like a missile. If I were Pitz, I'd be concerned.

"You know I'm older than Casey, right, Pitzy?"

He lifts her in his arms and spins her so her back is facing me. He winks at me and has that cheesy grin on his face.

Motherfucker.

And where the fuck did Casey go? He should be keeping these assholes in line.

Archie shoves Pitz out of the way once he releases Charlie, wraps his arm around her shoulders, and obnoxiously says, "So, I hear we're having a sleepover, Chuck. I have a Cali king in my room because I'm a big guy. In all areas. So, you can cuddle up with me."

"Griff, get your slutty hands off my sister," Casey says. With. A fucking. Laugh.

Raising his arms, Archie says, "I'm a hospitable guy, King. I promise I'll take real good care of your sis."

"Okay, Archie, before you get punched, come help me get my stuff out of the truck," Charlie says.

"You got it, sugar. Let's do this," he says while following her out the door.

Casey walks over to me with a look in his eye that I can't quite figure out. It's a cross between amused and concerned.

He puts his hand on my shoulder and squeezes a little. "Look, if it gets to be too much, having her in your space, just say the word. I'll switch with her. If I have to do an hour of stretching a day, I'll do it. Plus, Aunt Linds says the cot she's bringing over is more like a rollaway twin-size bed."

"Case, you're six foot four. Your legs will be hanging off that thing. I'll be fine, I promise. You know I'm not the one with the problem. I wish I …" I leave my thoughts hanging.

Casey knows me better than anyone, except maybe Charlie, and nods in understanding.

"Okay, brother. Look, I have to run out for a bit. Once Charlie gets her stuff out of the truck, can you help her get settled and take her to the store so she can get some food she wants?"

"Where the fuck you going?" It's not that I don't want to take her; it's more because I'm a nosy fucker.

"Noelle called, and she needs my help with something, so I'm going to grab a few things and head over to her place," he says while rubbing the back of his neck.

"Is she okay? Did Trey drop by again?"

"Don't worry about it. I've got it covered, but if I need anything, I'll call you, man," he says.

I nod, and we start walking out the door to the truck. Archie and Liam have already grabbed most of Charlie's things by the time we get out there.

"Nice of you two to join us," Pitz says as he and Archie pull some boxes out of the back of the truck.

"I'll follow you to your room, Beck, so you can show me where you want me to put my things. I can keep most of it in Casey's room though, so it won't be in your way," she says over her shoulder as she pulls out her duffel bag from the back of the cab.

"Nah, it's fine. I have a walk-in closet, and I don't have many clothes, so you can put your stuff in there," I offer and grab another bag and a small box.

I have to say, I'm impressed that my tone doesn't sound too eager. This all plays into my plan, so I'm not sad about it. Having her in my space? Yeah, it doesn't suck.

"Oh. Okay, thanks. What about the bathroom? You have your own bathroom too, right? Should I use the one in the hall or yours?" she asks as we all walk into the house.

When we moved into this house, we pulled straws. We all contribute to the rent equally, so it really was the luck of the draw. And my straw was the biggest. I got the largest bedroom that not only has a walk-in closet, but its own bathroom as well. Not gonna lie—it's a sweet setup as far as older houses go. A lot of the houses around campus aren't nearly as nice as this one. We got lucky. I'm sure it helped that the guy who owns it is a huge Walker University Stallions fan.

"Nah, you can just use mine. I mean, you won't really be here long enough to make a mess with all your girlie shit anyway. Plus, these guys are pigs," I say with a laugh.

"Pardon me. I'm exceptionally clean. I take hygiene very seriously," Archie says with a hand on his chest as he walks in front of us into my room. "I even clean up my ball hair, unlike you fuckers."

Holding up her hand, Charlie says, "Welp, I just lost my appetite, and I'm definitely not using your bathroom—ever —Arch."

"Chuck, baby, if only these fuckers took after my example, they'd pull more ladies too. Liam over here—he leaves toothpaste in the sink and also drinks out of the juice carton." He shifts the box in his hold to one arm and rests it on his hip, then points at Pitz and laughs.

Pitz interrupts by muttering, "Asshole."

Which just spurs Archie on further, and then he moves his arm to point at Casey. "And your brother—well, you grew up with him, so you know how nasty he is," Archie says while tossing a wink at Casey, who just rolls his eyes.

"In my brother's defense, he's actually not that bad," Charlie says.

Casey walks over to her and puts his arm around her shoulders. "Thank you, Char. Twins unite, motherfuckers."

"With that said, he does leave the toilet seat up, which I've suffered the consequences of multiple times. Do you know how bad that sucks? You wake up in the middle of the night to pee, you're half asleep, you pull your drawers down and squat to take a seat, and then your ass hits cold water. It's a horrible experience, and I do not recommend it. I'm just grateful he is diligent about flushing. Mom would literally gag if she walked by a bathroom that smelled like pee, so he learned pretty fast not to let that happen. Oh, and he does leave water bottles and candy wrappers in his room. He used to try to hide it from our mom, but I think she gave up on him once we got into high school." She pauses to take a breath. "Casey also likes to leave empty boxes in the pantry. Have you guys noticed that yet? He's the culprit, just so you know."

"Dude, Charlie, why are you dogging me like this to my boys? What about twin code, yo?" He looks at her incredulously, which just makes her snicker.

We walk into my room, and Arch and Pitz set Charlie's boxes in my closet. She walks in behind them, Casey behind her.

I head over to the bathroom to make sure it is, in fact, clean. And that I flushed the toilet and put the seat down. I remember one of those nights she fell into the toilet. I don't want to hear that screeching again. Ever.

When I come out of the bathroom, I see Charlie looking around my room. Not much is different from my bedroom at home, honestly. I have the same bedding, and I'm the same neat freak I've always been. I can't help it. I like order, and I like everything in my room to have its place.

I can tell by the look on her face that she's counting. She

counts in threes. Always has. Panels, windowpanes, anything she can find in threes.

I give her space as I let her work through her numbers, knowing it's something she needs.

Casey comes out of the closet and hugs Charlie. "I have to run out, but I'll be back later. Beck is going to take you to the store to get anything you need. Mom said she already deposited money into our accounts for groceries."

Charlie takes ahold of his arm as he starts to walk out. "Case, wait. Where are you going? Is everything okay?"

"Yeah, yeah, everything is fine. I just have to go get something for Noelle. I'll be back later, I promise. Want to watch *Game of Thrones* or something?" he asks.

"Uh, yeah, I guess. I'm pretty tired though, so it depends on when you get back."

"Heard," he says, then nods at me. "Becks, take care of our girl. Be back later." He taps the doorframe with his palm as he walks out of my room.

I know I won't change his mind about leaving since it's Noelle, but, shit, this is going to be awkward as fuck. But again, I'm not mad about it. I just need her to warm up to the idea of hanging out with me without wanting to kill me.

CHAPTER
FIVE

CHARLIE

THE FOUR OF US—ME, Beck, Archie, and Liam—watch as Casey leaves. I'm kind of wondering if I should go follow him out and offer to go with him. Noelle and I have always been friendly, but I'm not close with her like Casey is. I know something happened to her last year, yet I'm not sure what. She started dating some baseball player, and Casey was pissed about it. Beck may know more, but I'm not going to ask him. If Casey wants to tell me more, he will.

"All right, kids, I have business to attend to this evenin', so I'll see y'all tomorrow. Pitz, you coming with or you stayin' home tonight?" Archie asks.

"I've got a little something of my own going on tonight, but I might see you out. You going to The Point?" he asks.

"You know it. The ladies are waiting. I'll see you losers later," Archie says with a salute as he walks out.

"Charlie, Linson, I'm out. Oh, but, hey, can you grab me some chocolate milk at the store? It's my cheat treat," Pitz says.

"Only if you promise not to drink directly from the carton," I say.

"Scout's honor," he says while holding two fingers over his heart and winks at me, then turns and walks out, which makes me giggle.

I'm not a giggling type of girl, but Pitz is a cutie with his dimples and all-American guy looks. He can make any girl—and maybe a few guys—swoon with his charm. Not that I would ever act on it. He's truly just a friend. A hot one.

Beck clears his throat, and I spot him sitting on the edge of his king-size bed. I can't read the look on his face. I think we're both feeling awkward, and, well, I'm not really sure what to say to him.

I can't remember the last time we were alone together. Probably the end of August, going into our senior year. I remember the pleading look on his face. His hair fell over his red-rimmed eyes, and his hands were on his hips as I turned my back on him and walked upstairs to my room.

The thought makes my eyes water, so I turn toward the closet and say, "Did you see where they set the box with my bathroom stuff? I just want to get that out now so I can shower when we get back from the store."

"Uh, yeah. I think Archie put it on the top shelf on the left side of the closet. Do you want me to grab it for you? Is it heavy?"

"Nope. I can get it. I don't think it's that heavy. My towels and my hair stuff are in there. I'll grab my toothbrush out of my duffel too. I feel like I need to refresh a little after being in the car all day, dealing with the room drama, and moving. I'll be out in a few," I say while walking into the closet.

When I come out, Beck is gone, so I move to the bathroom with my box and place it on the floor, next to the second sink that looks unused. Then I go back out to the bedroom and grab my duffel bag, where I left it near the door to the room.

While I walk to the bathroom, my eyes roam the room. It's so typical Beckham. He's always been a neat freak, so his schematically Star Wars–themed bed, which is fitting for his engineering major, is tightly made, even after he sat on it. On the wall, there are only a few things. One calendar and a whiteboard with football plays on it. Knowing him, I'm sure he wrote out the plays as he memorized the playbook. He also has a small desk with a chair and a tall dresser. It looks like there are drawers that pull out from under the bed, providing additional storage.

But what has me slightly concerned is, where am I going to put this damn cot?

Twenty minutes later, I'm sitting in the desk chair after I brushed my teeth, washed my face, and brushed my hair, and I text Aunt Lindsay to see when she'll be here with the cot. It's been nearly two hours since we left the sorority house. She tells me she's waiting for Andy to come home, which could be a while. So, it should give me time to run to the store and get a few things.

"You ready to go?"

I spin in the chair to see Beck standing in the doorway. His arms grab hold of the doorframe at the top, making his arm muscles pop and exposing a hint of his abs and that stupid V that hot guys have. Oh, and he threw on a hat. Backward. It's like he's intentionally trying to destroy me.

"When did you change?"

Jesus, Charlie. What a stupid question. But he literally has me stupefied right now with all the skin he has showing.

"I, uh, changed my shirt real quick while you were in the bathroom. I guess we should make some kind of schedule or something for bathroom time and changing and stuff," he says lowly.

I stare at him while he stands there with his unassuming good looks. A lot can change on a guy in a year, and he has certainly matured physically—in the best way possible. Where he was once lean, he's now filled out with all sinewy muscles. I wonder if he still likes it when he gets his back scratched or if he's still ticklish when fingers run along the sides of his torso.

He calls my name to get my attention, bringing me out of my ab haze. "Charlene, you ready to go? We can grab a calendar while we're there so we can set up a schedule."

I look up at him and scowl. "Beckham, why do you insist on calling me Charlene? It's like you want me to hate you more."

"Then maybe you should stop calling me Beckham."

"Playing tit for tat is so beneath you. And why do we need a new calendar? You have one right here," I say while grabbing the one off the wall near the desk.

"Can you not touch my things? That calendar is my football and class calendar. They can't mix. We'll get a new one," Beck says with irritation in his voice.

I forgot how particular he was about keeping things organized. But I guess I am, too, with my counting.

Not wanting to stay in here with him any longer than I need to, I stand up from the chair, grab my crossbody bag, and start walking toward him at the door to the room.

"Ready. Let's go."

He just stands there for a minute, looking at me. Like he's trying to find an answer.

"They've gotten darker," he mumbles.

"What? What's gotten darker? Do I have something on my face?" I ask, running my hand over my face.

With a hint of laughter in his voice, he says, "No, you're good. More than good. Let's go." Then he pushes off the doorframe, turns, and walks away.

Not sure what just happened, I pull out my phone, tap on the

Camera app, put it in selfie mode, and inspect my face. I don't see anything I should be embarrassed about, so I turn it off, slide my phone into my crossbody bag, and follow him out the door of the room, but not before flipping the bedroom light switch three times.

It's a habit I started when I was a kid. Once my parents separated Casey and me into our own rooms, I had trouble sleeping and would count in threes—the squares in the door, shadows on the ceiling, anything I could group into threes. I'm not sure why it had to be three times, but it helped me get tired and fall asleep. I haven't been able to break my little ritual since.

As I'm walking toward the front door, I make a mental note to check out the house more when we get back so I know where everything is.

When we moved Casey in last year, it all happened so fast, and I didn't have much time to look around. Now that I'll be staying here, I need to get familiar with it a little better.

By the time I'm out of the house and I reach Beck's car, he's opening his door and sliding into the driver's side. Beck also has a truck, but his doesn't sit as high as Casey's, so I can get into it much easier, and it's a bench seat with no rear cab.

It's been a long time since I've been in his truck. The last time I was in it alone with him, things got a little heated. Okay, maybe more than a little heated. It was so fucking hot that the windows fogged up. I can still see the look on his face when he looked down at me as his cock thrust into my mouth. I bite my lip and close my eyes, then quickly shake the thought away. I don't need to look like I'm imagining him naked. I want to seem completely unaffected by being in this truck with him.

But then he does the thing …

CHAPTER
SIX

BECKHAM

"LEAN BACK," I say to Charlie as I reach across her body and pull the seat belt over her chest and hips.

My knuckles brush over the cotton of her shirt, and she inhales quickly as I lock the buckle in place.

When we were … us … I always buckled her into the car. Honestly, I think it was muscle memory just now that made me do it. I'd started strapping her in when I got my license. A subconscious thing maybe to feel like I could keep her safe.

"Why did you do that?" she asks, sounding a little breathy.

"Habit," I answer. That's all I'm giving her right now.

I don't want to tell her that having her in this car with me is making me crazy. Memories of her, of us laughing, listening to music. All the fucking and other dirty things we did in here. Yeah, it's all rushing in.

Hell, I damn near grabbed her in my room before we walked out. She came to stand in front of me, and all I could see were her pink lips, begging to be kissed. She has the perfect mouth for kissing. The bottom lip is just slightly bigger than her top lip, which is shaped like a Cupid's bow. I could see the flush in her cheeks and neck. And her eyes—yeah, she wasn't unaffected either. The freckles sprinkled across her nose and cheeks get me every time too.

And, fuck, now my dick is starting to get hard again.

I basically ran out of the house like a chickenshit so she didn't see my growing boner. Like a freaking middle schooler.

Trying to get my dick to calm down, I turn my eyes away from her and look out the windshield as I ask, "Where do you want to go? Grocery store or Target? But please, if we go to Target, can we not spend four hours there? I have to get up early for training, and we'll still need to set up your bed. Do you know when that's coming yet?" And now I said *coming*, which is making me think about coming down her throat. Jesus. What is wrong with me?

"Target is fine with me. I know what I need, so it shouldn't take me too long."

Because my lower head is doing all the thinking for me right now, I just nod and pull out of the driveway.

When we get to the store, she suggests we break off and meet back at the register. She tasks me with picking out a calendar.

"I don't really care what you get. Just something easy to follow," she says, looking over her shoulder while walking away from me to go over to the grocery side.

A half hour later, she meets me at the register area. I've been waiting here for the last ten minutes, and it took everything in me not to go find her.

"When did you get a cart?" I ask.

"Well, I got hungry, so everything looked good. Plus, I had a feeling you guys would end up eating half of it anyway, even though you're on a strict food regimen. But don't touch my macarons. They had the little pink ones that I like with the champagne-flavored filling." She points her finger at me, nearly poking my chest.

"You know I only like the pistachio ones. The rest are like eating cardboard." I take the items out of her cart and place them on the checkout counter, and see a few things I know she got for me.

"And how would you know what eating cardboard tastes like? My macarons are crying right now. You hurt their feelings," she says so seriously.

When I look up from the cart, she's holding the container of pink cookies like a baby and then starts laughing, which makes me smile. It's been a really long time since she's laughed with me. Yeah, I've heard her laugh and seen her smile for other people. But this one? It's mine.

"I didn't have a chance to see what was in the kitchen, so I just grabbed a bunch of different things. There's some mac 'n' cheese in there too. I wasn't sure how much you had left, but you eat it for, like, every cheat meal, so in case you're running low, you can have some of mine. I also got some stuff to make chocolate chip cookies, and I got the chocolate milk for Pitz."

Her face is turned toward the cashier, but I can still see a blush on her cheeks.

"Thanks, Boss."

This makes her whip her head up, and we lock eyes. Boss is a nickname I started calling her when we were kids because she liked to be in charge of anything we did, and as a result, Casey and I were never bored. Later, I called her Boss because I damn near let her rule my life because she owned me. And I loved every minute of it.

"What did you just say?" she practically whispers.

The cashier saves me from answering by telling us the total. Charlie reaches into the contraption on her chest and pulls out her wallet.

"What the fuck are you wearing? It looks like one of those baby carrier things."

"And there he is," she says, shaking her head.

"Let me pay for some of the groceries since we'll be eating some of this too. And I'll buy the calendar," I offer.

"Okay, that's fine. The calendar was your idea anyway. Plus, I need to save a little cash to order my meal delivery." Then, to the cashier, she says, "Can you cut the bill in half?"

The cashier just nods and types on the register to separate the bill.

"What's in your meal delivery? Like, shit you have to make, or is it premade?"

She finishes paying for her half of the items, so I reach over and swipe my card that I pulled from my wallet.

While she puts her wallet away, she explains, "I wanted to try the cooking kits, but I couldn't do that while living in the dorms last year. And I hated the cafeteria food. Once Brit started bailing on me, it just made sense to get the premade ones that I could just heat up."

At the mention of Britney, any headway we were making freezes. Charlie looks up at me and opens her mouth to say something, but shuts it.

The cashier scans my calendar separately, and I pay for it. Not another word is said between us.

CHAPTER
SEVEN

CHARLIE

"I SPOKE TO THE SCHOOL, and they can get you into the freshmen dorms. It would be a double, but at least you'd have your own place." Mom's suggestion echoes through the phone, making me groan.

"Thanks for trying, Mom, but I'd rather not take a chance on having an awful roommate again. In the meantime, I have a place to stay."

"I know. I just want you to be comfortable."

I smile as I balance the phone on my ear while sliding my jeans on. "If you're worried about me leaving Walker because it doesn't feel right, you're wasting your worries. I am not transferring schools again. Even if I have to sleep on a cot for the next three years, I'm finishing my degree at Walker."

She lets out a relieved breath. "That makes me so happy. I'll be even more pleased when this room situation is resolved."

I button my jeans and put the phone on speaker so I can slide on a tank top. "Same. Living with guys was not on my bingo card."

"How has it been, staying with those boys?"

How has it been?

The first few days of classes are always a little chaotic, and I'll be honest, I was a little worried that living in a house with four guys would make it even worse. But if anything, it's been really great. Archie walked me to the bookstore to get what I needed for my classes, Pitz showed me how to access the student portal from my laptop, and Casey has been my chauffeur since he's been pretty tight-fisted with the car keys. Beck, on the other hand, has been quiet. I haven't seen him around much the last few days, and when I have, he's kept to himself. Even at bedtime, he seems to stay in the living room until I'm asleep and then comes up to bed.

"It's been great, Mom. Really good so far." I wrap my hair into a ponytail and walk out of the bathroom, ready to start my morning.

"I'm glad. Well, I was just calling to wish you a great day. Tell your brother that I love him."

"Will do, Mom. I love you."

I shove my phone into my back pocket and walk over to my side of the room. You can easily tell which side is mine compared to Beck's because while mine has bags and boxes stacked haphazardly, his side is OCD central, where everything is in its place.

I'm placing my laptop in my bag when I notice a pink peony on the top of my comforter. I lift it to my nose and inhale the sweet scent. The stem has a jagged edge, like it was hand-picked.

Beneath the flower is a note. Short. Simple. Handwritten.

Have a great first day.
—Becks

To say I'm surprised is an understatement. It's something he used to do. Back when we were together. Back when we didn't screw the whole thing up.

My stomach does a flip as I try to sort out in my head why he would do this. I can't help but wonder what it means.

I tuck the note in my bag and leave the peony on the bed as I head to the kitchen.

"Morning," Casey says from his place at the table.

Beside him is Beck, dressed in jeans and a henley, looking too delicious for words, as usual. His head is down as he eats and skims through his phone at the same time. He doesn't look up or acknowledge my presence at all. It leaves me feeling a little confused and feeling more unsettled by this shift from hate to … friend-ish … to ignoring me. The problem is, I don't think I could *ever* just be friends with Beck. Once he kissed me behind the tree all those years ago, I was his.

It's just always been more.

The Walker University horseshoe is the central part of campus, not only where most of the class buildings are located, but also where you can find a minute to yourself on the lawn or to hang out with friends between classes. I've spent some time there this week, getting organized and just catching up on my reading. I'm trying to take advantage before the Oklahoma weather turns and it'll be too cold to be outside.

Today, there's an impromptu football game going on. Instead of lingering, I have to head over to Dell Hall, where I have a late afternoon class. It's in a building I have yet to be in, and based on the tour Archie gave me last week, it's supposed to be on the far side of campus.

Problem is, I can't remember exactly where he said it was.

I stop and look up at the name of the building in front of me and down at the syllabus on my phone. The names don't match. I scroll through my phone to call Casey. He doesn't answer. Figures. He's probably with Noelle again, per usual. Just like they were in high school.

I place my hand on my head and start walking farther down the brick path that leads to the next building, but I stop short when I recognize that building is an all-girls dorm. I remember that because of a funny story Archie told me about sneaking out of the third-story window last year, wearing nothing but his boxers because the girl he had hooked up with happened to be the roommate of another girl he had hooked up with. The girls called their resident assistant on him as an unwanted intruder, and he'd hauled ass down a water pipe before getting caught and subsequently losing playing time.

So, now, I'm standing on the back side of campus, lost and laughing to myself like a crazy person.

"You okay over there?" a male voice says behind me.

I turn to see a guy with brown hair and blue eyes. He has on a hoodie and oversize headphones around his neck. He looks kind of familiar, but I can't place him.

I drop my hand from my forehead and explain, "Can you tell me where Dell Hall is?"

He smiles. It's a sweet smile. The kind that makes you want to trust him.

"You must be headed to Robertson's lecture on Human Sexuality and Religion," he surmises.

I lift a brow. "How did you know?"

"Only beautiful, smart, and absolutely awesome women take that class," he quips.

I roll my eyes even though I'm totally flattered by his compliment. "That was cheesy."

"Cheesy usually gets me laid."

I let out a bark-like laugh. "Yeah, I don't think it's the lines."

He is drop-dead gorgeous. He wouldn't need lines like that.

"Didn't work on you?"

"Not one bit."

He laughs as he nods his head. "Figures. For the record, my lines never get me anywhere. I need to work on my game." He holds out a hand. "I'm Bo Callaway. I had that class but had to drop it because of football practice."

I take his hand with a smile. "That's how I know you. You're the rookie on the team. Heard you're gonna give Pitz a run for his money as QB."

"I'm flattered you've heard of me."

"Only because I'm Casey King's sister, Charlie."

"Ahh. Your brother's a cool guy. I'm sure he wouldn't like me too much if I left you here, stranded. Here, I'll show you where your class is."

Bo and I start walking. There's a path between the two buildings I was standing in front of. He leads me down to a third building situated behind them. I never would have noticed this path if Bo hadn't shown me.

"Where you from, Bo?"

"California. Pretty crazy, being so far away from home."

"You homesick?"

"Not yet. Coach keeps me busy, and I get to meet pretty little ladies like you." He shoots me a wink and a smile.

I laugh at his comment. He's a cutie.

"Trust me, Bo, I'm not your type."

"Guess I shouldn't be hitting on my teammate's sister. He'd kick my ass, I'm sure."

I give him a smile as he grabs the door handle and pulls it open. "Flirt away, friend. It's good for the ego."

"In that case, are you free this weekend? There's a party after the game. I'd love to hang out for a bit."

Just as the words are out of his mouth, Beck comes walking out the door. Yes, Beck, the man who left me a flower and a sweet note on my bed yet acts completely indifferent to my existence. And he's looking at Bo like he's going to tear his head off.

"Hey, Beck!" Bo says as he steps back, not reading the room. "This is Charlie, Casey's sister."

"I know Charlene—*well*," Beck drawls, and I narrow my eyes at him.

Bo smirks and nods his head. "Ah, okay. Well, I was just showing her to her class. She has Robertson's—"

"Go to practice, Bo." Beck's words are a command. "I got her from here."

Bo laughs and clasps a hand on Beck's shoulder as he walks away. "See you on the field, Linson." He looks at me with a smile. "Charlie, it was nice meeting you."

"See you around, Bo."

Turning to face Beck, he holds the door with his back as I walk through. My side brushes up against him as I do, and I notice the hardened muscle beneath his shirt.

Okay, fine, I might have purposely shifted my weight into him because, honestly, I've been dying to run my hand down his chest. And then down his abs and into his—

Focus, Charlie.

I saunter past him and stop because I don't know if I'm supposed to go right or left.

Beck places a hand on my forearm and pulls me to the left. "You're over here."

I follow him down the hall and to a stairwell at the end.

"I can find it from here. You can go to practice."

"I'm fine."

"Won't Coach be upset if you're late?"

"I said, I'm fine. I'll walk you up."

We take one step at a time. Beck is clearly not in a rush.

"It's quiet in here compared to other buildings."

"This is the only class in here right now. It's crowded before three."

"You have class in here a lot?"

"I have, uh, class on the second floor."

"Oh, I didn't realize you were taking any psychology classes. Do you have to take that for your engineering degree? Or are you taking it for funsies?" I laugh to try to lighten the mood and catch his gaze.

His eyes are locked straight ahead, but I see a smirk on the side of his mouth.

"No, not any classes toward my degree, but I took a class last year and hit it off with my professor. I go in to help him from time to time between classes and practice."

"Ah, that makes sense. Do you know anything about Robertson? Is he good, or will the next hour drag on?" I grimace.

"Which class is it?"

"Human Sexuality and Religion."

"Interesting. I have only heard good things about Robertson, so I'm sure it'll be good. Is that something you're interested in studying, or is it a requisite for your major?" he asks.

"Yeah, it's in my field of study, so I need to take it in order to get into Women's Sexuality in Modern Culture next year." I blush a little, not because I'm embarrassed, but because I know that particular class is whispered about around campus. It's pretty graphic from what I hear.

"So, you definitely decided on a psych degree? You'll be great, no matter what you do, but this fits you. You have great intuition, compassion, and curiosity about people." He mumbles a little at the last part as we reach the top of the staircase.

I look at the number next to the nearest door and see it's the room I need to be in. "Well, this is me." I turn to Beck and see he's already looking at me.

"Have fun, Charlene. I'll come get you after practice." He smirks.

"Oh, no, you don't have to do that. I can find my way back to the house now. I just couldn't find the building and happened to run into Bo." I don't know why I felt the need to add that.

"I don't doubt you can get back to the house, but I don't want you walking home by yourself as it gets dark. I'll pick you up, and we'll go home together."

We're locked in a stare, but I break first and look down at my shoes. "Okay, that's fine."

Beck nods, then turns and walks away. And I watch until he's out of sight. I mean … that ass deserves to be admired.

Class passes by quickly. The professor's presentation for the course is fascinating, but I also love that he's engaging with the students. It's not a big group, so I think it'll be fun and interactive.

And when I walk out of Dell Hall an hour later, just like Beck said, he's standing by the door to take me home.

CHAPTER
EIGHT

CHARLIE

THE FIRST WEEK of classes flew by, and this weekend, we have a sorority team-building activity.

When I rushed last year, it was a good way to get to know some of the older members in the house. We went to a working ranch in the area there and were assigned different tasks around the farm. It was so much fun, despite us mucking horse stalls. By the end of the day, we were all sweaty and tired, and we stank like literal shit, but as we sat around the picnic tables to eat, we were all laughing as if we were old friends.

This year, our activity is an obstacle course. When we got on the bus, the president of the sorority explained that we'd be doing different trust exercises while also completing the course.

I'm partnered with Arbor and Lily, who are also fairly athletic, so I feel like we'll get through the course pretty easily.

"Charlie, I'm dying here. You have to tell us what it's like, living with Archie Griffith. He's so fucking hot. I don't even care that he's the biggest player on campus. I would ride that pony anytime," Lily says and fans herself with her hand.

Arbor and I start laughing.

I throw my arm around Arbor's shoulders and lean across her. "Babe, I'm telling you right now, as much as I love Archie, I'm not sure you could handle him. He's a lot."

"Okay, but have you seen him naked yet? I've heard he's huge." Lily bends forward a little in the seat she's sitting in across the aisle of the bus, then holds her hands chest-width apart.

"Lily, OMG, get ahold of yourself." Arbor laughs but then turns to me. "Okay, but really ... is he?"

"Ladies, let's settle down." I can't help but laugh, then drop my arm from Arbor's shoulders. "I can't say that I've had the opportunity to catch a glance at anything on anyone, but I don't think of them like that anyway."

"Lies. I call complete fucking lies right now!" Lily shouts and slaps her hand on her leg. "There is no way you can look at those guys and not wonder, even a little, about what they have under their jockstraps."

"Okay, first of all, ewww. I do know how bad they smell when they come home from practice and haven't showered. And I might have gotten a whiff of said jockstraps in the laundry room. I promise you, it's not something anyone should experience."

Arbor puts her arm around my shoulders and pulls me into her. "Give us something, Char. A butt cheek? A peen outline? I definitely wouldn't mind hooking up with Liam Pitz. He's fucking hot, and he seems like he's actually a nice guy too."

"Oh, speaking of QBs, I met Bo Callaway the other day. Holy shit, is *he* hot! I could look at him all day. And he was super sweet. And to answer your question, Arbs, I can confirm that Pitzy is, in fact, one of the good ones. He's a bit of a player too though. I haven't gotten a peek at any of his parts, but he does like to walk around without his shirt on. He's got a couple of tattoos I can't quite make out and wouldn't mind a closer look at. Although I think my brother might lose his shit if I did."

"Charlie, who are you kidding? Casey probably couldn't care

less. It's Beckham you have to worry about. He would lose his ever-loving mind. That boy claimed you a long time ago," Arbor says, shaking her head.

I bring my legs up and fold them into me and wrap my arms around them. "I mean, maybe, but we're not together anymore, so he wouldn't really have a say if I did date anyone or hook up with someone. He knew I dated a guy last year and didn't seem bothered."

Admitting that out loud hurts a little. Not that I dated Tony to get a rise out of Beck, but I thought maybe he'd care.

"What is the deal with you two anyway? I know you broke up before we went into our senior year, but you never really said why. I have to admit, I was completely shocked when you told me."

I drop my head back onto the seat and sigh. "It just got messed up, and we both let it fall apart. I'm not even sure I can remember the reasons why now." I close my eyes and shake my head. "No, that's not true. I guess I mean that I'm not sure I believe what I thought I did then."

"Vague much?" Lily coughs out a laugh, and Arbor and I start laughing with her.

"Okay, I will give you this. Beck has been a little ... nicer to me lately," I say with a scrunch of my nose. "I'm not really sure if it's because he's trying to be civil since we're sharing a room or if it's something more. I've caught him watching me a few times around the house, and he did pick me up from my Human Sexuality and Religion class both times this week. It's nice, but also kinda weird. Not weird, I suppose. But it makes me feel weird or confused at the very least."

"And have you been *nicer* to him?" Arbor lifts a brow. "You haven't been a little bitchy? The day you moved to Walker, you looked like you were going to kill him with your stare."

I sigh. "It's hard for me to be around him when I was angry with him for so long. Angry with myself. It's complicated. All that matters is, right now, we are civil. Just a couple of exes, trying to be roommates."

I decide to keep the note and peony out of this conversation. In fact, Beck left a peony on my bed again. No note this time. Just a pink flower on my pillow. That's an us thing, and it feels like I need to keep it in our space. I also won't mention that I made him mac 'n' cheese the other night. I didn't make a big deal about it, just like he hadn't acknowledged the note and peony he'd left for me on the first day of class. But he did give me a soft smile and thanked me before I walked out of the kitchen.

"I never heard of Beck hanging out with any girls last year. I mean, we saw him at a few parties, and of course, there were girls around, but I never saw him with anyone. I don't think he ever got over you. Anyone with eyes can tell he still cares about you." Arbor nudges my shoulder with hers.

"Yeah, I don't know about that, but it's also not something I really want to think about."

"So, maybe you aren't over him either," she says and puts her hand on one of my knees.

Thankfully, the bus stops and saves me from having to answer, and we get off.

The day flies by. Arbor, Lily, and I complete the obstacle course like the champs we are. We made it over the climbing wall together, conquered the tightrope, caught each other in the trust falls, and army-crawled through the mud. There isn't a winner because it's a team-building activity, but we did finish each one first. We decide we'll reward ourselves with manis and pedis tomorrow.

After the physical challenges are done, we sit around in a big circle and introduce ourselves and say what lessons we learned from the day. I might have rolled my eyes when we sat down, but by the time it gets to me, I feel a sisterhood around me that I have never experienced before.

CHAPTER
NINE

BECKHAM

"YOUR RANGE of movement is limited. Let's work on some of those wrist flexions and extensions to create more flexibility," Sally, the team's physical therapist, says.

I wince as I stretch out my palm and feel the sting go up my forearm and into my shoulder. It doesn't always bother me, but I've been going hard in practice lately.

"You said you did this falling off a bike?" Sally asks with a pinch to her mouth.

She's right to be confused by my bullshit story because that's exactly what it is—bullshit.

"Yep."

In my opinion, it doesn't matter how I severed a nerve in my palm that nearly caused paralysis when I was only nine. It healed, and even though it hurts from time to time or goes numb on occasion, I can still get out on the field and play ball with my best friend, and I got a scholarship to take the burden off my dad.

So, yeah, a little pain is worth it.

"You say you're feeling okay, but you wouldn't be in this

room without an order from Coach." The physical therapist places her hand on my forearm and slowly pushes down my hand, which is hanging over the table, to stretch out my wrist.

I smash my teeth together to keep myself from telling her to fuck right off.

"Did you ever have surgery on your hand after the fall? It looks like you possibly had some tissue grafting, but did they ever do anything with the nerve damage?"

She takes her palm and pushes my hand up now and keeps her other hand on my forearm. Once the sting subsides, the stretch actually feels kind of good.

"No surgery on the nerves, but, yes, I did have some grafting on my hand."

"From the hip, I assume?"

I nod.

It's intense, having these conversations. No one in high school ever asked, nor did this come up when I was recruited to the team. But Sally is new to the program and has taken an interest in the teams' injuries, particularly mine.

"I'm not going to meddle, Beckham, because I'm guessing there is a story here, but just tell me something. Does Coach know the cause of this?" She releases my hand and grabs the bottle of Aspercreme from the table next to us. She gives me a pointed look while squirting some into her palm.

"He knows. But don't you worry about me, Sal. I'm great with my hands, and I can catch or carry any ball given to me." I throw in a laugh to lighten the mood.

The very last thing I want to do is explain to Sally where my scars came from. Coach knows the story, and he's the only one who needs to know.

"Okay, got it. It's my job to ask though—you understand that, right? And besides, we really need another championship year, so I'm counting on you, Beck." She squeezes my hand lightly once she's done spreading the cream from my hand up to my forearm.

"I got you, Sal. We're taking it all this season." I stand from my seat and stretch my arms above my head, then turn my torso left and then right.

"From your mouth, Beck. Now, go finish stretching. I need to start on my next victim." She laughs.

I hear Archie's loud mouth and then a slap in the hallway before Casey and Archie walk into the PT room.

Archie says, "I heard that. You gotta be gentle with me. My body is a temple, Miss Sally."

"Get in the tub, Griff. I want you to sit in an ice-bath first before we get started." She turns and looks at Casey. "Casey, I don't have you on my schedule today. Did you need something?" she asks while looking at her chart.

"Nope, all good here. Just coming to see if Beck was finished yet. I'm checking to see if he wants to grab some food." Casey is looking at me while he talks to her.

I mouth, *What?* and shrug.

"He's all yours. Beckham, do your stretches at home too. If you need help with the pressure, have your buddy here help you." She points at Casey with her pen in her hand.

"Motherfucker, this is cold. Excuse me for cussing, Miss Sally, but I feel like my balls just hit my throat," Archie barks out.

"High and tight?" Casey asks.

"Yep. But it'll be worth it. Right, Miss Sally?" He tilts his head in her direction, but is looking at us with his ever-present smirk.

Always a good time, this guy.

She rolls her eyes and shakes her head, making us all laugh.

"Thanks, Sal. I'll stop by next week if it's still stiff. Griff, enjoy the plunge."

I bend and grab my gear bag, then walk toward Casey, who is waiting by the door. I reach out my fist for a bump, and he taps his to mine. We start walking out of the field house. We hear Griff already asking for a towel before we walk out the door.

"Sup, brother? You want to grab some food?" he asks.

"Yeah, that sounds good. I haven't had anything since break-fast." I rub my stomach with the hand Sally just worked on.

"I'm starving too." He slows to a stop and reaches for the same hand. "So, are you ever going to tell me why you have those scars? I knew they were there, but honestly, man, I never thought to ask why. And I wasn't eavesdropping, but I did hear you tell her that Coach knows. So, I'm wondering why I, your best friend, don't know. Is there a story there?"

I sigh and look into his eyes. "Case, it happened a long time ago, before I moved to Troy. You know how my mom isn't in the picture? Let's just say, she wasn't a good mom and leave it at that. Besides, it doesn't really matter anyway. I'm good, man, I promise."

He nods, but he knows I'm not telling him the whole truth. What happened to me was fucking horrific, but he doesn't need to know the details.

"What are we eating?"

"I thought we could just run by the dining hall before we head home. It's on the way to my car. I couldn't find a spot near the field house earlier today, so I had to park on the other side, near my morning class."

"Okay, that's fine. When I left this morning, I didn't see you, and your car was already gone. How could you have not gotten a spot? I ended up walking to campus since my first class was close to the house, so I'll ride back with you."

He rubs the back of his neck. "Well, I wasn't home last night. I went over to Noelle's, and we fell asleep. I'd forgotten to set my alarm on my phone, and when she woke up for class, I realized how late I was and ran out of there like my ass was on fire."

I'm not going to get into his business with Noelle. She's important to him, and no matter what I say, he's going to do what he wants. I think he's feeling more for her than she is for him though, and I really don't want to see him get hurt. So, I just hum in understanding.

As soon as I walk into the dining hall, I see her.

I have no idea how I went an entire year being at a different school from her. It almost seems like a blur. And probably why I stayed hyper-focused on football and school.

She's standing by the staircase, looking at the bulletin board of events.

I elbow Casey and nod toward her, and we walk in her direction.

Charlie King has the most beautiful face I've ever seen. She's got that girl-next-door way about her. She's sweet, even when she's trying to be mean. And, man, can she be mean to me. But I want to gain her trust, and I know the first step is to allow her to get used to me being in her world again. I realized that when we were shopping at Target. I'd pushed her buttons that morning, but then we found a common ground. It felt normal again. Then she brought up Britney, and it was like we were right back where we'd started.

I knew she needed space.

Fuck, I need space.

And yet I can't stay away.

"What up, Char?" Casey grabs her around the neck and pulls her into him.

"Casey, seriously." She shrugs him off, but there is a playful smile on her face.

I know how happy she is to be near him. Hell, they're both happy. They are the kind of twins you read about. They finish each other's sentences. Communicate without words most of the time too.

"You hungry? Beck and I are gonna grab some food."

"No, I just ate. I was checking the boards to see if there were any potentials for housing. In case a room doesn't become available in the sorority house this semester."

What the fuck? She's not leaving the house.

Casey must see my expression because he asks, "Why would you want to move out? We're the best roommates you'll ever have. Come on. Admit it. We're a good time."

He grabs her shoulder and pushes her back and forth, making her laugh, and then she pushes his hand away.

"Ideally, I would like to move into the sorority house, and just thinking of moving my stuff multiple times gives me heart palps, but I can't stay in Beckham's room for the whole year."

Casey barks out a laugh. "Char, I think he's fine with you staying in his room. Indefinitely."

"Dude, what the fuck?" I glare at him.

She looks at me with a dejection on her face. I try to fix it so I don't sound like a complete asshole.

Clearing my throat, I say, "It's really no problem at all. Our schedules coordinate well, so it's fine, really." I'm not making this any better, but I can't come out and tell her she's not leaving.

Charlie nods at me, then looks at Casey. She brings her hand up and points her thumb over her shoulder. "I'm gonna head out, so I'll see you guys back at the house."

"Later." Casey waves, then starts to walk over to the food line.

I watch her walk away, and just as I start to follow Casey, I see her turn to look at me. Our eyes meet, and I nod my head and smile.

Later that night, as I walk into my bedroom, Charlie comes out of the bathroom—with only a towel wrapped around her body. I want to walk over and grab ahold of the knot keeping it together and yank it off her body. But I don't.

Instead, I politely look away. "Sorry. Do you want me to come back in a few minutes?"

"Oh, no, it's okay. I'll just get my PJs and go back in there to change." She's talking fast, like she tends to do when she's feeling awkward.

While she grabs her clothes, I walk over to my desk, pull out the chair, and drop my backpack onto it. I take out my laptop and plug it in on my desk to charge. After we ate, instead of riding back with Casey, I stopped at the library on my way home. I needed to get in a little study time without interruptions in the house.

Charlie comes out of the bathroom, dressed in her little shorts and T-shirt, which she calls PJs. She's so fucking gorgeous.

She settles on the cot and picks up a book from the floor next to it.

"What are you reading?" I ask.

Looking up from her book, she blushes a little. "Oh, um, just a book about the Mafia."

"Mafia? What about the Mafia? Like a biography or something? Is it for class?"

Clearing her throat, she says, "Well, no. It's a Mafia romance."

"Hmm."

I'm sure my mouth is hanging open a little because she then says, "Don't judge me, Beckham. I'm looking at it as research for my Understanding Romantic Literature class."

"Why would you need to take a class in that? You've been reading those dirty books since we were, like, twelve."

That gets a laugh out of her.

"You're right, but I chose the class as an elective, and I'm considering adding literature as a minor to my psychology major. I feel like they go well together."

I nod. "Makes sense. What do you think you want to do with that?" I ask for two reasons.

The most important is because I just want to know everything about her again. She hasn't talked to me like this in two years. I'm going to get anything I can from her while she's willing. And the other reason … when I succeed in getting her back —and I will—I want to make sure I do everything I can to allow us both to follow our dreams together.

"I think I want to teach at a college level. I don't really want to go into practice, and I don't really want to do research, so I think that's what will make the most sense for me. What about you? You still like the engineering track you're on?"

I shift my head back and forth. "Yeah, I do. You know math was never hard for me, so I get bored sometimes, but I like it overall. The NFL is my dream, but once my pro career is over, I want to have my degree in something other than sports management or broadcasting. Just not sure what exactly I'll do with it. I'm considering taking some architecture classes to see if I might like that too. But I plan to be in the big show for a long time, so I might never even get the chance to use my degree at all."

When I meet her eyes, she nods and says, "That's a good dream, Beckham."

I look away first, mostly to stop myself from getting up and bringing her to my bed. Eventually, we'll get there, but I know it's still going to take some time before she's ready to let me in all the way.

CHAPTER
TEN

CHARLIE

AFTER OUR TARGET run a few weeks ago, Beck created a schedule for the bathroom and private bedroom time for changing and studying. I will mostly go over to the sorority house to work in the study hall room, but on the chance I don't, I need space to think without thoughts of him distracting me. It's hard enough, smelling him all around me. And if it's not him, it's the peony. He's left one on my pillow every day. I've been placing them in a small vase on the kitchen table. We don't talk about them or even acknowledge their existence. It's like our little secret, although there's no doubt Casey knows where they're coming from and for whom.

I went back to the store today to grab some more groceries and a whiteboard to create a kitchen schedule for the house. We don't eat every meal together, but I thought it would be fun to have at least one meal a week as a "family." And also, I'm not going to get stuck with all the cooking and cleaning duties. Surprisingly, the guys are pretty neat and clean. At least in the main living areas. I'm not sure what their rooms look like.

That said, tonight is my turn to cook. I did get my premade

meals ordered, but these guys eat a lot, and despite the cheat food I picked up, they are on a pretty strict diet with the team nutritionist, so I need to accommodate that.

Archie is in the kitchen, looking at the whiteboard I put on the fridge. His hands are in the pockets of his gray sweatpants, and he's rocking back and forth on his heels. "So, this is going to be like a scheduled thing? We each have days?" he asks while nodding. "I dig it. What are you making us tonight, Chuck?"

"I have chicken marinating in the fridge, and then I was going to roast some veggies and red potatoes. That's all on the food plan from the team, I think, right?" I guess I should have asked Casey before I made a plan, but I figured I'd model what I saw him eat over the summer.

"Yep, that all sounds great. Did you check to see if we had propane in the grill? I think we do, but I'll go double-check," he says, already walking out to the back porch.

"Shit, I didn't even think about that. Thanks, Arch."

Walking over to the fridge, I pull it open and bring out the chicken, veggies, and potatoes. I set everything on the counter and open some cabinets in search of the cutting board. I know they have one because Casey took my mom's old one when they moved in. I can't find it in the lower cabinets, so I open one of the upper cabinets and see it on the second shelf. Lifting on my toes, I try to grab it, but I'm too short.

I mean, who puts a cutting board on a second row in a top cabinet? Oh, right, boys. Tall boys.

"Need a hand?" I hear a deep, gravelly voice ask behind me.

I turn my head slightly to gaze over my shoulder and see a shirtless Beck standing directly behind me. Close enough that if either of us leaned in just a little, we'd kiss.

"Uh, I think I can get it, but I might have to grab a step stool or something."

Beck smirks. "We don't have a stool, Boss. Let me grab it for you."

I pull my arm down and start to lean to the side to give him room to grab it, but he blocks me in with his body.

His left arm is on the counter, practically touching my hip, and his right arm reaches over me to grab the cutting board. Since I have a crop top on, I can feel the heat from his body radiating against my back, sending shock waves straight down my body and to my toes.

And he called me Boss again. There's something about that nickname that still makes my stomach flip.

"Thanks," I whisper.

"Anytime. So … what's cooking?" he asks so close to my ear that I can feel his breath tickle me.

Clearing my throat from being slightly flustered by his closeness, I say, "Grilled chicken and stuff."

He laughs. "Do you need any help with … stuff?"

The last thing I need is Beckham in my space, but really, it will make this go faster.

"Yeah, you can wash the potatoes for me while I cut the veggies."

"Don't you need to clean the veggies too?" he asks.

"Uh, yeah, good point. You do that while I get the chicken on a pan to take out to the grill. In fact, I'll go check on the grill, and you can start washing. Make sure you get all the black spots off the potatoes. No one wants to eat dirt."

"Huh, is that what those black spots are? I didn't realize that," he mocks.

"Ha-ha, funny guy. I'll be right back," I say, walking toward the sliding door that leads to the porch.

Archie is standing by the grill and texting on his phone when I walk outside.

"Hey, Arch. Do we have enough propane?"

"We have enough propane, and I started it for you. Should be getting pretty warm by now. Is the food ready?"

"Not yet. I need to cut up the veggies and potatoes, but I can get the chicken on while I do that." I lift up the grill hood and feel the heat immediately. "Yeah, I think this is ready. Thanks, Arch."

"Anytime, sugar. Thanks for making dinner. I'm starving. I haven't eaten in, like, two hours," he says, rubbing his stomach, which makes his shirt ride up, exposing his six-pack—or maybe eight-pack.

I haven't seen him shirtless yet, but I'm sure he's solid, like the other guys.

I pat him on the shoulder. "It's coming, big guy. I'll be back out in a few with the chicken. I don't expect you to man the grill though. I might be a girl, but I can handle some heat."

"I just bet you can, Little King," he says, laughing.

I shoot him a wink over my shoulder when I walk back into the house. Beck is standing at the sink, washing the potatoes, and the veggies are sitting on the cutting board.

"Wow, you work fast. Thank you."

He just nods while he scrubs a stubborn dirt spot on one of the potatoes.

"Oh, hey, I need a bowl to put these veggies in with some olive oil and seasoning. Where are the mixing bowls? Oh, and I need a pan to put the chicken on. I didn't see one when I was looking for the cutting board."

Wordlessly, he leans down, reaches in front of my leg, and opens the cabinet.

"It's in this one. I think we have a few different sizes. If you don't see one that works, I'll see where the popcorn bucket is. The pans—if you're talking about, like, a cookie sheet—are in the drawer under the oven. Like where your mom keeps hers," he says and then turns back to the sink to keep washing.

I bend down to peek inside the cabinet and find a medium-sized bowl I can mix the veggies in and a larger bowl for the potatoes. Pulling both out, I set them next to the cutting board. Then I go around to his other side, where the oven is, bend down, and pull out one of the larger cookie sheets. I found the foil in the pantry last week when I made meatloaf for the guys, so I walk over, open the door, and grab it.

Setting the pan on the counter, I start to roll out some foil and place it on top of the pan, then open the drawer in front of me to get a fork.

"We're running out of room on the counter here," I say with a slight laugh.

"Am I in the way?" he says with a teasing tone as he leans toward me.

Okay, if he wants to invade my space, I'll invade his right back. Two can play this little game he seems to be starting.

Pressing into him so our arms are now touching, I say, "I'm sure we can make it work."

His chest rises, and his lips part. I watch as his tongue darts out and licks his bottom lip.

I gently nudge him with my hip. "Just don't put your hand in my way, or you might get cut."

His body stiffens. I glance over at him, and he's got an odd expression on his face.

Then he glances down at his hand and flexes it a few times.

He looks from his hand to my face, and his demeanor shifts. He takes a step back and shakes his head, seeming to snap out of whatever was on his mind. "I'll keep that in mind."

I take my own step back and scratch my head.

The chicken is marinating in a ziplock bag, and I pull each piece out with the fork, placing it on the pan. "I'll be right back. I'm going to get this on the grill."

Beckham nods. "I'll be here."

Literally, what is happening right now? It seems like he's making some kind of effort to keep things nice since we're stuck living together. But I feel like I have whiplash.

I've been thinking more and more about how things between us ended so … abruptly.

Once upon a time, Beck was the boy who threw pebbles at my

window late at night just so I could come to the window and blow him a kiss. He said he had nightmares sometimes, and I was the only thing that brought him peace on those nights. I never asked what his dreams were about. I just wanted to be there for him.

After the breakup, he avoided me like the plague. Maybe that was him treating me the way I was treating him.

My heart was shattered, and I couldn't drop the wall I'd built around myself.

I know things won't go back to the way they were before, yet I'm trying to figure out if I should allow myself to become emotionally invested in him again or stay guarded.

Slowly, I feel that wall falling down.

Outside, I find Archie sitting in one of the outdoor chairs on the patio. Still on his phone, but no longer texting.

"Whatcha looking at?" I ask him.

Lifting the lid, I start placing the chicken on the grill.

"Sugar, that sizzle tells me this meal is gonna be top-tier." When I look over, he winks at me, smiling, then goes back to his phone. "I'm just looking at Instagram. One of my little brothers plays hockey on a junior league in New England, and he made the highlight reel from his game last night. He's badass."

"That's awesome. I remember Casey saying something about your brother, but I don't think we have ever met him, have we? Which one is this? You have a few brothers, right?"

"Yeah, I have five younger brothers. This one is Aiden. Our schedules don't really line up because he starts training around the same time I do. We talk all the time though. When my season ends, I try to make it to as many of his nearby games that I can. Out of all of my brothers, we're the closest and the most alike, so it's been tough, not being able to see him play the last few years, but it'll be worth it. Looks like he'll get drafted at the end of the season this year," he says with pride.

"That's amazing, Arch. And you'll enter the draft this year, too, so that's big time for your family. Two boys going to play professional sports. Pretty unique."

"Yep, my mama fed us well." He laughs.

"Sounds like it. Okay, I'm heading back in to get the rest cut up." I shut the lid, grab the pan, and walk back into the house.

Beckham has laid the potatoes on a paper towel next to the cutting board. He's still in front of the sink, leaning back, but he's got his phone in his hands now.

I set the pan down, roll up the foil, and toss it into the garbage bin next to the sink. Then I grab a knife out of the butcher block and start cutting some red pepper that's already sitting on the cutting board.

"You get the chicken on the grill?" Beck asks while pocketing his phone into his track pants.

"Yep, it's cookin'. Archie was just telling me about his brother Aiden, who's probably going into the draft this year. I guess he's a hockey player."

Beck nods. "Yeah, kid has sick skills on the ice. Seems to have a good head on his shoulders too. They get those kids young though. I hope he's ready for diving into pro life."

"How old is he? I thought he was only a year or so younger than Archie."

Shaking his head, he says, "No, he's a few years younger. I think he turns eighteen soon though."

Finishing the peppers, I move back to the fridge to grab an onion. I chop it up and add it to the bowl of peppers. "Can you grab the olive oil, salt, and pepper for me?"

"Yep." He turns around and pulls them out of one of the cabinets on the side of the range hood and sets them on the counter next to the bowls.

"Thanks," I say quietly.

"Do you want me to go check on the chicken?" he asks.

I shake my head. "No, I'll go out there in a second. I just want to cut the potatoes real quick and get them wrapped in foil."

He doesn't say anything, but stands close, watching me. Well, watching my hands.

I lay out a new sheet of foil onto the pan, then set it aside for the chicken. Rolling out more foil, I scoop up the potatoes I cut and set them on it. Then I drizzle some olive oil and sprinkle salt and pepper on them, and I wrap the edges of the foil together, making a packet. I set that to the side and do the same thing to the peppers and onions.

"Okay, I think I'm all set. I'm going to check on the chicken and get these on the grill." I pick up both packets and start for the door.

"Let me get the door for you, and I'll bring out the pan for the chicken if you're ready for that," he says from behind me.

I look over my shoulder and nod. "That works. Thanks."

So, I guess this is what it's like, living with your ex-boyfriend and being friends-ish. I just hope my heart doesn't start to get other ideas because while I can be civil with this new version of Beck—the roommate—I can't completely separate him from my old Beck.

After the food was done cooking, I called the guys in for dinner.

We're all sitting at the table. They're talking about their upcoming game, and I'm listening—sort of. I'm also lost in thought. My first exam is tomorrow, and it's open book, but I'm running through my coursework in my head, making sure I have everything I need annotated.

"What do you think, Char?" Casey asks, shaking me from my thoughts.

I look over to my left, where Casey is sitting. "I'm sorry,

what? I didn't hear you. I was just thinking through my exam tomorrow."

"I just said that we should go to that taco place after the game with Mom and Dad."

"Oh, yeah, that works," I say, nodding.

"My dad and Brooke are riding down with them, so they'll come too," Beck mentions.

"Sounds good. Do you boys want to come with us, or are you doing your own thing?" Casey asks.

Archie shakes his head and says, "No thanks, man. My dad might come up for the game, so I'll grab something with him after if he has time to stay."

"Yeah, I think my parents might come too. But I don't know if I want them to if I'm not playing. I wish Coach would announce who he's starting soon. I hate not knowing," Liam says.

Liam, who is the current starting quarterback, has some competition this season. Bo Callaway was heavily recruited by some of the top schools in the country. Of course, I only know this because I've overheard Casey and Beck talking about it. Liam is good, but apparently, Bo is Heisman material already.

Archie nods and puts a hand on Liam's shoulder. "I feel you, brother. Coach won't leave you hanging long. I hate to ask, but I have to. What are you going to do if he gives Callaway more playing time than you this season?"

With a heavy sigh, Liam says, "I don't know, man. I still want to go high in the draft next year. I won't be able to if I'm not starting."

"Heard. We're here for you, man. I just want to get this season going!" Archie says with a clap of his hands.

Casey drums his hands on the table and says, "Yeah, baby! I finally get my chance to stand with you fuckers on the starting line this year."

Liam raises his fist to bump Casey's. "You know I'll give you the ball if I'm QB, brother."

"That's what I'm talking about! I know you have my back," Casey says with a nod.

Archie grins. "This is awesome, boys. I'm into this family-dinner shit. I even dig the flowers. It's great having a girl in the house."

I blush and look over at Beck.

He shifts in his chair and agrees, "Yeah, the flowers are a nice touch, Charlie."

"Thanks," I state. "They make me happy. Really happy."

Beck leans back with a small, crooked smile on his face.

The rest of dinner goes by quickly. These boys eat a lot, and they eat fast.

I stand to go into the kitchen so I can start cleaning up. "You guys can bring your own dishes in, and I'll wash, but just remember that when it's your turn to cook, you clean it up too."

Standing from his seat, Beckham says, "I'll help you clean up."

Casey mumbles something I can't hear, but Beck responds with, "Fuck you."

And the guys all laugh.

I'm already scraping my plate in the trash when Beck walks in. "What did Casey say to you?"

He shakes his head with a smirk. "Nothing. Don't worry about it."

I let it go, and we work in silence for the next few minutes. After we load the plates and silverware into the dishwasher, I fill up the sink with soapy water to wash the pan and bowls I used for marinating.

Beck moves to stand behind me and puts his hands into the soapy water, right over mine, sliding his fingers between mine under the water. "Let me wash, and you can dry. Just like old times. Then I want you to tell me about your day."

I nearly drop the plate in my hands. Luckily, I keep it from slipping, along with keeping my surprised reaction to Beck's comment to myself.

"What could you possibly want to know about my day?" I dry the plate and leave it on the counter.

He hands me another. "What was one thing that made you smile today?"

With a half laugh, I bow my head. "Getting a sense of déjà vu."

"Yeah. This used to be our thing, wasn't it? Hanging with you, well …" He pauses briefly as he moves his hand right over mine. "Sometimes, being with you, it feels like old times."

My breath catches, and I can't speak, so I just nod and pull my hand out of his and continue drying the plate in my hand. I mean, if he's talking about old times, literally anything we did together, including dishes, turned into kissing, then making out, and eventually … sex. I don't think that's what he's talking about though.

And if I say the wrong thing, he'll go cold on me again.

That seems to be a new trait of Beck's.

Although I can't figure out exactly what it is I say that makes his moods shift so easily.

"Beck, I …" I can't find the words to answer him.

He stares at me with a look in his eye that I can't quite read.

He must see the confusion on my face, so he breaks the awkwardness. "It's okay. You can just admit it now. Being here, washing dishes with me, is your favorite part of the day."

Is it? Maybe. Or perhaps it was an hour ago, when we were cooking together and being close. Or even when I woke up this morning and saw him still sleeping but with a soft smile on his face.

I huff, "You wish."

We both start laughing. Like everything is normal. Like he doesn't keep saying and doing things to make me want to smile at him again.

When we were younger, I got into the routine of asking him about his day and to tell me something that made him smile. I'd started doing it because my mom would ask Casey and me the same at dinner, but also because Beck would get a distant look in his eyes sometimes, and I wanted to bring him back to me.

Bring him back to me …

A thought I shouldn't have anymore.

After the kitchen is clean, I go to the bedroom to take a shower and collect myself. Beck has me feeling out of my element, and I need a minute to regroup.

I'm lying in bed, reading, when he walks into the room.

"I'm gonna jump in the shower. Do you need to get in there before I do?"

"No, I'm good. Do you mind if I read for a while? I won't need a light. I have the backlighting on my Kindle, so it shouldn't bother you."

Beck shakes his head. "Nah, I'm good. I'll be out in a few."

When he comes back into the room, I can smell his body wash, which is the same scent as his shampoo and conditioner. He's a low-maintenance guy. He's used the same scent since middle school, and it makes me want to be close to him.

He pulls his covers back from his bed, plugs in his phone on the nightstand, and climbs in bed. I don't dare look directly at him, but I can see it all in my peripheral vision.

He moves around in his bed and then quietly says, "Thanks for dinner. I've … I've missed you."

Not sure I heard him correctly, I just respond with, "Welcome."

Then I stew on if what I thought I heard was that he admitted to missing me.

But that can't be right.

CHAPTER
ELEVEN

BECKHAM

IN THE MONTH since Charlie moved in and school started, it has been less awkward than I thought it would be.

The cot that Lindsay brought over, which is really more like a rollaway bed, is sitting against the only open wall space in the room—between the closet and the door to the hallway—which means I basically have a clear view of her while she's sleeping. And, yeah, I realize that's creepy, but it's been a long-ass time since I've been alone with this girl in a room.

I tug a shirt over my head and walk past her bed, which smells like her coconut shampoo even though she's not in the room.

The other day, she was in here, painting her toenails the deepest shade of pink, and she looked so damn pretty, just sitting at my desk with her leg curled up. She was biting her lip as she concentrated on painting one nail at a time. It took everything in me not to crawl across my bed and pull her by the ankles so she was splayed out in front of me and kiss up her body like I used to.

I let out a groan, just remembering how she'd tasted.

As I sat in bed, I tried to concentrate on my laptop and focus on the screen, pretending not to stare at her.

While my dick can't keep control of itself, my mind is in a good place when it comes to me and Charlie.

Things have changed since she moved in.

She's not the same girl she was when we were in high school. Charlie grew up while we were apart. I can tell by the way she speaks with confidence and that twinge of sass. She navigates campus alone in a way I never would have imagined. She used to need Casey and me for everything. I even like that she goes to the sorority house to spend time with Arbor and Lily. They're good for her. Not like Britney.

Damn, just thinking about Britney makes my fists clench. How could one girl ruin seven years of a good thing?

It's been easy, not talking about the past. I'm good at burying that shit where it needs to be. No need to bring it up. Let's move on, and everything will be good.

At least, that's what I keep telling myself.

And why would I want to worry about past pains when right now, in the present, is going way too fuckin' good.

I've got Charlie sleeping in my room.

My best friend lives down the hall.

And tonight, we won our first home game of the season.

I scored one touchdown and had one hundred thirteen yards rushing. My dad and my sister were there to see it, which made me happy. I know my dad loves coming to watch me play. We've come a long way, the three of us. Brooke and I didn't have the easiest childhood. Not because of my dad, but because my mom was abusive and a severe alcoholic.

Again, past shit I don't like to think about, let alone talk about.

Casey and Charlie's parents drove down with my dad and sister. And because we had an early afternoon game, we went out to dinner at our favorite taco joint with our parents, then met the rest of our friends back at the house.

Now, it's time to party.

While our place is one of the football houses on campus, we rarely have parties here. We made an agreement when we moved in that we would keep the place intact the best we could. So, we're heading out to one of the other football houses to party.

Charlie met up with some of the girls from her sorority after dinner, and I'm not sure if she plans to come to the party. I hope she does, just so I can keep an eye on her. The thought of her hooking up with someone else … yeah, I can't go there. I'm just hoping she makes her way to the party. I don't care if she brings her friends, but I definitely want her there.

With me.

"Yo, Linson. You ready to ride or what?"

Archie comes to my doorway, already dressed in jeans and a *Texas Forever* T-shirt. Charlie will love it because she is a huge *Friday Night Lights* fan. I know she loves that one guy, Tim something. Whatever. That shirt will probably end up in her pile of clothes at some point. She was always stealing my shirts.

Stuffing my wallet in the back pocket of my jeans and my keys in the front pocket, I pop a mint, and with one last swipe of my hand through my hair, I turn from my dresser and toward the door.

"Let's roll, Griff. You looking for anyone special tonight or whoever comes your way, brother? You had a hell of a game today, and you, my friend, deserve to find someone to celebrate with." I egg him on.

"Fuck yes, I deserve to celebrate. I'm covered in bruises from saving your sorry ass from getting pummeled," he says with a jab to my sore ribs.

"Ow. Fuck, Arch," I say, dodging another jab while we walk into the main living space together. "My cage is sore too, brother. Those motherfuckers were gunning after me the whole game. I swear they knew our plays before we ran them. We're lucky we pulled it out today."

"Dude, I'm glad it was you and not me," Casey says from the kitchen. "Anyone need a beer? I need to get my pregame on before we head out. I'm in the mood to blow it up tonight."

Archie and I both agree to the beer, and Casey comes into the room with two beers in each hand.

"You double-fisting, Case?" I ask.

"Did you think I was joking when I said I was ready to get lit? Let's fucking go, man! Where's Pitz? He coming with us, or is he out with that one girl he's been talking to?" Casey asks.

Archie nods and says, "He said he's going to meet us there, but didn't say where he was heading before the party." He takes a drink of his beer, then lifts it up. "Okay, boys, let's gather round."

Casey and I both laugh, knowing what's about to come out of his mouth.

"Let's bow our heads and send a prayer to the man upstairs." Archie drops his chin to his chest, looks at us, and says, "Do it, fuckers."

So, Casey and I lower our heads, look at each other, and smirk. Archie has his eyes closed now, like he's really thinking about what he wants to say.

"May your glass stay full. May your dick stay hard. And may you be in heaven (and by heaven, I mean, pussy) for at least a half hour before the Devil knows you're dead (and by dead, I mean, blow your load). Amen. Let's go, boys. Bring it in." Archie puts his fist out to bump mine, then Casey's.

"Are we walking over or driving?" Casey, still laughing, asks.

"I ain't driving. I'll just walk home later," I say.

"Fellas, I don't plan on coming home tonight. Feel? I'll get a ride home in the morning," Archie says with a wink.

"Dude, just remember to wrap it up. We definitely don't need any baby Griffs running around the world yet." Casey slaps his shoulder.

Archie walks out of the front door first, then Casey. I take my keys out of my front pocket, pull the door closed, and lock it.

The house we live in was built in the '80s and still has the original door handle on it, so I have to lift up on the handle and jiggle it to make sure the lock is in place. Then I step down from the porch stoop and jog to catch up to Casey and Archie.

"Beck, did Charlie say if she was coming tonight?" Casey asks.

"I overheard her talking with someone before she left the restaurant while you were talking to your parents. Sounded like she was going out with some of the girls from the house. I'll shoot her a text later and see where she is."

Casey looks over at me and grins.

"What, fucker? What's the smirk for?"

"Huh? Nothing, man. Nothing at all. Just funny that you're back to texting with her and she's been here for, what, a month?" Casey laughs.

"Fuck off, King. One of us has to keep an eye on her. You've been too preoccupied with Noelle to know what your own twin is up to." I don't mean to sound like an asshole, but he's hitting a sore spot for me.

Casey slings his arm around my shoulders. "Dude, shut the fuck up. You know I'm just playin' with you. I truly do appreciate that you're a stage-five clinger—I mean, friend to my sister." He removes his arm and leans forward toward Archie. "Am I right, Arch?" He punches Archie in the shoulder, who just turns around and looks at us with a smile.

Fucking asshole, always happy and shit.

"Whatever. And where is Noelle tonight? Will we be seeing her? Is that why you're in such a good mood?" I poke.

"Ha! I mean, she might show up tonight, might not. Who knows? I haven't talked to her since yesterday."

"You mean, you guys didn't text all night and she didn't wish you luck today? Wow, you must really be jonesing for her then, huh, buddy?"

Do I want to dig in to my friend? Not really, but now he has me thinking about where Charlie is more than I already was. Dick.

He doesn't say anything, just laughs me off, and we continue walking to the party and recalling the game we played earlier in the day. As we round the corner, we can hear the music coming from the house. Luckily, because we live on campus, and … well, because we're athletes, the party isn't likely to get broken up. Not only is the house literally vibrating from the music, but people are standing on the porch with drinks, and I think there might be a couple banging in the corner.

As we walk in, Archie holds up both arms and says, "Ladies and dicks, the party can begin. I have arrived! Let's get fucked up, motherfuckers! Cowboy up!"

He strolls in with a gallop and moves right into a group of girls who are dancing to the music. He puts his arms around one of the girls while another moves in behind him, so now all three are gyrating. Knowing Archie, I'm sure it's about to become real dirty. He'll likely have one girl—or both—in a bed tonight.

"Let's go find the keg," Casey says.

I nod and follow him through the crowded room and to the back of the house where the kitchen is, but my guess is that they have the keg in the backyard, where we hear some of our teammates yelling, "Chug, chug, chug!"

Two of our teammates and linemen, Chris Schuster and Dan Smith, are holding up our freshman kicker, Leo Morris, by his legs while he's doing a keg stand.

Morris taps out, and as he's brought back down, he spits out beer into the crowd standing near the keg and yells, "Let's fucking go!"

Casey and I look at each other and laugh. This kid is going to be so fucked up tonight. But we've all paid our dues, and now it's his turn. We'll keep him safe. As a team, we never let each other get into a bad situation. We watch out for our teammates.

"KING! Get over here, asshole." Schuster holds his arm in the air, waiting for Casey to reach up for a high five.

They slap palms and pull each other in for a bro hug.

"Dude, I saw your sister inside. I forgot she was coming here this year. Does she have a guy, or is she fair game?" Smith asks Casey.

One minute, I'm smiling, and the next, my gaze snaps to Smith at the mention of Charlie, and I swear I'm ten seconds away from punching my defensive lineman in the face.

"Charlie's here?" I ask, my interest in her whereabouts way too obvious based on these assholes' expressions.

Smith looks at Casey, then back at me and nods. "Yeah, she's in the basement, playing beer pong with some of the guys. She your girl, Linson?"

"What? No. We just didn't know if she was coming here tonight or not." I shrug.

"Yeah, uh-huh." He nods, then says, "Okay, boys, let's head into the house and get some shots!"

Casey turns to follow Smith and nudges my shoulder with a smirk.

"What?" I ask him.

"I'm going in to do some shots. Why don't you go find my sister? You know, make sure she's okay," he says with a laugh, covering it with his fist.

"Fuck off," I mutter as I walk away. To go look for Charlie.

CHAPTER
TWELVE

CHARLIE

WHEN WE GOT to the party, I didn't see my brother or the guys. I wasn't even sure if any of them were coming, but it doesn't stop me from looking for Beck and his beaming grin that he gets after a big win.

I should be annoyed that the first thing I do is look for him, but being around Beck hasn't been so bad lately.

Okay, fine, living with Beck has been awful.

Watching him leave the bathroom in nothing but sweatpants and a naked torso, still damp from his piping hot shower ... awful.

Having to watch his hands when he's doing his laundry and remembering what they felt like, wrapped around me ... the worst kind of awful.

"Come over here. I know these guys!"

Arbor knows one of the players on the team—a new guy I haven't met yet. He brings us down to the basement for a game of beer pong. Now, I'm not trying to brag, but I'm pretty good at beer pong.

It's a guy-and-girl team situation, so Arbor and I can't be on a team together. I'm paired with Brian Haney, whom I met briefly last season. He's a senior on the team this year and not likely to continue his football career after he graduates. Brian is a really nice guy, a lot of fun to talk to, and a killer beer-pong partner.

After a few rounds, I'm carrying my team—aka Brian—to a victory.

"Yo, Charlie, it's your turn, babe. You got this. Two more points, and we win!" he whisper-yells in my ear, thinking he's being quiet.

I fear he was dipping into the keg long before I arrived tonight. It hasn't hurt his game, but I could do without the beer spittle in my ear.

"Bro, Brian, I got this." I turn my crossbody bag to my back to give me a better range of motion. Then with the ping-pong ball in my right hand, I close one eye, lining up my target, and count to three. With a flick of my wrist, I watch that baby sail right into ... the back-corner cup, just barely staying on the table.

"Yeah, baby! That's my girl! Charlie, will you marry me and make me the happiest guy at Walker? I promise I'll take good care of you and I'll never stop you from playing beer pong." Brian is now shouting to the entire basement, which pretty much has our whole group down here laughing.

I mentioned to Brian that a guy I'd briefly dated at State—aka Tony—didn't like that my beer-pong powers surpassed his. It didn't help that I'd gotten partnered with one of his frat brothers and ended up beating him and another girl, who I found out later was his ex-girlfriend. Anyway, that's beside the point.

"Brian, you are the sweetest, truly. But I can't accept your proposal. Besides, if my next boyfriend doesn't *let* me play beer pong, is he really the one for me?"

"True that, true that. Hit me up," he says, holding his fist out for me.

Arbor laughs at Brian, then says, "Okay, guys, it's our last turn, so back it up and let us shoot our shot."

Brian steps back, but then starts to walk toward Arbor and

her partner. "Arbor, if you make this last shot, how about I take you out for dinner sometime? Make me the luckiest guy on campus."

Arbor huffs a laugh. "Bri, you couldn't pay me to go out with you. I think you've dated half the campus by now. Move away so I can shoot. Your distraction techniques won't work on me."

"You wound me. Well, if you won't go on a date with me, how about we just go up—"

He's standing close enough to her now, and she puts her hand directly over his mouth.

"Do not even finish that sentence. Step back, Haney. Watch and learn," she says, and then she takes her shot.

She misses, losing the game for her team, and she has to drink.

Brian basically leaps over to me, lifts me in a bear hug, and jumps up and down with me in his arms.

We're both laughing, and I can barely get the words out to have him put me down when I hear, "Haney, you'd better put her down before I make sure you can't play in the next game."

Yep, I know that voice.

I know that angry tone too. Though it's never been directed at me.

My feet hit the ground abruptly, and I stumble as Brian haphazardly lets me go. My elbow bangs harshly against the corner of the table, and all my body weight pushing on the tender tendon inside my arm makes me cry out in pain.

"What the fuck?! Did you have to drop me, Brian? Fuck, I feel like my arm is broken." I glare at him.

Beckham is at my side immediately. "Charlie, are you okay? Let me see your arm."

"I'll be fine," I mumble, trying to walk around him. The sharp, shooting pain is throbbing in my elbow and radiating up my biceps. I will not cry in front of these people down here, especially Beck, so I need to get upstairs and out the door ASAP.

"Arbor, I'll see you later. I'm going to grab some ice upstairs, then head home."

"Are you sure you're okay, Charlie? Do you want us to leave with you? We can walk you home, or you can come stay with us tonight at the house," she offers.

"I'll walk her home, but thanks, Arbor," Beck answers for me, which just pisses me right the fuck off.

If I wasn't hurting so bad, I'd say something about it, but right now, I just want to get upstairs and out of the house.

I wave at her so she won't hear the shake in my voice. I walk toward the staircase and start climbing the stairs toward the door at the top. I can feel Beckham behind me, but I can't seem to move fast enough. I'm mad, but mostly embarrassed that I got hurt in front of him.

Why did he have to be here? Urgh.

"You don't have to follow me, Beck. I'm fine."

"You're not okay. Let me get you some ice for your arm."

"I don't need a babysitter. This isn't the long walk from psychology class."

"You're right. It's more dangerous. A hurt, beautiful girl, leaving a house party alone late at night. Stop being so stubborn," he says, and I feel his hand touching my uninjured arm to stop me.

"Leave me alone. I'll be fine. I just want to go home." I try to yank my arm out of his grasp, but he pulls me to a stop before we reach the top of the staircase.

Our chests collide.

I still, half loving how authoritative he is over me and half resenting him for it. I look down at our feet and fight the urge to push him away. Like I've been doing for the last couple of years.

For some reason, in this moment, it's not coming as easily.

I blame my damn elbow.

I blame the last month and his ever-protective ways.

Beck places a finger on my chin and lifts my face toward his, forcing me to look up and into his blue eyes. "Come on, Boss. Just stop for a second and let me look at it."

His fingers run along my arm, and I get lost in the feeling of it. The way the rough pads of his fingers brush over my skin, sending waves of gooseflesh up my arm and down to my core.

He's standing one step below me, but it makes us nearly at eye level. He's so close that I can see the dark circle around the blue of his eyes. It's hypnotizing.

He's hypnotizing.

Beckham's left hand grabs my hip with a slight squeeze as his right hand trails up my arm before gently skimming my neck. Then he brushes his fingers over my cheek and tucks a piece of my hair behind my ear, lingering there until his hand moves to the back of my head, tugging me closer.

I can't stop staring into his eyes. I watch his heated gaze move over every inch of my face. Like he's memorizing me. Then he looks at my mouth, then my eyes, and back to my mouth.

"Charlie," he breathes.

I feel like there is a magnetic force pulling me toward him.

One tiny move, and our lips will connect.

My injured arm is tucked tight against my side, but with my other hand, I tentatively touch the biceps of his arm. The move forces me closer into him until our breaths are one as we drink each other in.

My heart is pounding in anticipation. He licks his bottom lip, and I shiver at the sight.

"Tell me what you're thinking right now," he growls, desperation in his voice.

I'm thinking a million things. How much I crave his touch and how having his hand on my hip makes me ache for more of it.

I'm thinking about how I've missed his kisses, so smooth yet consuming. It's taking everything in me to not steal one from him.

And I'm thinking how badly I've missed *him*. Despite the hurt, I want Beckham Linson.

"I'm thinking that the lines between us have blurred and I'm afraid we'll both get hurt."

"You're right," he agrees, and my heart drops. "You've done a damn good job of keeping me away. I should stay away. I should walk back down these steps and let you go."

I feel an ache in my gut as his hand loosens from my hip.

My eyes hold his, and I wait for him to release our gaze. Wait for him to do as he said and walk away.

Because Lord knows I can't.

He moves an inch, and I think he's about to step away. I brace myself, expecting him to leave, when, suddenly, his eyes flash back to mine, determined, and his hand grips my hip once again and pulls me in with a fierceness that takes my breath away.

"Fuck it," he says before crashing his mouth to mine.

I feel his tongue testing the seam of my lips, and they part on instinct as his tongue touches mine.

This kiss is hard, our tongues tangling, and his hand is firm on the back of my head, holding me in place. My fingers dig into his biceps, and I pull him closer to me so I can feel his chest brush against my breasts.

The pain in my arm is all but forgotten as I get lost in his kiss. The feel of his mouth on mine is like coming home. He tastes like beer with a hint of mint. I'm addicted to him, addicted to this kiss. I'm so lost in him that I barely register people moving down the stairs next to us.

His left hand moves to my ass, and he squeezes and pulls me into him even more. There's a throb growing between my legs, and I feel like I could combust just from this kiss and his touch.

I start to move my injured arm so I can wrap it around his waist. I'm desperate to feel more of him. But when I begin to uncurl my arm, I wince, pulling us out of our haze.

Beck leans his forehead against mine, breathing heavily. I

close my eyes and try to gain some control of myself—and I also try not to get teary from the pain in my arm.

When I open my eyes, Beck pulls his head away from mine, looking into my eyes.

"You okay, Boss?" He moves the hand from the back of my head and brushes his thumb lightly across my lower lip.

I can't say anything yet, my words caught in my throat. So, I nod. I know what happened, but for real … *what just happened?*

"I didn't know banging an elbow could hurt this much."

"You'd be surprised how easy it is to injure an elbow. Let's get you home," he says, pressing his lips to my forehead and holding them there for a few seconds.

We take the last few steps to the top. When we open the door, we see Casey, Liam, and Schuster in the kitchen, taking shots. Casey sees us out of the corner of his eye and does a double take.

For a moment, I think my face must look like I've just been thoroughly kissed—swollen lips, flushed cheeks—but then Casey's attention goes to me holding my arm.

"What happened, Char? You okay?" he asks.

"I'm fine. I just bumped my elbow on the beer-pong table. Hit it in just the right spot. You know, the one that hurts like a motherfucker? I just need to put some ice on it. I'll be fine, but I am going to head home. I came, conquered, and once again claimed my Beer Pong Champion title. My day is complete." I try to keep my tone light, but I'm feeling a little lightheaded from the kiss.

Beck reaches for my hand, twines our fingers together, and tugs me closer, like holding my hand is a normal thing. "I got her, man. Going to head home and crash anyway. I'm beat from today."

Casey looks down at our hands, smirks, and nods. "Thanks, brother. I'll be here for a while longer. I'll head back with Pitz unless he leaves with someone."

"Yeah, and you won't be seeing Arch again tonight for sure. I think I saw him head upstairs with a girl before I went to the basement to find Charlie," Beck says to Casey casually.

I look down at our joined hands and start to pull my fingers from his, but he lightly squeezes, holding me in place. His thumb moves once over the top of my hand, and I stop trying to pull away. With one last nod to Casey, we head out of the house together and walk home.

CHAPTER
THIRTEEN

BECKHAM

THE WHOLE WAY HOME, I keep her hand in mine. I don't think I'll ever let her go. I broke the seal, and now I want more of her. I've been patient with her, leaving her notes, special-ordering peonies, and buying more of those pink champagne macarons she likes. Trying to break down her walls and get her to trust me again. But there's no fucking way she's sleeping on that cot tonight. She'll be sleeping in my bed. With me. I don't even care if anything happens. I just want her with me, against me.

That kiss on the stairs ... I couldn't stop it. Her lips were just begging to be kissed. The little bow in her top lip, her puffy bottom lip—all mine. She tastes the same to me, like the strawberry lip gloss she's worn since sixth grade.

"Beck, slow down. My legs aren't as long as yours." She's teasing me—I can hear it in her voice.

"Sorry, I forget you fall behind. Just like when we raced as kids," I say, then look at her and wink.

"Hey now, I got you a few times. But once your legs got

longer than mine, it was tough to beat you. I still held my own though."

It feels good to joke around with her about the past like this. It's been a long time since we've been able to be completely normal around each other. We need to talk about what happened between us in high school because she doesn't know the full or true story. Despite the way I acted indifferently as a result of our breakup, I never really believed it was over between us. And I'm tired of waiting to claim what's mine.

Turning the corner toward my house, I slow my pace. I glance down at her and see she's still staring at our entwined hands.

"What are you thinkin' 'bout, Char?"

"I ... don't really know. I guess I'm wondering what's going on here. Beck, we haven't really been on the best terms the last couple of years. This seems kind of out of the blue, or ... I don't know ... I guess it's a little confusing. My mind feels like it's all over the place. But when you kissed me, it felt like nothing had changed at all."

There is hesitancy in her voice, and I don't like it. What happened was real. And she's not wrong; it felt like everything was back in place.

I stop walking and turn to look at her. Grabbing her other hand in mine, I search her face, seeking confirmation in her words.

"Charlie, every time I'm near you, I want to kiss you. I want to touch you. Just because we haven't been together in a long time doesn't mean you aren't still mine."

I bend my head down toward her and kiss her forehead. When I pull back, her eyes are fixed on mine with tears threatening to spill over. I bring my hand up to her face and trace my thumb just under her eye, where one tear has fallen.

Not wanting to seem too eager, I gently tug her toward the house. When we reach the door, I pull out the keys from my pocket and unlock the door. As we walk in, Charlie pulls her hand out of mine and walks toward the living room.

"Not so fast." With my hand on her hip, I guide her toward the kitchen and settle her against the kitchen counter.

I take a ziplock bag out of a nearby drawer and fill it with ice. When I'm done sealing the bag, I walk back to Charlie and stop in front of her.

Gently, I lift her arm and place the ice pack on her elbow.

She winces at the icy-cold feel. I hold it firm against her skin.

"Nothing cures a wound better than ice," I state.

"Is that a metaphor or something?"

I laugh. "I guess it could be. You've been icing me for years. But, nah, this is what my physical therapist recommends for injuries. You ever do a cold plunge? Now, that really gets the immune system going."

She smiles, and it warms my chest. "I think I'll stick to the ice pack."

We stay like this—me holding the bag to her arm and her letting me tend to her—for a few minutes before I remove the bag from her arm.

"Better?" I ask.

She nods lightly and moves her arm to test the range of motion. "Better."

I step away and toss the bag of ice in the trash.

Charlie runs her hand along her cheek, takes a breath, and moves toward the refrigerator. "I'm gonna get a water. Do you want anything? Are you going to bed now, or do you want to watch a movie or something?" Her words are spoken quickly, like she's nervous.

"Yeah," I state evenly, "I'll take a water. Why don't we watch something in my room? I'm exhausted, and my ribs are hurting a little from the game today."

I'm watching her to gauge her reaction to my suggestion. Her back is toward me now, so I can't see her face, but she stills for a beat as she's reaching into the fridge for the waters.

Pulling two bottles from the fridge, she shuts the door with her hip.

Turning to face me, she walks over and hands me my bottle. We stand there for a minute, just staring at each other. I take a sip of my water. She takes hers as well. I watch her eyes as she opens and closes the cap of her bottle … three times.

She needs time to process how she feels. She needs control.

Lucky for her, she owns me and this moment.

Charlie reaches out her free hand and grabs mine, breaking the silence. "Well, we'd better get you to bed then."

She walks us out of the kitchen and through the house with my hand still in hers.

When she opens the door to my room and looks back at me shyly, I give her a smile to break some of the tension.

"I'll let you pick the movie. I'll even watch one of your girlie movies."

"Aww, aren't you just the sweetest? You know which one I'm going to pick, don't you?"

She lets go of my hand, walks over to her cot, and drops her bag from her shoulder. I notice that she winces a little when she does it.

"Does your arm still hurt? I can go grab you some more ice. I might get some for myself too. I think I need to wrap my left side for a little bit to numb some of the soreness there."

"No, I'm good. It's just a little stiff now, but it'll be fine soon. I think I'll get changed and wash my face and stuff while you're doing that."

"Okay, I'll be right back."

I leave my room and go to the kitchen. While there is a part of me that feels like everything is the same or more so as it should be—us, together—I have a small amount of fear that she might try to push me away again. But one thing I'm sure of is that she kissed me back with full force. She won't forget about our breakup, but she can't ignore our bond and attraction to each other.

I grab one of the ice packs from the freezer and head back to my room. I walk in and go to the closet to get a towel to wrap the ice pack in. I already had an ice pack wrapped around me at the field, but I took it off before my shower. I don't think I need to wrap it with plastic wrap again, but a towel around it will keep my skin from burning from the cold.

Walking over to my bed, I notice the door to the bathroom is slightly open. I drop my water, the ice pack and towel on the bed and see Charlie through the crack in the door. She's bent over the sink, washing her face. She changed into a tiny pair of gray shorts and a white crop top.

Fuck me. I can see the bottom of her tits with the way she's leaning.

I'm getting hard, just watching her, and my pants are starting to get tight. I pull my shirt over my head and throw it into the laundry basket near the closet. I palm my cock through my jeans before I unbutton them, then pull the zipper down. While I'm pushing my jeans down my legs, Charlie opens the door. Her head is down, but when she looks up, she sees me undressing and pauses. Her mouth drops open a little, and—I'm not gonna lie—it makes me feel pretty fucking good about the way I take care of my body. I mean, not that I have a choice with football, but still.

I'm down to my boxer briefs now, and there's no hiding my hard-on. I palm my dick again and watch her eyes follow the track of my hand. I'm getting harder, the longer she looks, but I don't want her to feel pressured to do anything. I really don't care what happens, but she's gonna be in my bed. I can't watch her sleep on that cot for one more night. It's been killing me to be so close to her, to smell her, to hear her little puffs of breath while she sleeps.

"Boss, eyes up here," I tease, but also love that she can't seem to break away from looking at my dick.

"Hmm, what? Oh." She breaks her stare. "Oh my God, sorry. I didn't realize you were changing. Do you want me to go back into the bathroom? Sorry ..." She's looking around the room now, at just about everything but me. "Just let me know when you're done, and I'll come back out."

"Charlie, wait. It's fine. I like that you're looking at me." I drop my voice to a low hum. "I *want* you to look at me."

Closing the distance between us, I reach out my hand and brush some of the loose hair that's fallen out of the bun thing on the top of her head and tuck it behind her ear. She's glancing down at her feet, and I can see the blush in her cheeks now.

"Hey, it's just us. We're gonna get in bed." With my index finger, I tilt her chin up to make sure she's paying attention when I declare, "Together."

Her lips part, and there's a sharp inhale that makes her chest rise and press against mine.

I lean down until my lips are just above hers. "And, no, you're not sleeping on that fucking cot tonight. Pick your movie while I go brush my teeth." When I move around her, I glide my hands down her arms. "I'll be right back."

Clearing her throat, she says, "Okay, yeah, I'll pick something out. Um ..." She pauses and looks at the mattress. "I'll take this side."

Turning my head back to look at her, I say, "Yeah, you know I like to be closest to the door."

Although she doesn't know why I need to be closest to the door because I've never really told her anything about what my life was like before we met.

"Okay, I'll just, uh, grab my pillows and get comfy, I guess."

She's not shy, but I can still tell when my girl is getting worked up, and she is.

I don't reply, but I do smile, then shut the bathroom door. I take a piss—though it's challenging with a hard-on—wash my hands, then brush my teeth. When I open the door, I see her lying in my bed—as she should be. She's propped up with her back on her pillows behind her. She's wearing a little smile on her face now though, and she seems less ... anxious.

"I picked *She's All That,* which you know is one of my all-time faves."

I huff a laugh and nod. Pulling back the covers on my side of the bed, I sit on the edge and reach over to grab the ice pack and towel. I wrap the towel around the ice pack, then scoot back on the bed toward my pillows. "Here, can you hold this for a sec?"

Charlie takes the ice pack from me. "Ah! This is so cold. Why don't you lie down and I can prop it where you need it?"

I nod and lie down while she scoots closer to me on the bed.

"Okay, roll over to your side a little so I can fit this under you." She grabs her small pillow that she likes to hold while she sleeps and rests it on the other side of the ice pack. "There, that should hold it in place for a while. Oh shoot, I forgot my water bottle in the bathroom. Where did yours go?"

"Oh, right. Yeah, I put it on the bed with my ice pack, but it must have fallen off the bed. Can you grab it for me?"

"Yeah, I'll get it. Don't move." She gets up from the bed, goes into the bathroom to get her bottle, then walks over to my side of the bed. "I don't see it, so it must have rolled under the bed."

When she bends over, I can see right down her shirt. It's killing me not to touch her right now.

"Urgh, I can't reach it. I need to try from a different angle."

Now she's turned so her back is to me, and she bends over again, putting her ass within reaching distance. I'm so very tempted. Charlie has the best ass.

"I got it!" she yells out, snapping me out of my ass haze.

"Thanks, Boss. Now get back in here so we can start the movie."

"Okay, do you need anything else? I'm not hungry, but if you are, I'll go grab something."

"Lie down. I'm fine. I'm still full from dinner. Plus, I just brushed my teeth."

Walking back to her side of the bed, she gives me a little smile and says, "Okay, are you ready for this ultimate '90s classic?"

"You act like we haven't watched this a hundred times. I'll even tell you what happens," I say, but she cuts off the rest of my words with her hand covering my mouth.

"No! Beckham Linson, you will not spoil anything. Yes, I know the words to this movie almost verbatim, but you will not ruin it for me." She wears a little scowl on her face, but there is humor in her eyes.

Her hand is still over my mouth, so I lick her palm, which makes her squeal as she pulls her hand away.

"Beck! That's so gross!" But she's laughing.

My hand reaches out to touch her face, and I graze my fingers from her cheek to her lips. "Oh, come on, Boss. You used to like it when I licked you."

Charlie grabs my forearm and quietly asks, "Beck, what are you doing?"

I let her pull my arm down, but I settle my hand on her knee. My thumb brushes her skin, and it makes goose bumps appear on her legs.

"What do you mean, Char? I'm not doing anything. Are you cold? Maybe we should get under the covers," I say with a smirk.

"Okay, buddy, let's just watch the movie." She scoots back over to her side of the bed and fights with the comforter a bit because it got a little tangled when she was helping me with the ice pack.

The movie starts, and we both stare at the TV, but I can't concentrate on anything but the feeling of having her next to me. She's so close that I can smell her hair. Not gonna lie—seeing her shampoo and all the other girlie shit she has scattered around in my bathroom makes me happy. I don't even care that she's a little messy either. I like order. I like to be organized. I thrive on having a schedule. But Charlie, she's more of a works-best-under-pressure and chaos kind of girl.

I love it.

I love *her*.

Still.

Under the covers, our hands are just inches apart. I can't hold back anymore, so I extend my pinkie finger, looping it with hers. She doesn't resist; she curls hers around mine too. We sit like that for what feels like an hour, but it's probably just minutes. She keeps scooting further down the bed, so she's not really leaning on her pillows anymore but lying down, which pushes the comforter below our joined hands.

"Hey, Beck?"

My gaze breaks from our hands and up to her face.

"Yeah, Boss?" I turn our hands and entwine our fingers, but I pull them together and apart, just feeling her skin brush against mine.

"Tell me about your favorite part of today."

She's turned on her side, facing me now, which makes holding hands a little awkward, but I'm not letting go until she does. And I love that she's asking me about my favorite part of the day. When I asked her the other night, I didn't mean to upset her, but it was just something I wanted to know. And being in the same room together, that close together, it just felt right in that moment.

"Hmm ... I would say ... obviously, our win. Seeing my dad and sister. But my favorite-est favorite is being here with you." When I look up from our hands, I see she's staring at my mouth.

"Beck, I ..." She lets go of my hand and moves closer.

I want her to be closer, so I toss the small pillow that's wedged against my ice pack to the floor behind her. "I'll get it for you later," I say as I pull the melting ice pack from my side.

I turn my body slightly to put the ice pack on the floor by my side of the bed and hiss. The bruising will fade in the next twenty-four hours, but it will be sore for a few days. I took some big hits today.

"Are you okay? Are you in pain?"

She starts to sit up, but I grab her arm, halting her movement.

"I'm fine. I've had worse injuries. Now, come here. I want

you closer. We don't have to do anything. I just want to hold you."

I lie back down and pull her toward me. She rests her head on my shoulder and brushes her fingers over my chest. I watch her hand move over the tattoos—a horseshoe for luck and then the *A* that represents our high school mascot, Arrows, on my shoulders. Then the cross on my biceps, then down to my side, where I have a large eagle spreading its wings.

"You've gotten more ink since …" She leaves her words hanging, but I know she means since we were together because she's seen me without my shirt on around the house. "What is this one for?" She traces the four-leaf clover that's right over my heart.

She knows what it means to me, but I think she just wants to hear me say it.

"You know what it's for, Char, but I'll tell you anyway. When I was younger, I moved to this town and didn't know anyone. This girl wearing baggy overalls and pigtails in her hair came barging over to our house. In her hand was a four-leaf clover. She gave it to me and said it would bring me luck. Now, see, being in a new town, it was a big change for me and my sister, so I needed a little luck. And when I took it from her hand, I just knew that she was my lucky charm and everything would be okay."

I place my hand over hers on top of my four-leaf clover tattoo and hold it there for a beat. She tilts her head up to look at my face, and she smiles. This isn't a shy smile; it's a smile that tells me she's coming back to me.

Breaking her gaze from mine, she lowers her head and kisses the tattoo and then lifts her lips to the spot between my neck and shoulder.

Fuck me.

My hand strokes her back lightly, but I move it into her hair, grabbing her messy bun and tugging it a little to bring her eyes back to mine.

"Come here. I need to taste those lips again."

She rises up onto her elbow and leans over me, stopping right before our mouths can touch. The tip of her tongue peeks out, and she swipes it just at the center of her top lip. I'm letting her take the lead from here. I don't want her to feel rushed. I need her to come to me.

"Beck, I don't … I don't know what we're doing, but I don't want to stop."

"Then don't."

No sooner do the words leave my mouth than her lips are on mine.

This kiss is different from the one on the stairs earlier. This kiss is patient and unhurried. Almost like a test. She's taking her time. The strokes of her tongue against mine are smooth, and she sucks on my tongue just a little, driving me crazy. My dick has been hard since we kissed on the stairs, and now it's about to bust through my boxer briefs.

My grasp is still tight in her hair while my other hand plays with the loose neckline of her shirt. I pull it down a little and brush my fingers over the top of her breasts.

Her mouth is still open, and her lips brush against mine while she breathes out my name. "Beck, don't stop touching me."

"I'll only stop when you do, Boss."

She's got one hand on my shoulder while the other drifts further down my abs. She toys with the waistband of my boxer briefs, right next to where my dick has popped out of the top. Slowly, she moves her fingers over to my dick and wraps them around me.

I pull in a breath as she rubs her thumb over the head of my cock, smearing the pre-cum. She pulls back from our kiss, lifts her thumb to her mouth, licks it, and then slides it further into her mouth, sucking.

Even when we were young, Charlie has never been shy about sex or our bodies. We experienced a lot of firsts together, but it was never awkward. It was just … us. She always takes what she wants, and that alone makes me close to blowing my load.

"Charlie, baby, come up here and let me taste you too."

She pulls her thumb out of her mouth and shakes her head. Pushing herself up, she kneels and climbs over me. "Beck, I want this. I want you. I've been thinking about this since the night we went to the store. Before that, do you remember the last time we were together, alone, in your truck?"

She's sitting up, but her hips are moving, rubbing my dick right where it wants to be. Her hands are on my abs, softly stroking, teasing. Her shorts are thin, and she's definitely not wearing any underwear. She's soaked through them, and my dick is gliding right between her center.

My hands are on her waist, and I move them up her sides, lifting her shirt. I play with her nipples, pinching the already-hard peaks.

"Yeah, Charlie, I do. Goddamn, you are so fucking beautiful. Tell me. Tell me what you remember."

Pulling her hands from my stomach, she takes the hem of her shirt and yanks it off and tosses it to the floor.

"Beck, fuck. Pinch a little harder," she says as she slides back and forth on my dick. "My mouth was on your cock, sucking, licking, tasting. You were leaning back against your door, and I was kneeling between your legs. My hands were wrapped around your cock, sliding up and down in rhythm with my mouth. I swirled my tongue around your head, and when I heard you inhale, I looked up. I will never forget the way you gazed down at me. You looked at me like I was a goddess. Like I was your everything. And I believed it. I was so turned on by the taste of you and the look you gave me. Then you told me you were coming, but I didn't pull back. You came in my mouth, and I kept sucking and sliding my hands up and down your cock. I could feel you coming, and I swallowed it all. It was so fucking hot."

"Fuck yes, baby." I'm playing with her nipples while she rubs her core against my hardened shaft. "Are you going to come like this, or are you gonna come sit up here on my face like you did that night?" My hands are moving her hips, rocking her back and forth.

She shakes her head and places her hands on her breasts, squeezing. "No, I'm going to make you feel good. You're sore, and I just want to take care of you. Will you let me take care of you, Beck?"

"Hell yes, but you have to promise me I'll get to take care of you next time."

Instead of pulling off my body, she drifts down my legs, bringing my boxers down with her hands. She lifts up and pulls my boxers off my legs, then starts crawling toward my dick.

"That's it, baby. Crawl to me."

My dick's at full mast. Then she wraps her hands around me, and it makes me suck in a breath. It's been years since I've had her like this.

She leans down and twirls her tongue around the head of my cock while moving her right hand up and down my shaft. With her left hand, she cradles my balls, tugging lightly. She's licking me like a lollipop, and my eyes haven't left her face once. I'm burning this into my memory because, damn ... who needs the past when the present is so fucking sweet?

My hands go to her head, and I brush back the hair that's fallen from her bun. With one hand, I grip her hair in one fist, and my other palm holds her face. I'm letting her set the pace, but it's getting harder to hold myself back from pushing all the way into her mouth to gag her.

Like she can read my mind, she takes me all the way to the back of her throat and gags. Spit drips out of her mouth, making her hand glide easily along my shaft.

When she pulls her mouth off my dick, she looks up at me with a wicked smile. "Does that feel good? Your side ... I'm not hurting you, am I?"

Fuck no, she's not hurting me.

"Baby, the only way you're hurting me is by not having those pretty lips wrapped around my cock. Twirl your tongue around the head like you were doing before."

"Getting a little bossy, Beck? I think I like it."

Her tongue touches the tip again, but instead of taking me in her mouth, she kisses and sucks down the length, and it drives me fucking crazy.

"Turn to the side and let me touch you too. I wanna find out just how wet you are for me."

I pull the scrunchie from her bun, and her hair falls around her face. I gather it in one hand and tug lightly. While I'm still holding on to her hair, my head falls back when she takes me all the way into her mouth again. She moves her hand in tandem with her mouth. It's not gonna take long for me to blow.

She shifts her body so she's no longer between my legs, but on the side of me, never breaking her rhythm. I move her hair to my other hand so I can still see her face and slide my hand down her bare back and between her pussy. My fingers find her opening, and she's soaked. My middle finger runs up and down her slit, and she starts to moan around my dick.

I lift my head and look down at her, and our eyes connect. Her pace slows just a little, and I wonder if she's memorizing this moment like I am. Her eyes tear up, and saliva drips from her mouth, but this, right here … feels like something other than just sex.

This isn't fooling around.

This is more.

And I'm not letting her take it back. We're not going back to what we were the last couple of years.

Her pace quickens, and I match her with my finger sliding in and out of her pussy.

"You want more, Boss? Can I add another finger?"

She hums her approval, and I pull my middle finger out, then plunge my index and middle finger inside her tight hole. I feel her body start to spasm just a little, which brings me closer to my orgasm.

"Baby, I'm gonna come. If you want to pull back, you'd better do it now. You've had me so tightly strung. I'm not gonna last much longer." I'm practically panting at this point, trying to hold on to the last bits of control I can manage.

She pulls her mouth off of me with a pop. "Then do it, Beck. Give me all of it. I'm so close. Keep fucking me with your fingers. Let's come together."

Goddamn, this girl.

She's barely done talking before my balls tighten, and cum shoots down her throat. She moans, and I feel her pussy sucking my fingers in deeper as she starts to come.

Our eyes stay locked, making everything feel heightened. I can still feel her pussy pulsing around my fingers, like I'm sure she can feel my dick twitching inside her mouth.

Pulling her mouth off me, she has a soft smile on her face and says, "You can stop now. I'm so sensitive at this point that I don't think I could wring out another orgasm if I tried."

"Challenge accepted, baby," I say, then flip her over onto her back.

CHAPTER
FOURTEEN

CHARLIE

WE WAKE up the next morning, wrapped in each other. Beck has his arm around my waist, under his shirt I'm wearing, and his hand is cupping my breast. I take a minute to just breathe. Being back in his arms feels like home. It feels like it's where I belong.

I feel his dick between my ass cheeks, and I can't help but rub myself against it just a little.

Beck stirs with my movement, and he groans, "Charlie, baby, what are you doing?"

I do it again because ... well, I'm getting turned on by having him wrapped around me, feeling his hard-on, and hearing that gravelly tone in his voice when he calls my name.

Instead of replying, I take the hand covering my breast and guide it into my shorts, which I put back on before I fell asleep. Keeping my hand on his, I move our hands in tandem over my core. I can feel the wetness as he slides his fingers through my crease and up to my clit. He circles it slowly, and I can't help but start to move my hips, seeking more friction. Kissing the back of my neck, he moves down to the place between my neck and shoulder, which he knows drives me crazy.

"Right there, Beck. Don't stop." In all the years we were together, I never got the chance to wake up in his arms. I had no idea it would turn me on so much.

It feels so good, and if he keeps doing this, I'll come quickly. I need to feel his lips on mine. Without breaking our rhythm, I roll from my side onto my back. I slide my hands up his sculpted abs and chest, making my way to his neck, where I guide his mouth to mine.

"Kiss me."

Beck leans in. My hands are still on the sides of his neck, pulling him closer. He brings his lips to mine teasingly. The tip of his tongue begins to trace the seam of my lips. It's slow, deliberate, and it drives me wild.

I glide my tongue along his, and we savor each other. Our mouths are open while we entwine our tongues, and between this kiss and the movement of his hand in my shorts, I'm feeling feral.

"Beck, I need more."

"What do you need, baby? You want me to suck on your clit?" He pulls my bottom lip into his mouth and sucks. "You need me to fuck you? Tell me, Charlie." His mouth hovers over mine while he speaks, and he licks the line of my lips again.

This time, I softly bite the tip of his tongue, then wrap my lips around it and suck. It makes him groan, and he pulls his tongue out from between my lips.

"You need to be fucked."

He pushes up so he's leaning over me, his arm bracing him. With the hand in my shorts, he takes one side, then the other and slowly pulls them down my hips.

I lift my ass, and he grabs the front of my shorts and pulls them off, watching my face while he does it.

There is a question in his eyes. Instead of answering him with words, I reach down the front of his boxer briefs and wrap my hand around his dick. My hand slides up and down his shaft, squeezing at the tip, where I feel his pre-cum leaking.

"You'd better stop doing that, or this'll end before I get to feel your pussy wrapped around me," he says, pulling my thigh to open me wider. He moves his hand back in between my legs. He takes the wetness from my center and slowly slides it back and forth over my clit.

"Take these off," I say, tugging the front of his briefs down, and his dick pops out. "Mmm ... maybe I should have another taste of you before we fuck."

"Charlie, if I don't get inside you, I might lose my mind. I've been waiting for this for two fucking years." He holds himself steady on his arm, lifts his hips, and pulls his other hand off of me to slide his briefs off.

While I watch him undress, I sit up and take off his shirt that I put on last night.

"Fuck me, I need those tits in my mouth."

Beck leans down and licks the tip of one nipple and then wraps his lips around it and sucks. When I feel his teeth bite down, I slide my hands into his hair to hold his head in place.

"Harder, Beck. Bite me a little harder." I'm practically panting.

He pulls his mouth off my nipple and moves over to the other one. I'm so lost in this feeling that I think I might be pulling his hair.

Beck lets my other nipple pop out of his mouth, and he leans back on his heels. He takes one finger and slowly drags it through my center, then takes it and puts it in his mouth. "Fuck, Charlie. You are so sweet."

He moves between my legs, and I widen them further so he can position himself over me. On his knees, he leans back to look at me. I'm completely open to him now, and the look he gives me makes me feel like he might just destroy me.

Beck slides his hands up my thighs, then under them to grab my ass. He tilts my hips up slightly so his dick can reach my opening. With his hands still cupping my ass, he starts sliding his erection between my slit, which is now so wet that the friction from this movement might just make me come.

"Please tell me you're still on the pill."

"Yes, I'm still on it."

I rock my hips up slightly, and the tip reaches my opening. We both stop and look at each other. With his eyes on me, Beck slowly pushes in. We moan, and then I let out a breath I didn't realize I had been holding in.

He pulls back to his tip, then pushes back in until he's completely covered by me to his base. His eyes haven't left mine.

He stops moving and says, "Charlie, I've needed you. I've waited for you and hoped you would come back to me. I know you're here, but"—he moves his hand over my heart—"I want you here. I know we have so much to talk about—"

"Not now. Let's just be here together. I'm not ready to go backward. All I know is, in this moment, I am exactly where I want to be."

"There's no going back once we start this. I won't survive you leaving me again. You're mine now. And forever. You understand me?"

I see the intensity in his eyes, but also ... he's allowing himself to be vulnerable, and he deserves the same from me.

"Yes."

"Yes what, Charlie? I want to hear you say it. Say you're mine."

"I've always been yours, Beck." My heartbeat is going wild, and I'm not sure if it's because I'm so turned on or because of his words.

"Right answer," he says, pulling back, then pushing in with short movements, like he's teasing me.

"Beck, I need you closer." I slide my hands up his arms and stop at his biceps to pull him to me.

He releases my ass and braces his arms on either side of my head. Without disconnecting from my body, he straightens his legs between mine. He pulls out again, then pushes in. His face is right above mine, and our eyes lock.

"More. I need more." I lift my head just enough to kiss his lips, and he returns the kiss, making it go from soft to hard in seconds. "Don't stop, but go a little slower and keep kissing me," I pant.

He pushes into me again, and he circles his hips enough to put pressure on my clit, driving me crazy.

"Like that?" he asks with a smirk.

"Yeah, that feels good. You feel so good." I start moving my hips in tandem with his, and we kiss again, tongues tangling.

Our pace picks up, and my orgasm is getting closer. Beck pulls back from our kiss and tucks his head into the side of my neck. His mouth is open, and I can feel his hot breath on my skin.

"Are you close?" he asks, mumbling against my skin.

"Yesss. So close," I breathe. "Don't stop."

I can feel my muscles tighten around him, pulling him inside me more. Our pace quickens, to the point that we're almost out of control and our movements are jerky. His head is still tucked into my neck, but I need to look at him when he comes.

"Beck, eyes on me."

He lifts his head, and his mouth hovers over mine, but he's far enough back so that we can look into each other's eyes. When he looks at me like this, it feels like the most erotic moment of my life. I can feel him everywhere.

"Come for me, baby. Let it go. I want to feel that pussy choke me."

We're panting heavily, and our skin is slick. He touches the tip of his tongue to mine, our breaths joining. I don't know how the fuck I went two years without this. Without him.

"I want you to come with me. Come, Beck." My hands hold his ass, pulling him into me while my orgasm takes over, and I moan into his mouth. I lick his top lip while I'm coming down and feel him start to come.

"Goddamn, baby. I missed you so much."

His body is still jerking, which makes my body pulse again.

Neither of us moves as we soak in the last few minutes of this high. His head is next to mine, and I reach up and run my nails through his hair, which makes him shiver.

"I can't move," he mumbles.

Laughing, I tug on his hair lightly. "Well, we can't stay like this forever. I'm starting to get hungry, and I'm sure I need to brush my teeth."

"I need to eat and probably get more ice on my side, although I think you fucked all the pain out of me, baby," he says and tickles me below my ribs.

"Don't make me laugh! You're literally still inside me, and I just felt your cum drip out."

Pulling out of me, he rolls over, props his head on one hand, and slides the other down my stomach and in between my legs. With his middle finger, he circles my clit, then moves to my opening and pushes his cum back into me. "There. That's better."

"Beck, honestly, I'm going to be a sticky mess!" I reach down and cover his hand with mine, stopping his movement.

He brings his finger that was just inside me to my mouth and wipes it along my bottom lip, then lifts it to his mouth and sucks. "Hmm … my stomach is growling. I might just have you for breakfast."

"Stop! You're going to make me blush, and we need to get up. Do you want me to make pancakes? I got that protein pancake mix you guys like. I can add blueberries or something to them if you want." I push his shoulder softly so I can get out from under the leg he has over me.

"Okay, okay. I can't move yet, so why don't you use the bathroom first? Then we'll go eat and see who else is in the house."

Beck lies back and moves his arms behind his head while he watches me walk to the bathroom. "I'll never get tired of this view, Boss."

I look over my shoulder and give him a wink.

I hope I'm not making a mistake here.

CHAPTER
FIFTEEN

BECKHAM

IT'S BEEN a few weeks now since Charlie and I started hooking up again. We haven't really said anything to anyone, but I know our roommates know. Between the fact that we spend all our free time together, we have been laughing at our inside jokes that no one else gets, and the shit job I've been doing of keeping my hands off of her, they know.

We've won our last three games, and she's been there for every one.

I slipped by her and kissed her after our big win yesterday. Instead of facing the onslaught of questions, we got in my truck, and I took my girl to the service road by the tornado siren outside of campus.

Lucky for us, I'd never taken out the blankets and sleeping bags from my summer fishing trip with Casey, so we used those in the truck bed. We watched the stars shine in the big Oklahoma sky, talked about the game and school, and, well, fucked all night.

I can't get enough of her. I feel like I'm making up for the last two years without her.

When we got home the next morning, no one was awake, so we snuck into my bedroom quietly.

Today, however, it's back to campus and the real world.

It's a brutal practice in preparation for the game against our rival this week. My whole body is sore, and I can't wait to go soak in the ice bath after I shower.

I'm pulling my gear off at my locker when Casey walks over and sits on the bench in front of his locker next to mine.

"So … we gonna talk about it, or are you not going to tell me that you and my sister are back together?"

I knew it was coming, but I really wanted him to be the one to ask. Not because I'm embarrassed or I feel weird about it. Casey knows I love Charlie and never stopped. He also knows the true story of what happened and why I never spoke up when Charlie blamed me. Granted, he didn't know it was all connected to issues with my mom, but he knew my side—at least as much as I could share at the time.

"Do I need to tell you we're together? I thought it was pretty obvious," I say with a smirk.

"Dude, I don't need to know any details. I saw the kiss and live in the house, and even though my room is at the other end of the hall, I can hear just fine. I'm on my fifth audiobook this week alone, and I'm pretty sure Noelle is sick of me stopping by her place too. I've ignored it as much as I could because I know you two need this time together. I just want to know everything is okay. I also want to know that you are going to tell her what really happened. She needs to know."

His brow is raised, and I get it. He's on my side, and he has been loyal and kept things between us.

I sigh. "I know, but I feel like we're in a really good place right now. I just got her back, and I don't know if I'm ready to bring it all back up."

"I think you need to give Charlie more credit than that. She knows you. I think once you tell her what Britney did, it will really close that up, and you guys can move on without any secrets between you. You owe that to her and to yourself too. Look, you're my best friend, but you keep things locked up tight. I don't know if I fully understand why you didn't tell her to begin with, but I know you don't like talking about your feelings and shit." He snorts.

He's right. I don't like talking about my feelings. Neither of them knows this, but I've spent years in counseling, trying to learn how to cope with things that happened to me before we moved to Troy. Casey and Charlie don't know why we moved or why my mom isn't in the picture. I know, someday, I'll have to tell Charlie because I will be wifing her up and she'll need to know. I can't keep my secrets about my mom forever.

My current coping method is stuffing the pain of the past into a tiny little box in the back of my mind and ignoring it all so I don't have to think about it. And I've been on an intentional hiatus from counseling because of football. I can't focus on what I need to do on the field and also *find my feelings*. Not happening. I do make a point to check in with my therapist semi-regularly though; that's actually what I was doing that day I ran into Charlie and Bo as she was looking for her psych class. I know he's there when I really need to talk.

"I will talk to her eventually. We can't go into this completely until she knows the truth. There are days I'm still just mad at myself for not fighting for us, but I promise, I'll fix it all."

I hold out my fist for Casey to bump. He is more than my best friend; he's been like a brother to me. I won't ever let him down. Loyalty and honesty are everything to me, and Casey is the real-deal, forever kind of friend. He doesn't fully understand what he and his family have done for mine.

His parents know what went down with my mom and why we moved. They've never made me and Brooke feel like there was anything wrong with us because of it either. I don't even know when my dad told them because they've always treated us the same. Like part of their family.

Right before Charlie and I broke up, it was a really rough

time, and her mom helped me through it. My therapist said she was surprised I didn't have more complex feelings toward women because of what my mom had done to me. But Carol? I knew she was a good egg from the minute I met her. She was the kind of mom that moms should be for their kids. Something I never had.

"I'm going to head home and shower there. Are you coming?" I ask Casey while I rip off the rest of my leg pads, then grab my sweats and pull them on.

"Dude, no. I can't leave here without a shower, and you shouldn't either. You smell like ass." He laughs as he whips me with his towel.

I finish dressing and grab my wallet, keys, and bag from my cubby. "Ow, man. Honestly, I just want to get home so I can bang your sister before you all get back." I bark out a laugh, then duck as Casey tries to whip me again, but closer to my face this time.

"You'd better run, motherfucker. I don't need to know any of that!" Casey yells at me as I bolt toward the door.

I turn my head before I walk out and give him a wink, and he just laughs and mutters, "Fucker."

When I get home, I see Charlie in the kitchen. She's got a spoon in her hand, stirring something that I can't see yet.

I drop my bag by the door, then come up behind her and wrap my hands around her waist. "Smells good in here. What are you doing, Boss?"

She squeals and puts a hand over her heart. "Jesus, Beck. You scared the shit out of me." With her other hand, she pulls out an earbud. "I didn't hear you come in. You're just getting home? Where are the other guys?"

I skim my nose along her neck and place a kiss behind her ear. "They're still at the field house, getting showered. I wanted to get home to you and see if I could steal a few minutes before they got back."

"Yeah, before any of that happens, you need to shower. You stink!" She giggles.

"I was hoping you would join me. I'll give you a little massage, rub you down … in all the right places," I say, sliding my hands up and down her sides over her long T-shirt, making her shiver.

"Babe, while that sounds amazing, I think you need to focus on your own stink for now. Besides, I need to get the brownies in the oven. How about a rain check?" She turns her head and kisses me.

I mumble against her lips, "Are you sure? I can think of some ways to make you a little dirty."

Reaching around her, I swipe my finger into the brownie batter. With my other hand still on her hip, I turn her around to face me. She's so fucking sexy with her little smirk.

"Wanna have a taste?" I ask, then move my hand up to coat her slightly parted lips with the chocolate batter.

The tip of her tongue peeks out, and she touches it to the center of her top lip and then across her upper lip. When she starts to lick the bottom, I stop her.

"Uh-uh. It's my turn."

Leaning in, I take her bottom lip between mine and suck. When I pull back with her lip between my teeth, she moans, then grabs the back of my neck to pull me back into her.

Before she kisses me, she says, "Okay, but let's make it quick. I would absolutely die if one of them walked in on us."

I waste no time grabbing the hem of her shirt and pulling it off. She's not wearing a bra, and her little shorts are giving me plenty of room to play.

Dipping my finger back into the batter behind her, I take a hefty dollop and trace some around one nipple and then the other. When I look at her face, her cheeks are starting to turn pink, and her hands are gripping the edge of the countertop.

She whispers, "More."

I move the bowl from behind her to the side so I have better access. This time, I take two fingers and coat them in the batter and bring them back to her chest. Starting in the center between her tits, I trail my fingers down her torso. I stop just above the band of her shorts.

Using my other hand, I grab the front of her shorts and bend slightly to pull them down her legs. She steps out of them as I rise.

"I should probably clean up my mess, huh?" I frame her face in my hands, and she nods.

Moving my hands, I cup her breasts, lean in and twirl my tongue around one nipple, then suck it into my mouth. When I pull back, her nipple pops out of my mouth, and I kiss the tip before moving to the other breast. I repeat the movement, but this time, I bite down lightly, which causes her to bring her hands to my head. Her fingers slide through my hair as she lets out a soft moan.

"That feels so good, Beck. Holy shit, keep going."

"Oh, baby, I'm not even close to being done with you."

I lift my body, and her hands fall from my head. Then I reach back into the batter before I make my way down her chest and stomach with my tongue.

When I get to her center, I get on my knees and look up at her. Her eyes are glazed, and she's holding her bottom lip between her teeth.

"Open for me, baby." I smooth my unbattered hand down from her hip to her inner thigh while she spreads her legs. "That's better."

I lean in and place a kiss on her pussy. "So pretty."

One hand opens her center, and I lean in to kiss her clit. When I pull back, I look up at her again, but this time, her head is tilted back slightly, and her eyes are closed, her palms flat on the countertop.

With my brownie-battered fingers, I start at her clit and slide them down to her opening. Bringing my fingers back up to her clit, I slowly circle them, then lean in and lick.

"Fuck, Beck. Do that again."

So, I do. Running my tongue back and forth from her clit to her center. Her hips start to thrust, so I slide one hand around to her ass and help her move in sync with the swipe of my tongue.

"Are you gonna be a good girl and come for me, Charlie?" I ask when I pull away.

"So good. I'll be so good. I'm almost there, Beck. Keep going, but add a finger."

Is there anything hotter than my girl telling me what she wants? I think not.

So, I lick my fingers clean before I lean back in to circle her clit with my tongue and slide my index finger inside her pussy. I pump in and out and start to increase my pace with my tongue and finger, moving in time with her thrusts.

"Beck! I'm going to come. Fuck, don't stop," she demands, breathing heavy.

I pull my finger out and slide two fingers into her, finding that spot that makes her see stars, and I suck hard on her clit. My hand on her ass holds her in place as she reaches her orgasm.

Feeling her pulse around my fingers and tongue, I slow my movements. She's moved her hand back onto my head, holding me in place. As her hold softens, I remove my fingers and pull back.

When I stand, she reaches for me, bringing me in for a kiss. I slide my tongue into her mouth, twirl it around hers, and moan.

"I think you should make brownies more often."

COUNTER PLAY 119

"Beck, I didn't even get them in the pan. And now I have to start all over again since you mixed me in with the batter!"

Resting my forehead against hers, I tease, "But it was worth it, right?"

"More than worth it, but I think our time is up. I need to get dressed before the guys start walking in. And you still stink, babe."

"Okay, I'm going. If you make more, don't let them eat all the brownies before I'm out."

"I'll save you the best piece, Beck," she says and blows me a kiss.

I turn around and head toward my bedroom, but look over my shoulder and say, "I'm counting on it, Boss."

CHAPTER
SIXTEEN

CHARLIE

AFTER PUTTING my shorts and shirt back on, I wash and rinse out the bowl, then grab the other box of brownie mix from the pantry. Thank God for BOGO deals. This new batch can wait though.

Knowing he came home early to spend time alone with me just really works for me in all the best ways.

I check the clock and see it's been about thirty minutes since Beck got home. I'll put a pause on this until I get cleaned up. I'm sure there are still traces of batter on me and no doubt my clothes. I turn the oven off before heading back to the bedroom. I pull off my T-shirt and shorts again once I close the bedroom door and lock it.

I see the bathroom door is cracked and steam is coming out. He's listening to "I Feel Like I'm Drowning" by Two Feet. Nice pick and perfect for what I'm about to do.

I slide open the glass shower door, and he looks at me over his shoulder with a smirk.

"I had a suspicion you might come in here. And, baby, I'm so glad you did."

Stepping into the shower, I reach my hands around his waist to the front of his body. I glide one hand up his chest and the other down to his erection. He was either thinking about me before I came in or he really was expecting me to join him. Either way, I win.

Slowly, I start to stroke him. I'm gentle in my movements, and despite the heat of the water, he gets goose bumps. He starts to turn, but I pull him tighter into my body.

"Not yet. Let me play for a few minutes."

"No way am I letting you have all the fun. I want to play with you too, Boss. Now, come on. Let me have you." He puts one of his hands over mine, firmly stopping me from moving and squeezing his erection.

With one final tug, I let my hand fall. "Fine, but I'm calling the shots."

When he turns to face me, I have a smile on my face. Again, either way, I'm winning here, and I have no doubt we're both going to walk out of this shower happy. Two orgasms within thirty minutes—yay, me.

Beck combs his hands into my hair and looks at me with so much heat in his eyes. I bring my attention down to his length and can see the pre-cum leaking out already. This won't take long. Looking back up at him, I lean forward and kiss him. It's sloppy, wet, and greedy. I wrap my arms around his neck and pull him in closer to me.

He takes one hand out of my hair and moves it down my body, stopping at my breast to pull on my nipple—a move that he knows turns me on. It makes my center throb. I love it when he plays with my nipples. His hand finds my center, and he groans when he finds me still slick from my orgasm in the kitchen, his fingers easily slipping into my heat.

Beck breaks the kiss. "Baby, I think you couldn't wait to get into this shower with me."

"Listen, all you had to do was kiss my neck behind my ear, and I was ready. You play those dirty tricks on me, and I melt.

You have this special voodoo over my body. And now I want to taste you." My hands move down and over his chest, making their way to his erection. "Can I taste you, Beck?"

One of my hands takes ahold of him, and the other slides between his legs. I pull on his balls. He hisses, then leans in to kiss me hard. Our kiss becomes frantic and slightly out of control.

We're both panting when I pull back and drop to my knees.

He places a hand on my cheek. "Boss, I'm not sure we have time for this, and I need to be inside you—like, right now."

My response? I hum around the crown of his cock.

He tips his head and grumbles, "Fuuuck."

With one hand still tugging on his balls, I move my mouth up and down his length in tandem with my other hand. I only have the chance to suck him in a few times before he pulls me up by my elbows.

"I can't wait, baby. Turn around and put your hands on the glass," he says as he moves his hands up and down my body before reaching to the front and palming my breasts.

With his knee, he separates my legs, and I feel his cock sliding between my ass cheeks.

One hand still on my breast, he moves his other hand to my hip. "Tilt your hips and let me in."

I spread my legs a little more and lean forward so my hips tilt up to reach his erection.

"That's it, baby. Look at you, so wet for me. You couldn't wait for me to get inside this pussy."

The head of his erection enters me, and my breath catches as he pushes in. We've never done it like this before. Sure, he's been behind me on the bed, but never standing like this. It doesn't feel as deep, but more like a tease. He slowly moves in and out, and when I turn my head to look at him, he's watching our bodies come together.

"Fuck, baby. This is so hot. I'm not going to last long like this.

Does it feel good? I'm about to lose it," he says as he gazes at me with a feral look in his eye.

My words are stuck, so I just nod. I feel like I might cry, which makes no sense, and I'm slightly embarrassed. I cannot start crying while we're having sex. He must sense it—of course he does—because he gives me a soft smile and moves his hand on my breast to my jaw and pulls me toward him.

He places the softest kiss on my lips before saying, "I just want to stay here. Right in this moment with you."

This time, I can't help it, and a tear drops down my cheek. I kiss him with a smile on my lips, and I feel him smile back while our lips meet.

"Always, Beck. Always with you."

Pumping into me deeper now, he picks up his pace while holding my hips. Our eyes are still locked as we fuck. We know we don't have much alone time left, and our urgency grows to a boiling point. It's getting faster and more frantic. My legs are starting to shake from trying to stay in this position, but I need to come, and I'm afraid if we stop to shift positions, I'll lose it. So, I keep one hand planted on the glass, and with my other hand, I reach down to play with my clit.

"Oh fuck. You playing with your pussy, Boss? That's it. Keep stroking it while I go deeper. You feel so good, baby. Are you getting close? I can't hold it much longer. You feel too good." His breathing is ragged now, and he's ready to lose control.

"Ye-yesss … go a little deeper. I'm almost there," I pant.

"Fuck yes! Motherfucker …"

He groans out his release, and he squeezes my hips so hard that he might leave bruises. I hope he does because this is … hot.

He's lost in his release when I explode. White-hot shots of pleasure seep into every nerve in my body. My clit pulses under my fingertips, and I feel like my core is pulling Beckham inside me even more.

I don't know if sex with him is so good because it's us or if it's because it's been so long since we were together. Or since I've been with anyone really. Either way, I'm here for it.

My head leans on the glass as I come down.

I can still feel him pulsing inside me when he places a kiss behind my ear and says, "Us. Always us," like he read my mind.

CHAPTER
SEVENTEEN

BECKHAM

THIS WEEK IS our game against our rival, Chandler State. Because our games got to the point of violence and campus destruction in the past, we can't play this game on either campus. We play in a stadium that is considered neutral territory between our campuses. It's a huge event that is really similar to a playoff game. This game holds a lot of stakes, and it usually predicts who will win the division championship.

Our bus arrives at the stadium. Casey and I always sit together on the bus, so we walk together to the locker room, both with our headphones on. My head is down and bobbing to my hype playlist when I feel Casey nudge me with his elbow. I look up at him, and he tilts his head to the side, where we see Charlie standing with Arbor and Lily. We're not really supposed to break the line, but Coach is so far ahead that he won't notice me run over to her.

When I reach her, she's smiling with a slight hint of pink on her cheeks.

"Hey," she says loud enough over the crowd cheering for us. "You look good, Linson. That suit really works for me."

Arbor and Lily laugh next to us, and I look at them and nod.

"Ladies, thanks for coming out today. Charlene, you look like … mine." My eyes widen at the number on the front of her jersey. "Turn around. Whose name is on your back?"

"Well, you see … I have this one jersey that I usually wear—you know, with my name on it. But the girls thought maybe this one was more appropriate for tonight. What do you think?" She bites her lip and then turns around, moving her hair to the side to show me my name on her back, and she looks at me over her shoulder with a smile.

I grasp her elbow and turn her back around. Leaning in, I kiss her on the lips and whisper, "When we get home, you're wearing that jersey while I fuck you."

"Promise?" she asks.

Nodding, I pull her into me and kiss her again quickly, knowing I need to get into the locker room.

Casey is standing near us and shouts, "Linson, let's go. Bye, ladies. We'll see you later, I'm sure."

Arbor and Lily giggle and wish him luck as he starts to walk away.

Charlie pushes my chest to encourage me to start to move. "Go win me a game, Linson. And if you do, you'll get a prize when you get home later."

"Oh, baby, you'd better make good on that promise because I assure you, we'll win." I walk backward as I talk, and with a final wink at her, I turn and head toward the locker room.

It's not a complete blowout, but we are pretty much destroying Chandler State. This win will knock them out of playoff contention and secure our spot as the division champions.

We're in the fourth quarter with five minutes left on the play clock. Our defense is in right now, and State has the ball on the forty-two-yard line on third down.

Their quarterback snaps the ball, but our defense reads the play quickly, and two of our linebackers rush up the middle in a cross-dog blitz that State doesn't see coming. This block makes it fourth down, and with nothing left to lose, they run another play. One of our top defensive ends stops the play by leaping over the center and sacking the quarterback.

A whistle blows, and we see a yellow towel thrown onto the field. A false start is called on the defense and goes under review. We're all standing impatiently while the refs review the play on the monitor. A few minutes later, the lead ref announces there was no false start, and we resume play.

Running back to the sideline, our defense is hyped up, getting in our faces and smacking our helmets to pump us up. The energy on the sideline is like a playoff game. Wins against our rival team are a big deal. We're ready to lock this in and head home.

Pitz played the first quarter and did okay, but the score was neck and neck, so Coach put Callaway in.

Bo is an enigma. This kid is something special on the field. There's no doubt he'll go pro and likely before his senior year. I know he's already heavily scouted, and he's a true freshman. Barring any injuries, this guy will be a huge name in pro football someday.

Our offense runs out onto the field and gets into a huddle on the thirty-five-yard line. Bo calls a play-action pass, which is a fake pass off to me, but he'll turn to the other side of the line and throw the ball off to Casey. The goal is to get Casey as far down the field as possible and this play should give him the time to do that. It'll all happen so fast that it'll make the defense think I'm in possession of the ball and moving down the field.

We break and get into position.

Bo shouts, "Red one! Red one! Alamo!"

Then he claps, and the ball snaps from the center right into his hands. Bo turns to me on his right and fakes the pass. He spins around as I take off running down the field with my arms folded, as if I were holding the ball. From my peripheral vision, I see Casey pass the fifty-yard line and turn slightly just in time to catch a beauty from Bo. With the ball in hand, Casey takes off with one of the cornerbacks right on his heels. The cornerback reaches for the back of Casey's jersey, but Casey jerks out of his hold and makes it to the thirty-yard line before one of their safeties comes at him from his right side and tackles him.

Casey gets up from the tackle and runs back to the huddle. "Let's fucking go!"

He has a huge smile on his face, and we all slap his helmet and laugh. Casey has worked hard for this spot, and he's been proving himself in every game we've played.

Bo calls the final play. With one minute forty seconds left on the clock, he hands it off to me with Archie blocking the defender. I score the last touchdown of the game, securing our win.

As I rush off the field toward the sideline, I look up. Instead of seeing my girl waving her arms, my eyes collide with the one who took her away.

Britney.

CHAPTER
EIGHTEEN

CHARLIE

ARBOR, Lily, and I are jumping around in the stands, watching the team bounce around the end zone, celebrating their win. I'm so unbelievably proud of Beck, Casey, and all the guys. I know it'll be a big party on campus tomorrow night.

We decide to stick around so we can congratulate the guys after the award ceremony. A gold cowboy hat is passed back and forth between the teams for whichever one claims the win each year. The Stallions have had the hat for the last three years, so it'll return to campus with us. You would think it was a championship game with the way we celebrate this win.

Our seats are near the first row because we used my family tickets. My mom, dad, Beck's dad, and his sister watched the game with us, but they've already started to make their way down to the family waiting room to see the guys after the game.

Eyebrows were raised when our families saw I was wearing Beck's jersey and not my brother's. I don't really think they were that surprised though.

Arbor nudges my side and points down to the team bench, where I see Beckham waving his hand, motioning for me to come to him, so I go down as close as I can. The brick wall between us is low enough that he can reach me as I make the last step to him.

He's sweaty and smelly, but I couldn't care less. I lean down and wrap my arms around his shoulders and drop my head to kiss his lips. We laugh and kiss like there's no one around.

When I pull back and smile at him, he quietly says, "We did it, baby. The hat is ours for another year."

"I'm so proud of you guys! Casey must be going wild right now about his catch. I can't wait to see him. Should we go down to the family waiting area or go ahead and take off?"

Waving one of the stadium security staff over, Beck asks, "Where can I let my girlfriend and her friends enter the field for the award ceremony?"

I blink at his affectionate term. Yes, we're together again, yet we haven't had any official talks. His public proclamation feels good while I also feel like we're rushing back into something we haven't completely worked through.

My brain has all these thoughts while my heart is leaping out of my chest.

The man leans in so Beck can hear him over the noise and then waves me over. "Take this row all the way down until you reach the top of the locker room tunnel. There is a gate at the end, and I'll radio the guard down there to let you and your friends onto the field."

"Do we need an additional pass or anything to get onto the field?" I ask.

Beck pulls me in again. "Baby, you have my name on your back and a family pass around your neck. They'll let you in." He gives me one more quick kiss and turns to walk away, but looks over his shoulder and says, "Hurry up and get your sweet ass down on this field!"

I shake my head and smile, then turn to Arbor and Lily. "Well, you guys want to go with me or—"

"Are you out of your mind? Of course we want to go down

there with you!" Lily screeches. "I've had my eye on Chris Schuster, and I feel like he needs a congratulatory hump—or hug or whatever."

Arbor and I just laugh, and the three of us start to make our way to the entrance of the field.

When we reach the guard, he already has the gate open, and he lets us in with a nod.

We each say, "Thank you," as we pass, and Lily nearly trips down the steps because she's so excited.

"This your first time on the field?" I ask.

"College? Yes. In high school, I was a cheerleader, so I was on the field all the time. But this is so much more fun! I'm surprised the crowd didn't rush the field, honestly. Do we just walk over to where they are, or do we wait by the benches?" Lily asks.

Arbor cuts in and says, "We can go over to where the team is, right, Char?"

I'm in the middle of them so I grab both of their hands and look at each of them and say, "Let's go see those boys and congratulate them properly!"

And then we start running toward the team.

The team is still jumping around, high on their win. Bro hugs, bouncing, and cheering wildly. It's always great to win, but this was a big one, and I love to see these guys soak it up.

The announcer calls the coach over to where the camera crews are and where the hat will be brought out. Then the team gathers around.

The announcer asks, "Coach, how does it feel to win the Golden Hat four years in a row?"

"It feels real good. Real good, Hank. These boys played their hearts out today, and they put everything into their performance. We dominated on offense and defense. We never let them run us over. The seniors on this team …" He starts to choke up a little. "This is their final game against State. They not only won today, but they have *owned* this hat every season of their time at Walker.

That's something to be truly proud of, and I couldn't be prouder of all these guys."

The team surrounding him starts to cheer, and we can barely hear the rest of the coach's speech.

The announcer breaks in and says, "Let's get this trophy out here so you can take it back to Walker again!"

He steps back as officials bring out the Golden Hat to present it to the coach.

They hand it off to Coach as red and white confetti starts to rain down on the team and us. I look at Arbor, who is laughing and trying to catch some of the confetti in her hands.

"This is so much fun!" She drops to the ground and starts moving her arms and legs in a sweeping motion.

Lily looks at me, raises her eyebrows, and smiles. "Don't let us get run over, Charlie!" Then she drops down next to Lily.

"You two are wild!" I say, laughing.

When I look back at the team, Archie has the hat on his head.

He holds his index finger up and shouts, "There's only one! Only one, baby! Let's go!"

Then he takes it off and hands it off to Beck, who kisses the hat, then sets it on his head. I can't help but laugh at them as we watch them pass the hat around to each guy on the team. The photographers call out to the team and ask them to get together for a team photo. Some guys stand, some crouch, and some lie right down on the field. Coach stands in the middle of it all with a huge smile on his face.

Beck breaks away after the photos are taken and starts to walk toward me.

I turn to Arbor and say, "Be right back!"

Then I take off running to him. When I reach him, I leap up, and he catches me in his arms. I wrap my legs around his waist while he puts his hands under my ass, and I kiss him. I intended it to be a simple kiss, but he slides his tongue into my mouth, deepening it. I'm getting lost in the moment, but in the background, I hear some cheering and even see a flash go off in my peripheral vision.

Pulling back from the kiss, I hold Beck's face in my hands. "I'm so proud of you guys! I can't wait to celebrate."

"Oh, we'll be celebrating. Tonight, tomorrow, probably all week!" He laughs, then sets me down. "I have to get back to the team. I'll say goodbye to my dad and Brooke before we get on the bus to head back to campus, so I can tell them you left if you don't want to stay."

"Uh ... yeah, we'll probably head back to campus now that the stadium has emptied out a bit. Hopefully, traffic won't be too bad on our way home. Just tell everyone I said goodbye, and I'll call my parents on our way to campus."

I tilt my head up with my lips puckered, asking for one more kiss. He complies, then touches his forehead to mine.

"I'll see you at home." Beck turns to walk away, stops, and turns back. "Oh, and, Charlie, I expect you to be waiting in bed wearing nothing but my jersey." He winks, then turns back around and heads toward the rest of the team, who are standing together in front of the band, playing our anthem.

As I watch him walk away, I can't believe how we got back to this place so effortlessly. I guess it was inevitable that we would get back together, but thinking about where we were last year and the year before ... I would have said a big fat *hell no* if someone had told me we would be a couple again. And I know there are things we're avoiding that we will need to resolve if we're really going to make this work. I just need to find the courage to bring it up. I don't want to risk us falling back into a bad place. I know, without a doubt, he's meant to be mine.

When I walk back over to where Arbor and Lily are, they have an odd look on their faces.

"What's wrong?" Looking between them, I wait for someone to say something. "Arbs?"

She clears her throat. "I'm not sure how to tell you this, but I just saw Britney walking off the field with some girls."

I suck in a deep breath. Since we played Chandler, I wondered if she would make it to the game. I mean, it is one of the biggest games of the season for both teams. I just hoped I wouldn't see her.

"Which way?" I ask, standing frozen, stomach churning.

"Looks like she's leaving out the tunnel across the field from ours. You know what? Who cares? You can't let her get in your head. We probably shouldn't have said anything because she's irrelevant." Arbor waves her hand in front of her like she's brushing Britney away.

Lily walks up to me and puts her arm around my shoulders. "Babe, I don't know the story, but I'm guessing it has to do with Beck. But you seriously have nothing to worry about. That boy is so far gone for you. And besides, you're so much prettier."

I know she's trying to make me laugh, but the truth is, Britney is pretty. "It's fine, really. Let's just go back to campus. I didn't see her, she didn't see me, so it's like it didn't happen."

Arbor and Lily look at each other again.

Then Arbor looks at me and says, "Yeah, totally. I'm sure she didn't see you."

"Okay, ladies, let's get out of here. I want to hit some of the parties on campus and see if I can find my latest conquest." Lily hooks her arm around Arbor's, then mine, and we start walking toward the exit we came in from.

"Count me out. I want to be home when Beck gets back." With one last look at the team, then around the field to make sure I don't actually see Britney, we leave.

CHAPTER
NINETEEN

BECKHAM

"OKAY, boys. Where are we going to celebrate tonight?" Pitz walks over to Archie and slings his arm around his shoulders.

"No can do, Pitzy. I have someone to see, and I plan to celebrate all night long." He smirks and looks over at me and winks. "I think Linson has the same idea. Right, brother?"

Casey makes a gagging noise. "Dude, that's gross." Which just makes Archie laugh.

Shaking my head, I smile and finish packing up my bag. I can't wait to get home to my girl. The faster we can get out of here, the faster I can get to her.

"Let's move it out, team. We have a bus to catch," Coach yells into the room.

I turn to Casey. "I'll meet you on the bus."

He likes to take his time packing his bag, but I'm too anxious to sit around and wait for him.

When I walk out of the locker room, there are still some family members hanging out in the hallway. I saw my dad, sister, and the Kings before I went into the locker room to shower earlier and got to say goodbye to them then.

I turn the corner to exit the stadium toward the bus and hear my name being called. I almost don't look because I'm used to fans cheering for us or the opposing team's fans heckling us. But this voice ... sounds familiar.

"Beckham Linson!" I hear again.

Turning toward the voice, I see Britney standing with two other girls, who look just like her. Basic.

What the actual fuck is she still doing here?

I start leaving, ready to ignore her, but then I hear her say Charlie's name to one of the girls.

Walking toward her, I say, "You can keep her name out of your mouth. Go back to Chandler, Brit."

"I was just saying that I thought it was funny to see Charlie in your jersey after everything that happened last year."

Shifting my bag to my other shoulder, I sigh. I know I should just walk away and ignore her, but curiosity gets the best of me. "Why would that be funny?"

"Oh, you don't know?" She pauses. "I guess you wouldn't. I mean, why would she tell you about all the guys she hooked up with after Tony broke up with her last year?"

"Ha! Yeah, okay, Britney. Go home." I start to turn again, but she keeps talking, halting my track to the bus. Gripping the strap of my bag tighter, I turn back to face her.

"She slept with half of Greek Row, Beck. It was sad, really. I can't say I blame her for running home. I would be embarrassed, too, if I was rated the worst lay on campus."

She and her friends look at each other and laugh.

Here's the thing I think Britney is forgetting here. I've known Charlie a lot longer than she has. Not for a second do I believe anything coming out of her mouth. Does it still sting? A little, but only because I do know she was with Tony for a while. And I also think she dated him to try to forget me.

What really makes me angry though is that she is lying—again—and disrespecting my girl.

"Britney, I'll say it again. Go. Home. You're pathetic, thinking you could ever change my mind about Charlie. I have loved that girl since we were kids."

"What the fuck are you doing here, Britney?" I hear Casey say before I see him come to stand next to me.

"Hi, Casey. It sure is good to see you. You've gotten much better-looking since high school." She winks at him.

"Fuck right off, Brit. And don't even think about trying to mess with my sister again." He points his finger at her, seething.

"Settle down, Casey," she huffs. "Isn't it funny though—how easy it was for Beck to stand up for Charlie and not believe me?" Then she turns to look at me. "Too bad Charlie couldn't do the same for you in high school, Beck. I guess she didn't care about you as much as you do her. It was so easy for her to walk away from you. But I am curious about something. Why didn't you ever tell her the truth?"

Casey steps closer to her and her friends. "Take your manipulative, lying ass out of here. How did they let you stay anyway? You're definitely not anyone's friend or family. Leave." He nods his head toward the exit and grabs my elbow to pull me away. "Let's go. Charlie's waiting for you at home."

We drop our bags with the driver to put under the bus and are almost to the door when she shouts, "Bye, bye, boys. Tell Charlie I said hello. Was a shame I didn't get to talk to her at the game."

Casey flips her off and pushes me toward the steps. "Come on, brother. Ignore her."

"I'm good. I just can't stand that girl." I shake my head and settle into my seat.

Casey sits down and nudges my arm with his elbow. "I didn't hear everything she said, but just stay focused on you and my sister. You finally got her back. Don't let anything mess it up this time."

I nod.

Putting my AirPods in my ears, I drop my head back onto the headrest and close my eyes. I know it was all lies, but I do hate how I handled our breakup. She deserved the truth then, like she does now.

Soon.

We'll talk about it all soon so we can put it behind us.

She's mine, and I need to make sure she never doubts me or us again.

CHAPTER
TWENTY

CHARLIE

FEATHERLIGHT TOUCHES DRAG me out of sleep. I can feel fingers moving up my legs, causing goose bumps to sprout. I'm trying to wake up, but my eyes don't want to open. When a finger reaches my panties and tugs the center to the side and circles my clit, I moan.

Then I feel my jersey being pushed up to my collarbone, and kisses trail up my center, over my belly, in between my breasts, and then to one breast. The pull on my nipple finally spurs me to open my eyes. I look down and see Beck with a wicked look on his face. He's smirking, but he also has my nipple between his teeth. It stings, but doesn't hurt.

Beck palms my breast with one hand while his other holds him up so he isn't putting all his weight on me. He opens his mouth again and sucks on my nipple, which triggers a pulsing between my legs.

I bring my hands to his head, holding him in place. "That feels so good."

He pulls my nipple in one more time, then lets it pop from his mouth. "You're a good girl, staying in my jersey. Did you try to wait for me, Boss? Were you dreaming about me? Were you hoping I'd wake you up to wreck this pussy?"

His words make me blush, and I can feel the heat run from my face down to my clit. We've always been vocal with each other, never embarrassed, and we've definitely gotten more vocal with all the sex we've been having. Making up for lost time, I guess. Maybe it's because I'm still sleepy, but his words hit differently, and I'm starting to feel overheated. I let go of his head and grab the bottom hem to pull my jersey off, which stops Beck's exploration of my breasts.

"What do you think you're doing, Boss? I didn't say you could take my jersey off. I want to see my name across your back while I fuck you. You look so pretty, splayed out like this. Legs open, tits peaked, just for me. My number on your chest, my name on your back." He releases his hold on my breast and reaches for my hand, pulling it away from the jersey. "On, baby."

I just nod and bring my hands back to his head and drag my fingers through his hair, then down his neck and over his bare shoulders. I can feel his naked body against my legs, so he must have undressed before he climbed into bed. I'll never get tired of his body. It's like a work of art. With his arm braced next to my body, I keep one hand on his head, and with the other hand, I run my fingers lightly down his biceps, feeling the taut muscles flex from my touch.

"Beck, come here. Kiss me."

I try to pull him up, but he looks at me and shakes his head.

"I'll kiss you, Boss, but I need a taste of your pussy first. That game left me starving," he says.

He trails kisses down my stomach, stopping at my core. When he looks up at me, he swipes his tongue right up the center and circles my clit.

The deliberate way his tongue moves over me has me lifting my hips, trying to keep his mouth on me.

He smirks, then licks again. "You need something, baby? Tell me what you need."

I'm practically panting at this point. "I need you to put your fingers inside me and suck my clit. I need to come. Make me come, Beck."

He wraps his arms around my legs and opens me wider. Parting my folds with his thumbs, he holds me open and is relentless in his attention on my clit before dipping inside my center.

"Baby, you taste like perfection." Lick. "You came back to me, and I'm never letting you go." Lick. "I need you." Lick. "I want you." Lick. "You can't ever leave me again." He moves one hand to my entrance and slides his middle finger inside while he continues circling my clit.

"I'll never leave, Beck. Ever," I moan. "Please don't stop. I need to come."

My hips lift in rhythm with his tongue, and I feel like I'm on the verge of exploding.

"Come, baby. I need to be inside you, but I need to get you off at least once before I do. I'm trying to hold on here, but I can't do it for much longer. Come on, Boss. Give it to me."

He pumps his finger in and sucks my clit. The movement triggers my orgasm.

I'm still pulsing when I feel his cock slip inside. He pushes in hard, and I can feel all of him, up to his base. His hands are on either side of my head, and he's looking down at me.

"That was one, baby. I need two more."

Three. He wants three.

"I don't know if I can. You wrung me out, Beck. I feel like jelly right now." My breathing is heavy, and I still feel lost in all the sensations that orgasm gave me.

My hands travel up and down his back and to his ass, where I take hold.

Beck leans down and holds himself on his elbows, his hands cradling my head. "I got you, baby. Just feel me. Feel what you do to me."

He presses his lips to mine, gentle at first, but once our tongues tangle, the kiss gets wet, messy, and urgent.

"I'm so close, Boss. I need to get you there first. Play with your clit for me."

I move one of my hands from his ass to my clit, and my fingers circle until I find a rhythm, bringing me closer to coming.

"Just like that, Beck. Keep going just like that."

"Come, baby. I need you to come now!"

With our gazes locked, my hand moves faster, and I feel my orgasm come over me. As the throbbing subsides, I pull my hand away from my center and bring his head to me and kiss him. This kiss says everything I think we're both afraid to say. *I love you. I missed you.*

Breaking the kiss, he touches his nose to mine and then kisses my lips again lightly. "Two."

Then he slides out of me and lies next to me. He places my arm under his head and puts his head on my shoulder.

"Beck, I seriously don't know if I can go again. Don't you need to recoup a little? I mean, you just played a game and were hyped up from the win. You have to be getting tired." I giggle.

"Nah. I took a nap on the bus once everyone started to crash. I'd been thinking about you all night. I don't think you understand what seeing you in my jersey did to me. I couldn't wait to get through those four quarters so I could get to you."

He laughs as he pulls the jersey down and covers my breasts. Then, with his index finger, he starts to trace his number. Bringing my other hand to meet his on my chest, I link our fingers, and we just look at our joined hands. He pulls his hand from mine and turns my hand over and brushes his fingers back and forth on my palm. It's sensual, and it starts to turn me on again.

Beck turns his head and kisses my neck and jaw. He moves back to my neck and sucks, which makes me pull my head away.

"Beckham Linson, if you give me a hickey, I will literally kill you."

He starts to laugh and dives headfirst back into my neck. "Okay, baby, but it's too late."

"BECK! Ohmigod. I have chapter tomorrow at the sorority house, and now I'll have to cover it up. Hickeys are tacky, Beck." I mean, I wouldn't care if they were on other parts of my body, but the neck? No. "Urgh, and my brother will see it, you ass!"

Barking out a laugh, he slides his hand under my jersey and grabs my breast. "Oh, come on. You know you like my mark on you. *Property of Beckham Linson.* Wear it proudly."

I cover my face with my free arm and groan.

"Baby, it's fine. It'll fade in a few days," he says with a smile. "Now give me those lips. I still need that third."

His hand trails down between my legs, and two fingers slide through my center. I'm still slick from him coming inside of me less than ten minutes ago. And truthfully, it feels good. I wasn't sure I could get close to being ready again, but here we are. I melt for this man.

Our kisses aren't fast. We take our time. With his fingers sliding in and out of me and the slow, intentional kisses, I'm ready, and I feel needy to have him inside me again.

Beck pulls his hand from my body and sits up. He reaches for my arms to pull me up. "On your knees, baby. I need to see my name on your back while I claim that pussy. Hold the headboard and tilt that perfect ass up." His voice has a gruffness to it, which really works for me.

I turn around and do as he said. Grabbing the headboard and tilting my hips up, I look over my shoulder to find Beck roaming his eyes over my body, jaw clenched. He reaches out and runs his hands up the back of my thighs, over my ass, and under my jersey.

"I don't know where I want to start. I want to lick you from behind, but I need to get inside you, baby. I want to see that ass bounce when I drive into you."

His words and his touch make me shiver. I can't take my eyes away as I watch his hands move over my body.

Grabbing the bottom of the jersey, he pulls it tight. "*Mine.* It took you a while to come back to me, but I've been patient. It drove me crazy, not seeing you every day last year. Wondering who you were with, what you were doing. I needed you here. This was our plan—to be together through it all. Everything is back in place now, baby. Can you feel it?" His hands are skimming up and down my back. His touch light.

My heart feels like it's in my throat from his words, and I break my eyes from him and hang my head. Because I feel the same. And I'm angry because we wasted so much time apart, and for what? We have to have this conversation. I need to know what happened because I don't have the answers.

But right now, I need him to stop teasing me.

"Beck …"

"I know, baby. I need you too."

He smooths his hands over my ass and pulls my cheeks apart. I'm slightly startled, and for a hot minute, I wonder if we're trying something new. I hear him groan.

"Someday. Not today," he says as he brushes his finger over my hole. "Spread your legs wider."

I tilt my hips back a little more and spread my legs.

"Just like that."

Still holding my cheeks apart, he slides the head of his cock up and down—from my clit to my ass. I have to admit, it does feel good. But I'm not sure I'm ready for that yet.

On his down slide, he pushes inside me. "Fuck yes, baby. Suck me in, just like that. Fuck. I'm not going to last." He moves one hand to the center of my back, and his other hand moves to my hip. His fingers dig into my hip as he starts to lose control.

Letting go of the headboard, I move my hand to my clit so we can reach our climax together. My fingers circle, rub, circle, rub. The feeling of him inside me and the pressure on my clit bring on my orgasm.

"Beck, I'm coming," I pant out.

He grunts as he pumps inside of me faster. "I'm right there. Right. There. Fuck!"

I feel him spill inside of me as my own orgasm sends shock waves through my body. Beck pulls me up, still inside me, and brings my back to his chest. I can feel his heartbeat pounding through his chest, and his breathing is still ragged.

He puts his forehead on my shoulder and breathes out, "Charlie, I ..."

Then we hear three—yes, three—bangs on the wall and a, "Please be done now! I need to bleach my ears and never look at either one of you again. But now I need to go jerk off."

"Sorry, Pitz." Beck laughs, and his whole chest vibrates.

Me? I'm completely mortified.

"Ohmigod, Beck!" I pull away from him, even though he tries keeping me with him. "I cannot believe that just happened! You know they're going to talk about this at breakfast in the morning."

"Babe, it's three in the morning. We don't have to be at the field house until two this afternoon, so we're all sleeping in. But it might be a lunch conversation." He laughs.

Scooting off the bed, I grab my little pillow and throw it at Beck. I go into the bathroom to clean up. There's no way I can go to sleep with all of his cum dripping from me. And I need a minute. I suspected the guys had heard us before, but I didn't realize how clearly we could hear Pitz through the wall. His hookups aren't usually here.

I take care of business and am standing at the sink, washing my hands, when Beck comes in. Still completely naked. He stands behind me, arms coming around my waist. I'm watching his movements in the mirror, and his gaze meets mine. There's a soft smile on his face as he rests his chin on my shoulder.

With our eyes locked, he mouths, *Three.*

And we both start laughing.

CHAPTER
TWENTY-ONE

CHARLIE

"LET'S SEE THE NECK. Is it healed yet?" Arbor examines me as soon as I enter the sorority house.

The last time I was here, I was in a turtleneck despite the warm fall weather, and she knew exactly what I was hiding.

"Turns out, cold spoons help. Thanks for the tip."

"That would be my mom's advice. Although I'm not really sure I want to know how she knew that would work. Come on. Let's go upstairs."

I came over to the sorority house to study and hang out with Arbor. Since I've been at Walker, we have been able to spend more time together. Lily and I also get along great, but Arbor and I have history, so it's been much easier for me to bond with her, especially since we've known each other since we were in diapers.

Arbor and Lily's room is one of the larger rooms in the house. There are two twin beds, two desks and chairs, a small couch, and one lounge chair. They've decorated their room in purple and blue with lots of floral prints. They're style is similar to mine, but I prefer pink.

When I finally get my room here, I can't wait to decorate it. All the pink. All the peonies. I found a wall sticker that's one giant peony, which will basically take up my entire room, but I can't wait to put it up. It'll go with my peony comforter perfectly.

My thoughts pause when I start to realize that my finally moving in here means I have to move out of the house. Away from Beck. I mean, I know I can stay over there whenever I want, but the thought of not waking up in his arms now … yeah, it causes a little ache in my chest.

Arbor plops down and is sitting on her bed, books spread out in front of her.

I look up from the book on my lap, which I'm clearly not reading. She's looking at me, head tilted, twirling a piece of hair around her finger.

"Char, now that you and Beck are back together, can you please shed light on what the heck happened back in the day?"

"It's something that feels so ridiculous. I try not to think about it."

"I just remember him always being around after they moved to Troy. You guys were inseparable. Then you guys all came down for a game our senior year, and you wouldn't even look at each other. I asked my mom if she knew, but she would never say. So, I don't know if she really didn't know or if she wasn't supposed to say. I know it's not really my business, but—"

I cut her off, "Arbor, it is your business because you are my friend. More than a friend. We're practically like family. The truth is, I think we each have a version of what really happened. It's actually something I've been thinking about a lot, and I know we need to talk about it, but I can't figure out how to bring it up."

"You know he's totally obsessed with you though, right? I mean, he's always looked at you possessively, but it's gone to a whole new level. It's totally hot, BTW. I wish someone would look at me like that." She laughs. "I've always been a little jealous of you and your relationship with him. Not in, like, a mean way, but more envious, I guess."

"Did you have a thing for Beck? I wouldn't blame you if you did, but I've always wondered. You definitely look at him." I smile and wiggle my eyebrows at her.

Shaking her head, she says, "No, no. I mean, I appreciate a fine-looking man, but he's always been yours. Not that he would have looked anywhere else either. That's why I guess I don't understand how you guys could have broken up."

Arbor might be able to help me work through how to approach this with Beck, so I may as well tell her my version of events. I take a deep breath and look at her.

She waves her hand in a *well, come on* motion, so I release the breath I was holding and start.

I suppose if I'm going to have this conversation with Beck, it might help to sort out my thoughts now. "You remember my friend Britney?"

"Yep, hated her," she says and shrugs. "Mostly because I didn't like the way she looked at you behind your back. Britney was the typical mean girl, in my opinion. Your friendship didn't make sense to me."

As I listen, I nod.

My mom had similar concerns about my friendship with Brit. I swear I think moms just know this stuff. The first time I brought Brit over, my mom was friendly, but the minute she left, she told me she didn't care for her. That was her polite way of saying she didn't like someone. I should have listened.

"Okay, so Britney was at my house one day. We were up in my room, hanging out, and she went downstairs to get a drink. When she came back up to my room, she told me what she'd heard down there. Beck was talking to my mom, and Beck looked upset, I guess. He was talking about not wanting to see someone. She heard him say he didn't know what to do about it and that he wasn't sure how to tell me."

I stop talking and look down at the book in my lap.

I start flipping through the pages and continue, "She told me I couldn't trust him and that he was lying to me about something. That he probably wanted to break up with me, but didn't know how to tell me. So, naturally, I spiraled. Looking back, I think it's stupid that I believed her, but at that time, Beckham had been distant. He had been at football camp for most of the summer. He came back, but then he left again for a few days and hadn't told me where he was going. I really didn't think much of it because that was us. I trusted him—until she put that seed of doubt in my head."

"What a bitch. I'm sorry, Char, but honestly, she's a bitch."

The look on Arbor's face makes me laugh.

"Oh, I know. And when I confronted Beck about it, he just stood there and didn't say anything. I felt like he was gaslighting me. Making me feel crazy for thinking these things, yet didn't have a solid response for where he'd been or what he had talked to my mom about. He got mad and walked away. All my mom told me was that there was more to the story but to give Beck space, so I assumed what Britney had said was the truth. Casey tried to intervene, but I was too stubborn and hurt by that point. As you can imagine, Casey wasn't a fan of Brit either. Then, I guess … the silence between Beck and me just broke us. It hurt me more than I've ever told anyone."

Arbor shakes her head and points at me. "Girl, you know there has to be more to it, right?"

I nod. "I know, but we've never talked about it. And then I heard rumors that he'd tried hooking up with Brit, and when I asked her about it, she said he had come on to her and she'd turned him down out of loyalty to me."

Hearing myself say this out loud makes me feel embarrassed by how gullible I was and how I took her word for all of it despite knowing Beck more than anyone else did.

"When senior year came around, Beck and I didn't even want to be in the same room. He came for his recruitment trip here with Casey, and once they committed to Walker, I didn't feel like

I belonged here because, honestly, I felt kind of left out. Casey and I used to be inseparable, and it seemed like he was choosing Beck over me. Which is totally stupid. They both wanted me to come to Walker, even if Beck didn't say it. It had always been our plan."

"So, that's when Brit convinced you to go to State with her? When you were feeling like they were leaving you behind?" she asks.

"Yeah, but I never felt good about the decision. From the time I sent in my paperwork to State, it was like this dark cloud hung over me. And when we got to school, she basically ditched me for the girls she'd met when she rushed. When I went Phi Chi and she went Theta, I knew our time hanging out together was going to dwindle. And I didn't like any of her friends anyway, but I also didn't really connect with any of the girls in my house. Which was why I started making the trips down here to stay with Casey. I missed him—and Beck ... even though I didn't tell anyone that part.

"So, by the end of the school year, I knew I had to leave. Brit had been doing some sneaky shit too. She would take my clothes and then completely tricked me into thinking I'd lost them. But then I'd see one of her friends wearing something of mine, and I even found one of my sweaters in the back of one of her drawers. Not that I was snooping, but when I was packing to move out, I checked just to see where half my things had gone, and sure as shit, at least one was in her drawer. Oh, and she would guilt me into buying things for the room, like snacks, laundry supplies, you name it. She would use her mom's single-parent status as a weapon to get me to feel bad for her for asking her mom for things. It was gross."

There's more to the story, like how depressed I got, but I'm embarrassed by the whole thing when I say it out loud.

"Okay, that is really gross. Well, I'm so glad you're here and that we get to spend more time together. And I know our moms are happy you're here. And besides, we have the very best house on campus." She winks.

She's not wrong. Our sorority house is not only huge, but it's also gorgeous. The house is white brick with a wide front porch. There is a large eagle sitting in the front, which is our symbol. Inside, it has a beautiful foyer with meeting and common areas on either side. There's a huge kitchen, which is stocked with snacks and drinks, and we have a cook who makes us three meals a day. Because I'm not living here right now, I don't eat here very often, but I appreciate that it's here when I need it. Much better than cafeteria food.

A large, winding staircase leads to the second floor where the rooms are, and there's another set of stairs that lead up to a third floor with more rooms. My room, when it's ready, will be on the third floor, but I'm hoping to move to the second floor before next semester. Room selection is based on GPA, and we have a mandatory GPA guideline as part of our bylaws. I'm doing well in my classes right now, so I don't think it will be a problem.

But again … that means I'll be away from Beck.

"But, Char, back to Beck. You need to talk to him. I'm not an expert in relationships, but what you guys have is special. Don't lose it again."

She gets up and comes over to the chair I'm sitting in. She grabs my hands and pulls me up into a hug.

"You're right, Arbs. I know you are. I just don't know how to start the conversation."

"I mean, again, no expert here, but maybe naked?"

We both laugh.

"What's so funny?" Lily comes into the room, backpack over her shoulder.

"Just telling Charlie to get Beck naked before they have a serious talk." She starts laughing again and nudges my shoulder.

"Speaking of Beck, I need to get going. He's picking me up here so we can run some errands." I start packing my bag.

"But I just got back! Can't you stay a little longer? I wanted to tell you about that guy I hooked up with last weekend." She looks at me, her lip sticking out in a pout.

"I'm sorry, girl. We have to go get my parents an anniversary gift and pick up some things we're running out of."

Arbor is still standing next to me, and I give her another hug after I put my backpack over my shoulder. Then I walk over to Lily and give her a hug.

"We'll hang out soon. And you're coming to the game with me this weekend, right?"

"You know it. This is the last game before playoffs, right?" she asks.

"Yep, this game will give us the division championship, and we'll move on toward the big show! OMG, can you imagine going to the national championship game? I want to see the guys hold that trophy!"

I feel like my heart skips, just thinking about it. All the guys have worked so hard this season. It hasn't been easy. Living with them, I get to see all the injuries, aches, bruises. But they never really complain.

"Ladies, I'll see you later." I open the door, hold up my hand and wave, and shut the door as they both say goodbye.

Beckham

The sorority house is just a couple of blocks away, but instead of walking over to get Charlie, I drive so we can head out to get her parents a gift, and I also need to pick up a few things from the store.

I park outside the house, and when I see her walking down the front steps, I can't help but smile. This girl lights up my world. I know her room must be close to being ready, but I don't want her to leave my house. My bed. At this point, I might just try to convince her to stay anyway. The guys love having her around, too, so it just makes sense. Besides, it's taken a lot longer than they anticipated to get her room ready, but I guess when you start banging around walls in an old house, you get a few surprises.

Charlie opens the door and hops up onto the seat. We lean into each other on instinct, and I brush my lips against hers.

"Hey," she whispers.

"Hey, you. How was your study session with Arbor?" I reach over to grab the seat belt and buckle her in.

Her hands are raised, elbows bent, as she stares at me with a smile as I buckle her in.

"What?" I ask.

"Come here," she says.

I smirk. "What? Why?"

"Because I have to tell you something. Now, come here." She turns her body toward mine and wiggles her index finger toward her.

I lean in, and she wraps her hand around my neck and pulls me in for a kiss. She slips her tongue inside my mouth, twirling it around mine, and it makes me groan.

"I missed you too, Boss. Should we just go home instead?" I wiggle my eyebrows.

She giggles and pushes me away. "Beck, no. I will not let your body distract me. We need to get my parents something. They'll be down here in two days, and we don't have any other time to go. And you know Casey won't go pick something out."

"Hey, you started it. I was just giving you an alternative plan."

I straighten up and slide back into my seat. Foot on the

brakes, I shift the gear into drive. I look over my shoulder to make sure no traffic is coming and pull away from the curb.

The drive to the mall takes us on the highway, away from campus. I have the music on, yet it feels awfully quiet in here. I look over at Charlie.

"So, I know you want to go to that one home store with the fancy hardware stuff for a platter to engrave for your parents, but I need to run over to Target again. The rash guard the trainer uses has been making my skin break out, so I want to stop and get the kind I've always used."

She's playing with the hem of her T-shirt and looking out the window. "Okay, sounds good."

"I don't have a rash, but I like to use the rash guard under my shoulder pads and the back plate straps."

There's a country song playing that she likes. I make it louder, expecting a reaction from her. Instead, she just sighs a little as she looks off into space. I can tell when my girl has something on her mind.

I continue, only to gauge her distraction. "Some guys just wear a shirt under the pads, but it still rubs my skin raw. I'd like to prevent that from happening. Doesn't feel too good."

Taking my right hand off the wheel, I place it on her left knee and squeeze. She doesn't look at me, but she places her hand over mine and links our fingers. I feel like there's something she wants to say, but won't. I'll get it out of her by the end of this little shopping trip.

We park in a spot not too close to the entrance. I get out and swing around the front of the truck to her side.

I open the passenger door for her and reach over to unbuckle her. As I release the strap across her chest, the backs of my fingers graze her breasts.

"Beck," she warns.

"Hmm? What, baby? Do you need something?" I smirk.

She just shakes her head and smiles.

There's my girl.

I settle in close to her and lean against the doorframe. Brushing my fingers on her chin, I bring her face toward mine. "Hey. You okay? You've been kind of quiet."

Her hand reaches up and takes hold of my wrist, but she doesn't pull it away. "Yeah, I'm fine. I was just talking to Arbor about some things today, and it's got me thinking, is all."

Okay, now I'm on alert.

"What kinds of things? School stuff or something else?"

I don't want to assume it's about me, but I get this feeling in my gut that it is. My intuition isn't usually wrong; it's something I learned to trust at a young age. I had to protect myself and my sister.

"Beck, I think we need to talk." She eyes me warily.

I know that tone. It's the one she used when we broke up two years ago. "Oh, fuck no. I'm not doing this again."

"No need to get defensive, Beckham. I just want to talk."

"Fine," I say as I run my hand through my hair. "*Charlene*, what would you like to talk about?"

She scoffs. "See, this is why I didn't want to say anything. It's going to break this bubble that we're in. But, Beck, I really think we need to discuss why we broke up. I think we have two different ideas about what happened, and I feel like, in order for us to move forward, we need to have the conversation."

Her eyes are looking into mine, like she's trying to read me. I'm really trying not to close off. My first response is to shut down and not talk. Which was how we got to where we were two years ago. My therapist told me it was okay to let people I trusted see who I was. And I do trust Charlie. It's just that the stuff she needs to know, I'm not ready to talk about it.

Instead, I nod. "Okay, tell me what you think happened, and I'll tell you what really happened."

"Beck, I really don't want to fight or upset either one of us. You keep saying things like I'm yours and we're forever, and I believe you, but I can't have this hanging over our heads. Can you? Do you really want to move forward together and have questions?" Her eyes are wide as she studies my face for a reaction.

"No, you're right. But seriously, tell me what you think happened. I can already tell you that whatever Britney told you was a lie and not at all the truth." To give her some comfort and show her I'm not mad, I hook a piece of hair that came out of her messy bun and tuck it behind her ear.

I can see her gathering courage to say what she needs to say.

"Okay, well, it was after you got back from football camp before school started our senior year."

I nod, listening.

"And you left almost right after you got home, and you hadn't told me where you were going, just said you had a family thing. I never questioned it because, well, I trusted you."

I nod again.

"Britney was at my house and said she'd overheard you talking to my mom. She said it seemed like you were talking about a girl, and then she heard you say that you didn't want me to know and you weren't sure how to tell me." She sighs.

"Then, when I asked you if you were cheating on me and wanted to break up, you completely blew me off with really no response other than, 'If that's what you want to believe, Charlene, then I guess you don't know me at all.' Then you left my house. So, I took your response as Brit telling the truth.

"Then, two weeks later, Angie James told me that you and Brit were all over each other at Mike Brown's party. I couldn't go because I'd gotten really sick—do you remember?" she asks.

"Yeah, I remember it all. But you didn't really believe I'd hooked up with her, did you? I mean, baby, you knew I couldn't stand her. And Angie was a liar too. She was always trying to stir shit up between you and Britney, too, because she was jealous that Brit was hanging out with you more than her."

"Well, that's what I thought, but when I asked Brit about it, she told me you had been coming over to her house after practice and hanging out. And then you tried hooking up with her at the party and she rejected you." She takes a deep breath in and holds it, waiting for my reply.

"Okay, well, first of all, Brit was completely delusional. I never stepped foot in her house, and I sure as shit never made a move to hook up with her. So, that's that, Boss. That's the truth of it. She was jealous of you, and she lied to you. She took an opening that Angie had given her and ran with it.

"I hate to say this, but you know she only became friends with you because she liked Casey. She was after him hardcore. Brit was sending him tit pics, and ... well, other pics, and he would ignore her. So, I guess she figured if she became friends with you, she could get closer to Casey. When that wasn't happening, she got mad and turned her attention to me. And for the record, after the first tit pic she sent me, I blocked her ass."

I'm completely avoiding giving her the whole truth, but I can't bring myself to tell her about my mom yet. So, I'll make it about Brit. Everything I'm saying is the truth, but it's really just skimming the surface.

I did have a conversation that day with Carol, and it was about my mom. I did ask her not to tell Charlie because I needed to be the one to tell her. But that wasn't what Brit heard or told Charlie. So, I let it fall apart, like a chickenshit.

"Charlie, the only thing you ever needed to know and believe was that I loved you."

"If none of that was true, why didn't you fight for me? Bang down my door and make me listen to the truth?"

Her words hit me like a sledgehammer.

"Why would I when you believed the worst about me?" I swallow and give her two years of pent-up emotion. "I hurt you by not being completely up front with you, but you destroyed me when you believed I'd betrayed you."

"Beck," she stutters, her bottom lip quivering as she comprehends my words.

Charlie takes three deep inhales and pats her thigh at the same time. The lock button on the car is nearby, so she leans forward and hits it three times for no apparent reason. Then she hits unlock. Three times.

Her eyes drop to her lap, and tears spill down her cheeks. "I lost two years with you because, deep down, I think I always felt what we had was too good to be true. It still feels like that. Even now. Makes me wonder if I try to sabotage it because I'm afraid I can't control it."

I take a step forward, lift my hands to her jaw, and wipe her tears with my thumbs. I will her gaze to look up into mine.

"I never fucking stopped loving you, Boss. Even when you ignored me or gave me sass. And even when you got together with that fucker, Tony. I mean, babe, seriously, he was a piss-poor replacement for yours truly." I try to make the conversation lighter.

"Are you kidding me right now? I don't even want to think about the girls you were with while I was gone last year! I bet you and Archie just traded girls. In his room one night, yours the next. Urgh, I can't even."

My hand is resting on the cushion behind her, and she tries to push me away, but I don't let her.

"What are you talking about? I never fucked anyone else. Tempted a few times, sure—"

"Spare me the details!" she cries.

"What I was saying was that I never got far with any girl who came on to me because she wasn't you. I know you were with Tony, and it absolutely fucking tears me up to think about it. But that whole time, I couldn't go through with fucking some random girl because none of them were you." I slide my finger down her chin and tip her face up to look at me.

Tears are pooling in her eyes, and all I want to do is wipe them away. I told Casey I would have this conversation with her, but I still can't get the words out that I need to say.

"Baby, let's just put this behind us and move on. You heard me when I said I love you, right? I have never stopped loving you. I waited for you. I waited for you to come back to me. I knew it would happen, but you needed to be ready to let all of this go. Can you let it go now?" I plead.

Sniffling and wiping the tears that have fallen, she nods. "I love you too, Beck. I never stopped either. I'm just so mad at us now that we've talked about it. I think, deep down, I knew she was lying, but you had pulled away that summer, and I felt like what she'd said made sense. That you didn't want to be with me, but didn't know how to tell me. So stupid." She pauses, shaking her head. "I'm sorry for doubting you, Beck. And I'm sorry for believing her. She drove a wedge between us and my family. I don't know if you know this, but I wouldn't speak to my mom for, like, two months after we broke up. She refused to tell me what you had told her. I was so mad, but you know my mom. Can't stay mad at her for long."

I nod, knowing already that Carol kept my secret. Even begged me to tell Charlie when they weren't speaking. I think she pulled everything out of her arsenal to get Charlie back into her good graces. It made me feel guilty as hell.

Leaning in, I kiss her lips. I can taste the salt from her tears. I hate that I made her cry. I have never wanted—and never want —to be the cause of her tears.

Pulling back, I use my thumbs to wipe away the rest of her tears. "Let's go home, baby."

She nods and leans in to kiss me again. "Yeah, I'm not really in the mood to go shopping now. I'll figure something out for my parents."

With one last kiss, I close her door then walk around the front of my truck. My head is down, but I can feel her eyes on me. When I reach my door, I look up and give her a smile to let her know everything is okay. That we're okay. For now.

CHAPTER
TWENTY-TWO

BECKHAM

A FEW WEEKS have passed since our conversation in my truck. I've tried to show her every day how much I love her. I still leave her little notes. And I even found a florist that keeps pink fucking peonies in stock, so I still surprise her with those as much as I can. With all these little things I'm doing to prove myself, I can tell she feels better about putting the past behind us.

But the guilt is eating at me. I need to tell her all of it, but the timing never seems to be right. The team is in the middle of playoffs season. We won our division after Thanksgiving, so we're prepping for the quarterfinals now. Since our game is just after Christmas, we have to stay on campus during the holidays. Most of our families have come to visit, but our free time has been limited. Classes are over until January, but our training, studying film, eating, sleeping—that's all we have time to do really.

My dad and sister and the Kings came down for a few days. They rented a house near campus, and we had a small Christmas celebration with them two days ago. Liam's parents came up for the day a few days ago too. Archie's though, they couldn't make it. With the size of his family and the ages of his brothers, it's hard for them to get away. I think his parents are planning to be at one of the playoffs games though, depending on how far we make it.

Tonight, Charlie's put together a Secret Santa party for us. She got a tree for the house and tried to make it look nice, but Liam and Archie added beer-tab garland, and they taped unrolled condoms to the tree one day when she was at class. Dumbasses didn't think about the heat from the lights and the latex condoms, and a few melted right off the branches. Charlie suggested that they were better off just hooking them on the tree because they wouldn't be able to use them anyway if they were exposed to heat for too long. After she said it and looked over at Liam, he had a grimace on his face.

She said, "Please tell me you aren't actually plucking them off the tree and using them."

"I mean … maybe? But, look, in my defense, I didn't think about the lights being an issue. If you think about it, it's really your fault. You got a tree with fire hazard lights, Little King." He stood there, pleading his case, and we couldn't help but laugh.

Fucking idiots.

I do hope he was joking though. He's a smart guy, but sometimes, we don't think with the right head.

Liam also decided it would be a great idea to have an Elf on the Shelf. But instead of the little guy in the traditional elf costume, he bought the Snoop on the Stoop and Martha on the Mantel elves. The first night he brought them home, he propped them right on the bookshelf next to the TV. The Snoop elf has a joint hanging out of his mouth, and the Martha elf looks all prim and proper. I have to admit, shit's funny.

When we woke up the next day, we found someone had leaned Snoop against the toaster in front of a piece of paper with oregano scattered on top while Martha was hanging from a mixer attachment, dangling over a mixing bowl with flour inside. It was funny until Archie turned the mixer on.

"Look, Martha's a stripper."

But then poor Martha got tangled in the attachment and lost an arm.

Charlie's also been taking care of a lot of our meal prep since we're gone most of the day and dragging ass by the time we get home. But for tonight, I offered to get us a premade meal from the grocery store in town. It comes with ham, mashed potatoes, stuffing, gravy, mac 'n' cheese, some green beans thing, and some rolls. The guys and I are getting it all warmed up, so all my girl has to do is sit her pretty little ass in her favorite chair and watch Christmas movies.

She wanted her girls to come over, but Lily went home for break, and Arbor and her family went away on vacation, so they won't be coming. Charlie and those two have gotten really close, and I'm glad because Charlie really hasn't had true loyal girl-friends before.

Casey invited Noelle to come down for the night, so we included her when we picked names for Secret Santa. She could go stay at her apartment in town, but she's going to stay with us tonight after we open gifts. I heard Casey on the phone with her earlier, insisting on it. I can't wait for the day he finally tells her how he feels about her.

From the kitchen, we have an open view into the family room. Charlie is sitting in her chair and turns to look my way, catching me staring at her. She blows me a kiss, which makes me smile, then turns back to watch her movie.

"Let me know if I need to come in there and rescue dinner."

"Chuck, we got this under control. I'm like Betty fucking Crocker. You know I make the best meals in the house on my days." Archie moves to stand next to me. Oven mitts on both hands, raised in the air.

He's a big guy, so seeing him in gym shorts, a T-shirt, and oven mitts is pretty fucking funny.

"Excuse me! I'm the best cook in the house, Arch. How dare you?" She scoffs playfully. "And for the love of God, pull your hair back so I don't have your hair in my food."

Archie folds one arm across his stomach and slides one mitt off. He grabs the other with his now-free hand and sets the mitts on the table behind us. "Sugar, my hair doesn't fall out. These locks make every girl on campus jealous. But for you, I'll tie it back."

His hair isn't really long, but it is long enough that he can pull the sides back. And he just so happens to have a ponytail holder around his wrist, which he pulls off to tie his hair back. Charlie has turned around again, watching us.

He winks at her and asks, "This better, Chuck?"

"Much. Thank you. Besides, now I can see your handsome face." She winks at him.

And I've had about enough of the winking. "Okay, let's break up the winking, you two. Arch, go check on the ham. Boss, kick those feet up and watch your movie. Do you need more Christmas in a Cup?"

It's Charlie's favorite holiday drink. It's basically homemade hot chocolate mixed with RumChata. Not gonna lie—it's electric.

"I'm good for now. If I have too much more, I won't be able to eat dinner. Thank you though, babe."

She blows me another kiss. And I wink at her. I'm the only one who gets to give her winks, dammit.

I turn around and clap my hands. Casey and Liam are just standing around, shootin' the shit, while Archie and I are doing all the work.

I walk over to Casey, grab his shoulder, and steer him toward the table. I give him a little shove. "Bro, go set the table or something. You're just getting in the way, standing here." I look over my shoulder and point at Liam. "And, Pitz, put the rolls on a cookie sheet so we can warm those up too. No one likes cold rolls. The butter won't melt."

Thirty minutes later, the table looks as good as it can for a houseful of football players and one beauty, but the food is hot, and I can't imagine spending this day with any other group of people.

After dinner, Casey and Liam cleaned up the kitchen since Archie and I had done most of the food prep. I moved Charlie over to our oversize couch in the family room. I tried getting her to lie on me, but she refused because she would have to distribute the gifts.

Noelle arrived just as we were finishing dinner. Not sure why she was late, but I thought I heard her say Trey's name. Now she's sitting at the table, picking at some leftover ham, while Casey does the dishes.

As much fun as all of this is, I'm ready to take Charlie back to our room and get some dessert. I will never get tired of seeing her sprawled out on my bed, legs open, pussy wet and waiting for me.

"Beck, did you hear me?" Charlie squeezes my thigh that she's resting her hand on, and when I place my hand on top of hers and start moving it toward my dick, she pulls her hand back and gasps. Her mouth falls open, eyes wide, and she leans into me. "Babe, you cannot be serious right now. We have gifts to open. Get control of yourself." She pops a kiss on my lips and giggles.

"I need you, Boss," I whisper. "It's been, like, two days since I was inside of you."

She doesn't respond, just laughs again, grips my leg, and squeezes.

"You guys about done in there? I'm dying to see what everyone got for their person!" Archie shouts to Casey and Noelle.

Charlie stands from the couch and walks over to the tree. She bends down, and I can't help but stare at her ass. The waistband of her jeans has dipped down, and I can see the top of her thong. I swear she's trying to kill me.

Casey, Noelle, and Liam come into the room. Liam takes the chair next to Archie, a small table between them. And Casey and Noelle take the other half of the couch. They're sitting close, but not close enough to touch. Her legs are pulled up to her chest, her arms wrapped around them. She's facing Casey, and they share a smile. I haven't seen her much lately, but this is the first time I've seen her truly smile in a while.

"Okay, I'll just do a random selection. Remember, you can't tell your person it was you until after we're all done opening gifts." She points to each of us while she talks.

My bossy girl.

"Ma'am, yes, ma'am," Archie shouts and gives her a salute, which makes her roll her eyes.

She hands one to her brother. "Casey, yours is the first one. Open it up, then show everyone what you got," Charlie instructs, then turns back to the tree.

He tears into the paper and pauses when he opens the top of the box. I'm not sure who got Casey, but I know it wasn't me or Charlie. So, really, it could be anything, and by the look on his face, it's not something he wants anyone to see.

He looks up, mouth hanging open. "You can't be serious."

"What is it, Case?" Noelle reaches for his arm to see in the box, but he quickly pulls it away from her.

"Uh, it's just a flashlight. Inside joke because, you know, I don't like my room to be dark."

He slaps the box lid back on and looks around the room, mouthing, *Motherfuckers*, to all of us.

His gaze lands on me, and I shrug. I didn't see what was in it, but after he said flashlight, I have an idea. And from the way Liam's shoulders are shaking as he tries to hold in his laughter, my guess is that he's the one who got it.

Charlie walks over to Archie next and hands him his gift, then hands one to Liam. "Open them one at a time, so we can see."

Archie opens his, and it's a box of Magnum condoms. He smiles, looks up at each of us, and shakes his head. I see him mouth something, but I can't figure out what he said. I don't miss Liam's foot nudging Archie's though.

"Thank you to whoever got me these. I appreciate your concern for my safety." He holds the box up and nods, letting it drop into his lap.

"Is it my turn?" Liam asks, practically bouncing like a little kid.

"Go ahead." Charlie gestures to the box in his hands, and then she turns back to the tree.

This box is a little bigger than the others, so I can't imagine what it could be with our twenty-dollar limit, but Liam legit looks like a kid on Christmas morning with the way he's tearing through the paper.

With the paper off, he holds up the box in his hands, turning it around. "I'm not sure what it is or who it's from, but I love it!" He keeps one hand gripped on the side of the box, and with the other hand, he smacks the top of the box. "Love. It."

"Baby, why don't you open yours next?" I ask her.

I want her to open hers because it's a gift from me. I have a few other things for her for Christmas Day, but I know she'll like this one.

"No, I want to go last. You know I love watching people open gifts."

It's true; she does love seeing people happy.

She hands Noelle a gift.

Noelle looks up and smiles at her. "Thanks, Charlie. Hmm … what could this be?" She opens the small envelope in her hands. "Oh, I love Bath & Body Works! Thank you to whoever got me this!" Holding it in both hands now like it's a golden ticket, she brings it to her chest and has a big smile on her face.

Charlie leans down and whispers something in Noelle's ear, which makes her drop her head back on the couch cushion and laugh.

"I don't think you were supposed to tell me, Charlie. Wasn't that *your* rule?" Noelle keeps laughing, taking hold of Charlie, who is also laughing, and brings her in for a hug.

She walks over to me next since we're the last two who haven't opened gifts yet and hands me mine. It's a thin box, the shape of a rectangle, and lightweight. I have no idea what it could be or who my person is. I rip off the paper and see a notepad-type thing in a box. I'm not really sure what it is, so I pull it out of the box.

"Oh, this is cool. It's like a digital notebook or something. You can write in it, and it will sync to your calendar or notes on your phone or computer. This is awesome." I hold it up and glance around the room. "Thanks."

"Okay, since Charlie is the only one left, I'm just gonna tell you that's from me, man." Archie is turned toward me, holding his arm up for a high five. "Dude, I saw it and knew it was perfect for you. You are the most organized person I know. I thought it might be useful in class or whatever."

To be honest, I'm a little surprised the thought that went into this gift. I love Archie, and he's one of my closest friends, but he's the funny, laid-back one. Sure, you can count on him for anything, but this gift actually does match me perfectly. I love notebooks and calendars and shit. I like knowing what to expect and when. My therapist said it was because there had been a lack of routine and structure when I was little. Maybe so.

I stand, and instead of giving Archie a high five, I pull him in for a hug and slap his back a few times. "Thanks, man. I love it."

Pulling back, I look at him, and he's just nodding with a proud smile on his face.

"You all think I'm just another pretty face with an amazing personality, but I see you all," he says. He gestures with his fingers from his eyes to everyone individually, which makes us all laugh.

"I guess it's my turn!" Charlie has her gift in hand and holds it in the air.

She makes her way over to me and sits on my lap. I wrap my arms around her and rest my chin on her shoulder.

She unwraps the box and sees a blank frame.

"Turn it around and press Start," I instruct her.

Flipping the frame, she presses Start and turns it back over. Pictures of us start floating through the frame. Image after image of us at various ages. The one thing that's the same in all of them is, my arm is always wrapped around her. Some of the pictures have Casey in them too.

"I just wanted you to remember that, no matter what, it's always us. You are—and always have been—the very best part of my day. I love you, Boss."

I bring my hand up to her jaw and turn her face toward me. Her eyes are shiny with tears, and I lean in and kiss her, then rest my forehead against hers.

"Hey, wait. Did that follow the twenty-dollar limit? I feel like some of you broke that rule." Casey reaches over and grabs the frame out of Charlie's hand. "This is pretty cool though, Beck. Top choice, brother," he says with a nod and hands the frame back to Charlie. "I want to see the rest of the pics later though."

"Beck, I love it so much. I love you so much." She kisses me again, and without breaking the kiss, she turns her body to straddle me.

"Whoa, whoa, whoa, break it up. We still need to say who we bought for. You can maul your girlfriend later, Linson." Liam stands from his chair. "Okay, so, Casey, I bought for you. I don't know why you don't want to show the class. I thought I was helping you out. Clearly didn't think it through with Noelle being here and all. But seriously, dude, it's awesome."

"Casey, just show us what it is." Noelle grabs Casey's arm and tugs.

His head is down, and he's shaking it back and forth. "Pitz, I will find a way to get you back—I swear it." He opens the box, reaches in, and pauses. "Noelle, please don't think for a minute that I'll be using this. My hand works just fine."

She giggles, but looks confused. "What do you mean?"

Casey holds up what looks like an actual flashlight, but it is, in fact, an adult toy for men. The top of it looks like, well, a pussy.

I can't help the laugh that comes out. "Sorry, Case, but that's funny."

He looks over at me incredulously. "How can you think this is funny under the circumstances? My sister is in the room, and my best friend, who happens to be a girl, is sitting next to me. Not. Funny, bro." He waves the toy toward Liam.

"I don't get why you're mad, dude. I got you some lube, too, but since that technically put me over twenty, I figured I'd give that to you later. But, hey, before you use that, make sure you trim. I've *heard* that if you get your ball hair stuck in there, it feels like a wax. Hair rips right out." He makes a jerking motion with his hand, eyes wide.

"This is a super-fun conversation, but I think I'm ready to move on. Charlie gave me my gift, and I gave Liam his. My gift might not be as entertaining as your gift for Casey, but I thought you might like to use it after your games. It's a foot massager." Noelle walks over to Liam, who is sitting back in his seat, and pulls it from the box. "See, you just slip your feet inside this little pillow and turn it on. And before anyone says anything about the limit, I got it on sale."

Liam follows her directions and slides his feet in. "Babe,

Noelle, I hate to tell you this, but it's not working. Could be why it was on sale."

"How are you a leader on the team?" she asks while shaking her head.

Liam scoffs. "I'll have you know that not only am I one of the best college quarterbacks, but I also have a 4.0. There's a whole lot going on here." He gestures up and down his body with a laugh.

Pitz and Archie definitely make this house fun when we're all together. I'm going to miss Archie next year. He's one of the reasons I committed to Walker. Sure, I'd always wanted to go here, but there is no one better than Archie Griffith on and off the field. And I'm still hoping Liam sticks around, but this playoffs run, our coach has had Callaway starting, and I'm pretty sure Coach intends to start him in the quarterfinal.

"You're not bad to look at—that's for sure." Noelle giggles and turns back to sit in her seat.

I look over to Casey, and his jaw his slack.

"I'm sorry, but who are you, and what have you done with my best friend?" He mocks.

Noelle looks at him with doe eyes. "What? I can't appreciate a good-looking man? Don't make me go all feminist on you, Casey King."

Holding his hands up, he says, "Okay, you got it. I'm just surprised to hear you say something like that."

"Leave her alone, Case. She's having fun. A little flirting never hurt anyone. Am I right, Noelle?" Charlie winks at her, and Noelle smiles in response.

"Okay, so I think we're all clear on who gave who what, yeah? King, thanks for the condoms." Archie looks around, nodding his head. "I hate to break up this party because it really has been fun, but I do have a prior engagement. I'll be back before practice tomorrow." He walks toward the front door.

"Bro, where are you going? You've hardly been here between

practices and classes." Casey turns from his seat on the couch and leans over the back to face Archie.

A smirk kicks up on Archie's face before he looks at Casey. "It's all good, man. I just have places to be." He doesn't bother with a jacket despite the thirty-degree weather, but he does pull a beanie on his head and looks toward my girl. "Charlie, this was a real good time. Thank you, sugar." He nods at Noelle. "Noelle, pleasure as always. You should come around more." Then he looks around the room at the rest of us. "Dicks, I'll see you tomorrow at practice." Then he pulls on the door and walks out.

Casey turns back around and looks at me. "Do you know where he's going and where he's been lately?"

I shake my head, so he looks at Liam.

"Pitz, you know?"

Liam starts to busy himself and brushes off Casey. "Nah, I have no idea. Let's get this cleaned up. I want to watch *Christmas Vacation* again before I crash."

After we clean up all the wrapping and Casey goes to grab extra blankets and a few pillows for Noelle, we all settle in our seats. He tried to get her to stay in his room, but she refused, not wanting to make him sleep on the couch.

With Charlie tucked into my side and everyone in their spots, I tilt my head back to rest my eyes for just a few minutes.

CHAPTER
TWENTY-THREE

CHARLIE

MY HEAD HAS BEEN RESTING in Beck's lap since the wet-carpet incident in the movie. We're now in the part of the movie where Cousin Eddie is emptying the shitter in the sewer. This scene never gets old, and it always makes me laugh.

I look up at Beck, but he is sound asleep. I look at Liam, who is also sleeping. Then I turn to look down at the other end of the couch to see Noelle sleeping too. Casey is wide awake though, just like me, with a smile on his face.

"I love this part." Casey glances over at me.

"Same. No matter how many times we watch this movie every single year, I never get sick of it. It's like my comfort movie." I nod and look over at my twin. I notice that Noelle's legs are across his and he is holding her feet, which are covered by a blanket. "So, Case"—I'm trying to keep my voice quiet so I don't wake anyone—"are you ever going to tell"—I stop and point at Noelle—"how you feel? Or are you just going to pine for her forever?"

"Shhh ... Jesus, Char. Say it a little louder, for fuck's sake." He gives me a glare.

"All right, I'll stay out of it. But I do want to see you happy. And, Case, this situation hasn't made you happy. You can't keep up the loyal-buddy act forever."

He sighs. "I know, but timing has never worked in our favor, you know. It'll happen if it's supposed to happen. In the meantime, I'm going to be her best friend. The person she can count on."

I feel Beck's hand brush down my arm, so I lay my head back on his lap and look up at his face. "Hey, babe. You fell asleep on me."

He brings his hand back up to my face and takes a small piece of hair in between his fingers, then tucks it behind my ear. "I wasn't sleeping. I was just resting my eyes."

Casey and I both start laughing. Since we were kids, Beck has always said that. He never wants to admit if he fell asleep.

"How about we go to bed? Clark will still be here tomorrow." I sit up and then stand.

I turn around to face Beck, grab his hands, and try to pull him up, but he's like dead weight.

"Beck, come on." I laugh.

"Go ahead, baby. Pull me up. Start now. Pull," he says and leans further back into the couch.

I stop pulling and bring my hands to my hips, a pout on my face. "Not fair."

He doesn't reply, just leans forward and wraps his arms around my legs and lifts me when he stands. The movement makes me fall over his shoulder before I can catch myself.

"Beck!"

Beck says nothing; he just smacks my butt and says, "Good night," to Casey over his shoulder.

When we get to the bedroom, Beck leans down and drops me onto the bed. He braces himself on his hands, bends his head, and kisses me. "Be right back." Then he turns to walk into the bathroom.

I'm still in the same position when he comes out.

"Boss, why are you still dressed and on top of the covers?"

"I need to go to the bathroom and brush my teeth. Help me up."

I hold out my hands and reach for him. He grabs my hands and pulls me up and into him. He wraps his arms over my shoulders and gives me a gentle squeeze.

I step back and walk to Beck's dresser to grab a shirt to sleep in.

He mumbles, "Thief."

I turn my head back to him and wink.

By the time I'm done, which couldn't have been more than ten minutes, I walk out of the bathroom and find Beck sleeping. He's on his back, one arm spread out over my pillow and the other above his head. Not gonna lie—I was hoping for some of that fun he was talking about earlier, but I think the best thing I can do for him right now is let him sleep.

CHAPTER
TWENTY-FOUR

CHARLIE

AFTER THE QUARTERFINAL GAME, we spent New Year's quietly celebrating their win. I know some of the guys partied when they got back, but Beck and my brother stayed in. Sure, they had a few beers, but the training doesn't stop. Even just a little bit of alcohol can hurt their performance.

We had to travel to Pennsylvania for the semifinal game. Walker is favored to win by a pretty large margin, and in the fourth quarter with two minutes left, I think it's safe to say whoever bet on Walker winning is pretty happy right now. If we win this game, we'll go to the national championship.

I'm wearing my Linson jersey again, but it's freezing here, so it's on over two other layers of clothes. Since that first time I wore it this season, I haven't worn my brother's number. It literally drives Beck wild when he sees me wearing his name on my back.

His dad and sister are on one side of me, and my parents are on the other. My mom is holding my hand rather tightly, and I have to squeeze her hand to signal her to ungrip my grippers a bit before I lose feeling in my fingers.

"Sorry, honey. You know how nervous I get. I swear it doesn't get easier, watching them take those hits out there."

My dad leans over and reassures her, "Carol, they're fine. The clock is running out; they'll be done here in a few minutes, and then we can celebrate."

Mom nods, and we all stand as the clock winds down.

I let go of my mom's hand and turn to face her. "I'm going to go out onto the field. Are you guys coming or going back to the hotel?" I ask.

We're staying at the same hotel as the team, and even though families got to see the players briefly before the game, we haven't really gotten to see them the past few days. I can't wait to wrap my arms around Beck. They must all be so pumped. One step closer now with the final seconds on the clock.

My dad leans around Mom. "I think we'll make our way down there, but if it gets too hectic or people start rushing the field, we'll just go back to the hotel and wait to see the boys there."

"Okay, I'm going to start making my way over to the gate. Mr. Linson, Brooke, are you guys coming down?"

Beck's dad looks like an older version of him. Dark hair, blue-gray eyes. He's always been kind of quiet, but kind. Brooke has the same hair color, but her eyes are dark brown.

He looks down at Brooke, who is nodding.

"Yes, I want to go see Beck on the field!"

"Field it is," Mr. Linson says. "And, Charlie, stop calling me Mr. Linson and call me Ryan. I've known you practically your whole life, and now you're an adult. Let's make the awkward stop now." He smiles at me.

"Righto." *Righto? Who am I right now?* "I'll just meet you down on the field then. Do you want to come with me, Brooke?"

Ryan answers before she can respond, "I'm going to keep her with me in this crowd."

Brooke rolls her eyes. "Dad, I'm almost seventeen. I'm pretty

sure I can handle myself in a stadium. That has security. In literally every corner. We'd just be walking right down this row."

Ryan sighs and looks up. "We'll meet you down there,
Charlie."

I mouth, *Sorry*, to Brooke, hug my parents, and walk down
the row to the gate.

Beck is standing on the sideline, and he looks back to the
stands just as I walk behind him. He's close enough that we can
touch, but he tilts his head toward the direction of the gate. I nod
in understanding.

When I get to the gate, a small crowd is forming, and I wave
at the faces I recognize. Most family members have passes
around their necks, and those who don't are fans trying to get
down onto the field. They like to try to blend in with family to
get through security.

"Umph. Good Lord, these people are pushy." A lady with
shoulder-length sandy-colored hair is standing slightly in front
of me. She turns her head to look at me when she realizes I
heard her.

I laugh because, yeah, they can be. And I'm about to push
through this crowd, too, so I can get to Beck.

"This is my first time at a college football game. It's all so
exciting, but I'm not sure I could handle these crowds at every
game," she says as she reaches over to grab the handrail next
to us.

When she looks at me again, there's something about the way
she smiles that looks familiar. I feel a little like I might be staring
at her mouth, so I shake my head.

"Oh wow. That's so fun! Your first game? You'll never forget
it. This was a big win for us. Onto the championship game now!
Go, Stallions!" I lift my hands up waist high and wiggle my
gloved fingers.

She laughs at my gesture, but the smile on her face drops
quickly. "You here to see a boyfriend or something? Or are you a
fan?"

"Oh, yeah. Well, not just my boyfriend, but my brother plays too." I turn my back to her and look to where I see Casey standing near the bench. Next to him, Beck is squirting water from his bottle into his mouth. His dark brown hair is falling on his forehead from being wet with sweat. I point at Beck, then look over my shoulder to see if she sees where I'm directing.

She swallows, and she looks back at me. "You pointing at number twenty-four?"

I nod with a prideful grin.

"So, funny story. I'm actually here to see your boyfriend."

"I'm sorry, what? I don't think I heard you right. You're here to see *my* boyfriend?" I ask, confused.

Why would she be here to see Beck?

She clears her throat. "I'm his mom. Beckham Linson? He's my son. I wanted to surprise him. I haven't been able to come watch his games since they're so far away. But I figured with them playing here, I wanted to at least try to see him, even if it was just for a minute. I'm not really sure how these things work." She chuckles, but it seems forced.

"You're his mom?" I state in disbelief as I get knocked into by the person behind me. The woman helps me from falling, and as I regain my footing, I just stare at her.

She nods.

Now that she says it, I do see the high cheekbones and blue eyes of Beck on her face. He's always favored his father, and in the many years I've known him, I've never seen any pictures of his mom. But I do see some similarities in their features.

Snapping out of my shock, I shake my head. I don't really know what to say because I've never really heard much about his mom, other than his parents divorced when he was little. "Sorry, I'm just a little stunned. I didn't realize you lived here. I'm sure he'll be surprised to see you." I grab her hand from the railing.

"Do you know how I can get to him? I'm a bit overwhelmed right now."

I tuck her hand onto my arm. "Here, just hang on to me. You can come down to the field with me."

She squeezes my hand gently. "Really? You would do that for me? It would mean everything to me just to say hi to him. It's been so long since I saw him."

Part of the security team is starting to move toward the gate, and I watch them as they appear to be waiting for a signal. I feel her squeeze my hand lightly.

"For sure! Brooke is here, too, so you'll get to see them both!" I smile, but when I look at her, her smile drops.

"Ryan must be here then too?" With that question, she starts looking around. She's biting her bottom lip with her top teeth.

Trying to break the tension, I smile. "Yeah, he is. I guess that might be awkward though, huh? Oh, by the way, I'm Charlie."

She answers distractedly, "I'm Stevie."

"Nice. Like Stevie Nicks?"

"Something like that." She tries to smile, but it doesn't reach her eyes.

The sound of the gate opening has me turning my attention away from her. With her hand still in mine, I move her behind me and step up to the guard. I hold my badge, and he nods, but as we start to walk by, he grabs Stevie's arm and tells her she has to get back.

I'm standing on the step below her, so I turn and look up at the guard. "She's with me. She's Beckham Linson's mom."

He looks at my jersey, then my pass again and waves us through.

We reach the grass near the end zone, and we're told to wait there. I can feel the heat on her hand in mine. It's starting to sweat.

"Are you nervous to see Beck?"

He's never talked about his mom to me, so I don't really know much about her. I guess I always just figured because they lived with their dad that she didn't really want to see them or something. They didn't go spend time with her like other kids of divorce.

She doesn't look at me, but she nods. And when I lightly squeeze her hand, she looks up at me and pulls her hand from mine.

"Oh, I'm sorry. I'm sweating all over your hand." She tries to say it lightly, but I can see she is nervous. It's in her eyes.

I offer her another smile, and as I start to speak, we hear the announcers begin the award ceremony. The security on the field starts to usher us to the podium area. As we get closer, I see Beck standing on the stage, along with Archie, Bo, and a few seniors. I find my brother on the field and go to stand near him. I turn my head to the side and look at Stevie to make sure we didn't get separated.

I lean into her and point at Casey. "Ahh, there's my brother. Let's go over near him until Beck comes off the stage."

Again, she doesn't say anything, but she nods.

When I reach Casey, I grab his biceps and squeeze. He turns toward me, and when he sees it's me, he lifts me up into a hug. He's laughing, and I'm laughing.

"Congrats, Case! I'm so proud of you guys! You killed it out there!"

"Thanks, Char! Isn't this awesome?! I can't believe we're going to the final show! Dude, did you see that last catch Beck made? It was a beauty." His face is animated as he speaks, his excitement radiating off of him in abundance.

It's freezing out here, but I can still see the heat coming off of his body. I'm sure he doesn't even feel the cold right now.

The announcer starts talking again before I can answer. I look over to find Stevie, and she's standing slightly behind me. I reach back for her arm and pull her a little closer.

She smiles, but her eyes haven't left the stage. I pull my attention from her to the announcer as he begins to speak.

"I'd like to take a moment to congratulate Dawson on a

wonderful season, and their fans certainly gave us a great atmosphere today. But the day belonged to the Walker Stallions!"

The crowd around us cheers, and I can hear the roar of the fans that remain in the stadium. Archie is standing right next to the announcer, and Coach Pettys is on the other side. Archie raises his arms, waving them up and down to try to get the fans to cheer louder. When he does, he knocks the hat he was given off his head and laughs. Beck is next to him and bends down to pick it up. He tries putting it back on Archie's head, but it falls off again, and they look at each other and laugh.

A well-known sports broadcaster steps up to the microphone. "A huge thank-you to the Hanson Organization for sponsoring and hosting this event at this beautiful stadium in Pennsylvania."

"Coach Pettys, it's my honor to present to you the Keystone trophy!" The man hands the trophy to Coach and steps away as Coach moves to the microphone.

Coach hoists the trophy in the air, and confetti starts to rain down on the stage and in the area where we're standing. The crowd roars again, and he lifts the trophy up and down.

"Today is worth celebrating. The credit goes to all the young men who played their hearts out today. They worked hard, played smart, and stayed one step ahead of Dawson all day."

As he speaks, the players behind him dump a bucket full of confetti over his head.

Coach laughs. "Much better than getting soaked! But, yeah, these guys are the best. Unbelievable, resilient. We executed what we prepared for, but we've still got a lot of football left to play. It all comes down to the players, and we're gonna be ready for Southeast in the championship game!"

The announcer steps in again. "You came out strong, but that second half of the game, you completely dominated the field. What was the key to getting everyone locked in and ready to play this semifinal game?"

"Well, everyone came together. I have a great coaching staff, but it all comes down to the players. Walker!"

The crowd replies, "Stallions!"

"We have a commemorative football to present to you for your win today." He hands Coach the ball, and Coach steps back slightly.

"We still have a few other trophies to hand out. Let's start with the Offensive MVP of the game, Bo Callaway! Bo, you're a true freshman, which is unbelievable, considering you've accomplished so much this season and in this game. With six touchdowns and two hundred eighty-nine passing yards, how do you feel about this win?"

Bo steps up to the mic. "Thanks. Well, first, I have to thank God for giving me the strength to bring this win home for Walker!"

The crowd cheers.

"And my family, the coaches, my teammates—this couldn't have been done without them. These guys have my back. But we came out here hungry today. We wanted this win, and we never gave up. We're gonna be ready for Southeast!" Bo holds the trophy up and steps back.

The announcer turns to one of our senior defensive ends, Josh Schumacher, next. "Josh, you are today's Defensive MVP! With four tackles, one sack, and one forced fumble, you helped keep Dawson away from that end zone."

Josh takes his MVP trophy in hand. He's a quiet but intense kind of guy, so I'm curious about what he's going to say, if anything.

"Thank you. It all comes from my Lord and Savior. But we never give up. We keep going to work every day and put it all on the field."

The announcer asks Josh a few more questions and congratulates the team again, and some of the players stay on the stage, getting pictures with golden keys hanging from key chains in their mouths. A few start to leave the stage, and I lose sight of Beck, who I've yet to make eye contact with.

I grab hold of Casey's arm, and he leans down to hear me over the noise.

"Mom and Dad are still making their way down here. I'll stay out here until you guys go back, but I want to see Beck first."

He nods and motions to where Beck is coming down the steps of the stage. Casey puts his arm in the air to signal Beck our way.

Beck spots me and smiles, but then stops walking, and the look on his face changes. I'm not sure what's going on, but when I follow his gaze, I see he's looking at his mom. She's still standing next to me, but her hands are in fists, and she's biting on her lip nervously.

When I turn back to Beck, I see him charging toward us.

"What the fuck are you doing here?" He points accusingly at his mom, and then he turns to me. "Why are you with her? Is this some kind of joke?" He turns to his mom again. "Does my dad know you're here? Does Brooke? You shouldn't be here, and I don't want you here!" He's trying to keep his voice down, but his teammates are starting to notice, and Casey has now turned to see Beck's clearly agitated body language.

"Whoa, man. What's going on?" Casey asks.

Beck points at his mom. "Her. That's the woman who birthed me."

Casey whispers, "Oh shit." He turns to Beck and puts his hands on Beck's chest. "Okay, we got this. What do you need me to do?"

I'm watching this whole thing transpire, and so many questions are running through my head, but I can't form the words to speak. "Beck ..."

He looks at me with a sneer. "Why are you with her, Charlie?"

"I ... I just met her. We were both standing at the gate to come down to the field, and she saw your number on my jersey.

She said she was your mom and that she was here to surprise you. I ... didn't know!" I'm starting to feel panicked because the anger radiating off of Beck is palpable.

He turns to his mom, Stevie, and points at her. "You have about five seconds to turn around and leave before I have security escort you out of here."

Just as he says that, Ryan and Brooke approach from the side.

"Beck! What's going on? Stevie? What the hell? You're not supposed to be here."

I look at Stevie, and she has tears running down her face, her hands covering her mouth.

She's looking at Brooke. "Brookie? Oh my God, you're so beautiful."

Brooke is standing there, similar to the way Beck is. She's locked in place, and the look on her face is stone. She hasn't said a word, but I see Beck come to stand next to her when Ryan walks toward Stevie.

He reaches out to her, but doesn't touch her. "Let's go, Stevie. Don't ruin this celebration by embarrassing him like this right now." Ryan turns to Beck. "I got this, Beck. Go celebrate with your team." He turns back to Brooke. "Brooke, you stay with Charlie, and we'll meet you in the waiting area." Then he turns back to Stevie. "Start walking."

"Ryan, I just wanted to see him for a minute. I haven't seen him or Brooke in two years! Just give me five minutes. If they don't want to speak with me, I'll go." She starts to walk toward Beck and Brooke, and Ryan takes her arm this time.

"Nope. Not happening. You will not lay a single finger on my kids again." Ryan is trying to stay calm, but his face is starting to turn red.

"Ry—" she starts.

"NO! I said, no. If you don't start walking, I'm going to call your parole officer. You aren't supposed to be within ten feet of the kids. Ever." He's leaning down into her face now, trying to stay quiet, but those of us near them can hear what he's saying.

Then they turn and start walking off the field in the opposite direction of the locker room.

I'm still so confused about what's going on. Why don't they want her here? Why can't she be near them? Clearly, I did something wrong by bringing her out onto the field with me.

"Beck—" I walk over to where he is standing with Brooke and reach for him.

"Not now, Charlie. Not here. I'll speak with you later." He leans down to whisper something to Brooke, pulls her in for a hug, then turns to walk off the field toward the locker room.

Casey has moved beside me and places his arm around my shoulders. "Char, let's give him a minute, okay? I don't know a lot about this situation, but I do know it's not good. I'll make sure he's okay. You take Brooke back toward the waiting area, and we'll meet you there."

Brooke is standing there, still in a state of … shock? Anger? I can't really tell.

I shrug off Casey's arm and reach for Brooke. "I'm so sorry, Brooke. I have no idea what's happening, but I'm so, so sorry."

Brooke looks at me and nods.

"Let's go wait for your dad with my parents."

"Right, yeah. Okay, let's do that. Umm … where do we go?" She trembles a little.

I turn back to Casey. He's shaking someone's hand, but looking at me.

He mouths, *Go*, and points to the area where we can leave the field.

Taking Brooke's hand in mine, I lead us to the exit.

Neither of us says anything as we walk toward the family waiting area. Ryan is already standing with my parents. His back is to us, but his arms are spread out to his sides, and he's shaking his head. My parents are facing us, and my dad is nodding while my mom's mouth hangs slightly open.

As we get closer, I catch the end of what he's saying.

"I'll talk to him and tell him he needs to explain all of this to Charlie. I'm sorry about this. I had no idea she was coming."

My mom spots us and moves toward me. "Charlie, are you okay?" She pulls me in for a hug and squeezes me. Her face is over my shoulder, but I feel her reach out to Brooke while I'm in her embrace. "Brooke, honey, are you okay?"

"Oh, yeah, I'm okay. I think I'm just a little in shock from seeing her. It feels like it's been so long."

I can barely hear her with the noise in the hallway.

Ryan turns away from my dad and turns to Brooke. "Why don't you go back to the hotel with the Kings? I'm going to wait for Beck to make sure he's okay."

"How will you get back if we have the rental car?" she asks.

"Tim will take the rental, and I'll catch an Uber back to the hotel when Beck gets on the bus." He looks at my dad, who nods.

My mom releases me and turns to my dad. "Tim, let's head out now."

"Yep, let's go, girls. Ryan, we'll see you at the hotel in a bit." He places his hand on Ryan's shoulder and squeezes.

None of us says a word on the walk to the car or on the way to the hotel.

But now ... it feels like a dark cloud is hovering over what should be a celebration. And I'm not sure if Beck will want to see me at all.

CHAPTER
TWENTY-FIVE

BECKHAM

CASEY'S BEEN TRYING to get me to talk since we got on the bus, but if I do, I might blow. But I won't. Not right now. I refuse to let that woman have any power over me. And honestly, it's more the fact that I saw her with Charlie that messed me up.

I knew being back in Pennsylvania was going to be hard, but I tried to stay focused on the game. Knowing my family was there, that Charlie was there, helped me to forget about the reasons why it was difficult, being here. I didn't even know my mom had gotten out of prison, although we had known she was up for parole again in August. I'm guessing my dad knew she had gotten out and didn't want to tell me because of the playoffs.

I sure as shit didn't expect her to come to my fucking game. I wonder how she even got a ticket. They weren't cheap, and I'm sure she's had trouble getting a job with her record.

Coach pulled me aside before I got on the bus and asked me what had happened. He knows my family history and knows about my mom. I told him she was here, and he told me to let him know if I needed anything. Right now, I need to be anywhere but here.

All the guys are still hyped up from the game as we pull into the hotel. There are people standing outside, waiting for us to arrive, decked out in their Walker gear. Most of the people are family members, but there are some fans staying at the same hotel too.

I'm seated by the tinted window, watching everyone outside, cheering and celebrating. Casey nudges me to get up so we can disembark, but I wave him off.

"I'm good. I'll wait for everyone to get off and then come in."

"I'll wait with you. I'm not letting you sit in here and walk in there alone. You're my best friend, Beck. I've got your back, man." Casey sits back down in the seat and lifts his fist for a bump.

I make a fist and bump his hand and nod once. I look back out the window to look for Charlie. I want to see her so bad, but also don't. I have to explain it all now whether I want to or not. I can't brush this under the rug anymore. And if I want a future with her, she needs to know it all.

Once everyone is off the bus, Casey and I get up to leave. We have to get our bags that the driver set out for us from the undercarriage. Our bags are the last two player bags left. We grab them and head into the hotel. Most of the family members and fans have gone inside now. A lot of them are still hanging around the lobby though. Some of the guys have stopped to talk to people, and I see Coach hugging his wife and kids. Everyone looks so fucking happy.

Casey is walking beside me and nudges me to get my attention. He tilts his head toward a seating area, where we see Charlie sitting by herself. She looks upset, and I hate that I'm the reason for it. I'd rather not have this discussion here, so I'm hoping to talk about it when we get home, but I have a feeling I won't be so lucky.

"I'm going to drop my bag and go see my parents. You good?" Casey asks as we get closer to where Charlie is sitting.

"Yeah, I'm good. Will you take my bag up with you to the room?" I turn to him, and he reaches out his hand for my bag. "Thanks, Case. I'll be up after I talk to her."

"Okay. We can talk about all of this after you speak to her, but I do think it's past time you tell both of us the whole story, don't you?" He looks at me, eyebrows raised in question.

"I know. It's just a part of my life I try not to think about."

"Brother, it's Charlie. Nothing you say will change the way she feels about you. You guys are in a really good place. Now, go over there and don't make my sister cry." He nods and turns to walk away.

I watch him as he gets on the elevator. I can feel Charlie's eyes on me now. I can't avoid this anymore, so I walk over to her. She's sitting in a chair, and there's an empty one with a table between them.

Her hand is on the arm of the chair, and I reach over and grab it.

"Hey," I say quietly.

"Beck ..." She starts to speak, but stops and swallows.

I'm sure she wants to fire out so many questions.

Her hand is still in mine, and I pull her up. "Come on. Let's go take a walk."

It's still pretty cold outside, and I don't have a coat on over my suit, but I can't feel much of anything right now. But I do make sure she grabs her coat from the chair.

"Your gloves in your coat?"

She nods, lets go of my hand, and puts on her coat. As we get to the doors, they slide open, and a gust of cold air hits us. I hear Charlie gasp next to me.

"It's not that bad. We won't stay out here for long."

"Beck, what's going on? Are you, like, breaking up with me again? I've been sitting here, losing my mind. I'm so sorry I brought her onto the field with me." She's speaking rapidly, showing how nervous she is.

We walk toward an open seating area outside the hotel and sit on one of the benches. There isn't really anywhere else to go. The hotel is located somewhat close to the stadium, but it seems like they probably use this hotel for conventions or something. We could find a place in the hotel somewhere, but some of the things I need to say, I don't want anyone to overhear.

"Everything's okay, Boss." I squeeze her hand to try to reassure her.

"Beck, I need to know what happened with your mom. I feel like I'm missing a lot of pieces of the puzzle here. What did your dad mean about her parole officer? Was she in prison?" Her eyes widen in question.

"I was four years old the first time I remember my mom hitting me, spanking me, slapping my face. I don't remember what I had done, but I will never forget that first hit. Brooke was just a baby, and she cried a lot. I remember feeling like my mom wasn't okay. Because I was so little, the only way I could understand it at the time was that she just wasn't herself, probably because that's what she would say to me." I pause and take a deep breath in and exhale.

"My dad used to travel a lot for work, so he would be gone on long trips. I don't know if him being away made her mad or what, but she was left with two babies to take care of, mostly on her own.

"Don't get me wrong; I don't blame my dad for any of this. He didn't know what was happening until the end really. When he came home, it was like she was a different person. She was happy and loving to me and Brooke, but when he was gone, we got spanked a lot. She would forget to feed us. She wouldn't change Brooke's diapers. I pretty much potty-trained Brooke on my own.

"And then, when I was six, she forgot to pick me up from school one day. Brooke was still in preschool then. After an hour

of waiting, I walked myself to the preschool—which was probably about four miles away, thinking about it now. So, for a little
kid, that was far.

"When I got there, I had to be buzzed into the building. The
director came to the door, and when she saw me, she opened the
door, looked around the parking lot, and pulled me inside. She
asked where my mom was, and I told her I didn't know. She
took me back to Brooke's classroom and brought me some juice
and a snack. Brooke … she was just fine. She was happy to see
me. I saw the director say something to the teacher and walk out.
About an hour later, my mom came into the classroom. Her hair
was all over the place. She looked like she had just gotten out of
bed, and she smelled funny.

"It was the first time I knew that my mom had been drinking.
That I understood what that meant. She had probably been
drinking before then, too, but I was too little to notice.

"The director came in behind my mom, and I remember she
looked upset. My mom got Brooke's bag together and told me to
grab mine. The director drove us home. Again, I was little and
didn't really understand what was going on, but I knew something wasn't right.

"Of course, I found out later that my mom had been drinking
all day and passed out. She didn't hear the alarm she had set for
herself to come get us. The director went to our house when she
couldn't get ahold of my mom or my dad, worried something
was wrong. Then she'd brought my mom to the school because
she was still too drunk to drive.

"When I was seven, I had been watching Brooke because my
mom was asleep. When I went into the kitchen to get us a snack,
Brooke fell off a chair. She had stood on the chair to try to reach
something off one of the bookshelves and lost her balance. Her
arm was broken, so I had to wake my mom up to tell her we
needed to go to the hospital. Again, my dad was gone at the
time. I have no doubt that when we got there, the doctor and
nurses knew she was drunk or had been. She smelled so bad."

I pause for a minute and look at Charlie. She has tears streaming down her face. I reach over to wipe her cheeks, and she grabs my wrist.

"Beck," she says on a shaky breath, "I didn't know. I'm so sorry. I didn't know." She shakes her head, and tears start to fall faster.

"When we got home from the hospital that night, my mom was so mad at me for not watching Brooke properly. She tied me to a chair and put me in the closet. She left me in there all night. I hadn't eaten, and I wet my pants several times throughout the night.

"The next morning, she opened the door, sober, and started crying when she saw me. She apologized over and over again. Begged me not to tell my dad about what had happened. Promised it would never happen again.

"Of course, the spanking and slapping never stopped, and as we got older, the hits got harder. I would try to insert myself in Brooke's way to protect her. I was bigger and could handle much more than she could." I lean forward, rest my elbows on my knees, and fold my hands together.

Telling someone I love that all this happened to me … is hard. I've never talked about it outside of my family and therapy. Tim and Carol know a little, but I never told them all of this.

"The final incident was when I was eight. My mom was in the kitchen, making something for dinner. I was sitting on the couch in the family room, doing my homework. I wasn't allowed to watch TV until it was done. I wasn't paying attention to where Brooke was, but she walked into the kitchen at some point, and I heard my mom scream. When I looked up, my mom had Brooke's hair wrapped in her fist and was pulling her toward the stove. I jumped up from the couch and ran into the kitchen. I grabbed my mom's arm and was able to pull her grip from Brooke's hair."

I look over at Charlie. Her hands are covering her mouth, and she's still crying.

"My intention was to get her to stop altogether. Instead, she grabbed me by the wrist and pulled me over to the stove. There was a frying pan with oil in it. She was still screaming at Brooke, who had gotten into my mom's makeup. Her face was covered in it. To teach her a lesson, she was going to burn her hand. But she burned mine instead. She put my hand right in the oil. I tried to fight her, but she was still too strong for me. At first, the pain from the burn didn't register. I was kicking her, trying to pull her arm off me with my other hand. Brooke was wrapped around her legs. Nothing was stopping her though. About the time I started to smell the skin burning, I began to feel the pain. We were all screaming at that point. I'm honestly surprised none of the neighbors ever heard us. Screaming was a common occurrence." I huff out a laugh.

Charlie stands up and squats down in front of me, resting her hands on top of mine. "Beck, I don't even know what to say right now. I can't believe this happened to you. To Brooke. How could a mother do something like that to her children? But also, why didn't you ever tell your dad?"

Something about the tone of her question sets me off.

"Why didn't I tell my dad?" My voice is rising, and I can feel my heartbeat speeding up. It's not like I haven't been asked this question before, but the way she asked makes me feel stupid and weak.

"Because my mother would threaten to starve and beat us if we did! Before he came home from a trip, she would be all sweet with us. Pretend to be the perfect mom. She would stop drinking the day before he came home. WE WERE CHILDREN, Charlie! The person who was supposed to take care of us hurt us almost every. Single. Day. She would gaslight us, manipulate us. So, she was not only physically hurting us, but she was also emotionally abusive. I obviously didn't know the terms for all of it until I had to go to counseling, but that's what she did." I pull my hands from under hers and stand.

"So, what happened then? When did she go to jail? I'm trying to understand the timeline of all of it. Help me understand so I can help you."

She reaches for my hands again, but I pull away.

"Help *you* understand? To this day, *I'm* still trying to understand how a mother could do this. And you want me to help you understand?! It's taken me years of therapy to get over some of the stuff we went through. I thank God every day that Brooke doesn't remember as much as I do."

I start to walk away, but she grabs my arm. I can't look at her right now. If I do, I might start crying.

"Charlie, you just don't get it. You. Casey. Your family. And, hell, football. All of you helped me forget. You allowed me to have a place to push the past behind me, but now she's out. My past has collided with my present, and there's no going back."

"Let us be that for you now. We're still here for you."

I pull my arm out of her grasp. I shake my head and clench my jaw.

Seeing my mom today, looking into her cold eyes, brought it all back. It doesn't matter that, on the outside, she looks like a typical suburban mom. She had the fucking nerve to smile and act like she was the nervous one when, really, I was the one trembling on the inside. Just one glance, and I could feel her hands on me as she'd pummeled me with pain. The scars on my hands were on fire, and there was nothing to do to put them out. My mother—my very own mother—is the one who did this to me. Who made me hate myself for merely existing.

It's been years since I've seen her. I did a great job of keeping that hatred inside me away, but one encounter with her, and it's all back.

I'm nothing.

I'm bad.

I'm not worthy of love.

I claw at my scar as I pace in front of Charlie, trying to explain the basic fact that we will never be the same.

"You and Casey grew up with two parents who loved you

unconditionally. And I'm so glad you didn't have to go through what we did. But you won't ever really understand."

"Beck! I'm sorry, okay? I don't know what to say. I feel absolutely sick that you guys went through that. You've never told us anything about her, so I'm trying to process it all. I'm sorry. Please stay and talk to me."

She's pleading with me, but I need to be done with this conversation.

Charlie is all things good in this world.

She doesn't deserve to be brought into my nightmare.

"Charlie, go back to your room. We'll talk when we get home. I need some space right now. Seeing you standing next to her? All I could think was that the best part of my life was standing next to the worst part of my life. I thought maybe it was a sick joke or a hallucination from all the adrenaline from the game. But there she was, poisoning just one more good thing in my life."

"Don't let her destroy what we have. She was a horrible mother, but you're an amazing man, Beck. Please don't let anything she said or did ruin who you are."

"It's everything I am. Don't you get it? Even you never thought I was good enough or else you would have never believed Britney. Which she was sure to remind me of when I saw her after the game against Chandler."

"Wait, *what*?"

"You thought the worst of me once too."

"Beck, please. That was two years ago, and we already hashed that out. I told you I was sorry."

"There was a reason you believed it. I was never worthy."

"NO. Please. You can't think that about yourself."

She grabs my arm again, but I pull away.

"I gotta go."

I walk back into the hotel and don't look back.

CHAPTER
TWENTY-SIX

CHARLIE

MY TEARS HAVEN'T STOPPED.

Once Beck started to tell me what had happened to him as a child, I completely lost it. The pretty little woman who stood next to me had done all of that to her babies. I want to know what happened, but I'm not going to chase him. He will have to come to me when he's ready.

I never put my gloves on when we went outside, but I pull them out to wipe the wetness from my face. I don't want my parents to see me this upset. But also, I'm kind of mad at my parents right now for not telling us. There's no doubt in my mind they know what happened.

Walking through the lobby, I see a few of the guys on the team with their families. I spot Archie with his parents. They're laughing, and his arm is wrapped around his mom, who I met yesterday. Then I see Liam and Bo talking on a couch. I can only imagine what they're talking about.

Once I'm in the elevator, I press the button to our floor three times. As the elevator climbs, my level of panic skyrockets.

What if he goes silent on me again—or worse, what if we

break up again because of all this? I just can't help but wonder if this will put another wedge between us.

The elevator stops on my floor. As I walk down the hall, I grab my key out of the lanyard around my neck. I popped it in there before we left for the game. When I open the door to the room I'm sharing with my parents, I see Casey sitting on the bed I slept on, facing my parents, who are sitting on their bed, backs to me.

When the door closes behind me, my parents turn around.

"Charlie, come sit down with us." My dad motions me over to the bed.

My mom grabs my hands when I sit down next to Casey. "Honey, are you okay? Did you get to talk to Beck?"

Nodding my head, I look up at her. "Yeah, I did. He told me some things about his mom, which I'm guessing you already know." Then the thought hits me. "Mom, did you know all of this when we broke up two years ago? Is this what you couldn't tell me?"

"Charlie …" she sighs. "Honey, this isn't a pretty story, and it wasn't mine to share. Ryan wanted Beck and Brooke to have a life where their mother's darkness didn't overshadow their light. Moving to Troy was a fresh start for them, and we honored that. If you or Casey were going to find out, Beck needed to be the one to tell you. I really thought he would have before something like this happened. And I really thought he would tell Casey first, but I guess he never did. I'm sorry you had to find out like this."

"Mom, I was broken two years ago. I thought he was seeing someone else and lying to me. I would have understood. I could have tried to help him. Instead, I turned my back on him." I pull my hands from hers and stand.

"Charlie," Dad starts, "sit down. We want to talk to you about this calmly. You're upset, and we understand that completely. Ryan gave us permission to tell you both everything that happened before they moved to Troy. But I'm not going to talk to you about it unless you sit and listen." He points at the spot I was sitting in, next to Casey.

If Beck won't give me the answers, I want my parents to tell us all of it.

"We should be celebrating their win, and he's somewhere in this hotel, upset."

Casey grabs my hand and squeezes it gently. "He's back in the room. He came in when I was leaving to come here."

I look at Casey and notice he changed from his suit to sweatpants and a T-shirt, which has the Walker mascot and the Hanson Organization logo on it with the trophy and the date commemorating today's win.

"Tell us what he told you, Charlie, and we'll tell you anything you don't know," Mom says.

I tell them everything he told me up to the hand burn. As I'm retelling them everything Beck told me, it dawns on me that the scar on his hand must be from that burn. Why didn't I ever ask him about that? I assumed it was a sports injury or something. Although I don't think he would have told me unless something like this had happened before.

When I stop talking, I look at Casey. He's leaning against the headboard, head tilted, eyes closed. I know my twin, and he's got to be hurting as much as I am. I reach over and grab his hand that's by his side.

"So, I guess tell us everything you know from there. He didn't finish telling me what happened or how she got arrested."

Dad looks at Mom. "Do you want to tell them, or do you want me to?"

With a deep breath and an exhale, Mom begins, "The day she was arrested, Ryan was supposed to be gone for one more day, but he hadn't been able to get ahold of Stevie for two days. Things like that had been happening more frequently, and he was starting to worry. When he asked Beckham if everything was okay when he was gone, Beck never said a word. But Ryan came home early that day, and he could hear the screams from the driveway. He ran into the house, and Stevie had Beck's hand in the frying pan. Ryan said he could smell the flesh burning. He ran over to Beck, pulled him out of her grasp, picked him up, and ran him over to the sink. Stevie stood in shock while Ryan ran cold water over Beck's hand. He told her to call 911, but she wouldn't move. He called over to Brooke, who was still pretty little at the time, and told her to bring him his phone that he had dropped by the door. Once she did, he pulled her behind him to block her from Stevie." Mom stops and moves her gaze from mine to my dad.

My dad nods and takes over. "So, Ryan called the police. Once he got Beck's hand wrapped and the kids safely on the couch in the family room, he moved Stevie from her spot, still by the stove, to one of the chairs in the kitchen. He tried to get her to speak, but she wouldn't." He sighs.

"The paramedics arrived first and began to treat Beck. Next, the police arrived and started questioning Stevie. Ryan hadn't noticed it when he came in, but there was an almost-empty bottle of vodka on the counter near the stove. I guess she had taken to drinking vodka, even during the day, because she thought it was harder to smell on her breath when she picked the kids up from school."

"I'm literally flabbergasted that no one ever caught on to this happening in their house. Like, why on earth didn't a teacher or the freaking director of the preschool contact Ryan?" The longer I listen, the angrier I get. I know I shouldn't be mad at his dad, but I just can't imagine that people didn't know.

"I know, honey. It makes me sick, thinking about the whole thing. I just love Beck and Brooke so much. I can't fathom anyone wanting to hurt them—or any child. And there was a teacher who reported it, but after an investigation, there was no evidence of neglect. But that day of the incident, after she was questioned, she was arrested for child endangerment. While she was awaiting trial, an investigation was conducted in the home. Ryan had to go through evaluations, social investigations, and therapy for the kids, for him. He lost his job because he couldn't travel anymore. After nearly two years, she was convicted, and they were basically free of her, so they decided to move. Ryan wanted to get the kids out of there because too many people in the community knew what was going on and what had happened, and he needed a job." She reaches over and puts her hand on top of Casey's, which is still holding mine.

A tear drops down my face. Picturing Beckham and Brooke in that kind of home breaks my heart. Ryan is a great dad, and I'm trying really hard not to be angry with him right now.

"I just don't understand something. How does a father not know his wife is hurting his kids? When he was there, didn't he see bruises or signs that something wasn't right?"

Dad leans forward. "Charlie, alcoholics get really good at hiding and lying. Ryan found liquor bottles all over the house when they were packing up to move. Under clothes, in laundry soap boxes, under sinks. She had even filled a spray bottle with vodka. And he said she'd confessed to drinking Benadryl or mouthwash when he was home so she wouldn't completely detox. Addicts will do absolutely anything to hide their addictions."

He continues, "Apparently, she'd struggled with mental health issues before they were married. I guess her father had also been an alcoholic, so it ran in the family. She said she just couldn't deal with Ryan being gone all the time and couldn't handle the kids. When she went to trial, she confessed to everything she remembered doing to the kids. Some information about the abuse came from the social investigation with Beckham. They wouldn't allow him to testify because he was so young, but they had enough at that point to convict her anyway. She was sentenced to fifteen years; she lost her parental rights and was ordered to go through counseling and a rehab program at the prison."

Mom says, "The day that Britney overheard Beckham and me talking, he had just gotten back from testifying at her parole hearing. Because he was over fourteen, he had been permitted in the hearing. He asked for them to keep her in jail. When he had gotten back, he came straight to our house. He wanted to see you, but when I told him Britney was there, he didn't want to stay. He was pretty upset, and I think had she not been there, he might have told you about it then. I'm so sorry I couldn't tell you both, but because of some of the legal issues still pending, I couldn't say anything without their permission."

She looks from me to Casey. "Case, did you have any idea any of this happened to him?"

Casey shakes his head. "Beck isn't really one to talk about feelings. He's always been quiet about his mom. He only made a few comments in passing about how she was a horrible mother and that they were much better off without her." He sits up and places his palm on my back.

"We're his family, Charlie. We have to be patient with him. Trust me, I want to go up there to our room right now and ask him so many questions, but we have to let him deal with this in his way. He's not going anywhere." He brings his hand up to my shoulder and squeezes it.

All of this tonight has been a lot to deal with. Like Casey said, I want to run up and be with him, but I also want to show him that I respect him by honoring his request for space. The worst part of all of this is that Casey and Beck should be celebrating tonight's win with the team.

"Maybe I should go back early tomorrow and stay with Arbor for a few days. Give him some space. He has a lot going on right now, and he needs to focus on getting ready for the championship game." I turn to look at Casey. "What do you think I should do?"

He holds his hands up. "Char, I don't know what to tell you, honestly. I know he'll be pissed if you leave, but you're right. He needs to focus on getting ready for Southeast. Maybe go stay with her for a few days and see how it goes. I think I'll head back up to our room and check on him. If he wants to be alone, I'll go find the guys." He swings his legs to the side of the bed and stands.

"Oh, wait. Beck mentioned seeing Britney at the game against Chandler. Did you see her too?"

Casey sighs and hangs his head. "Yeah, I saw her." He looks up at me. "I wondered if he would say anything about it or hoped he would at least tell you."

"Why didn't you tell me? We tell each other everything."

"Because, Char, it doesn't matter that we saw her or what she said. What matters is that you two love each other. Britney is irrelevant. It's time to let it go."

"Arbor and Lily saw her too, but I can't believe she would seek out Beck. But you're right. It's time to let it go. I love him, he loves me, and she'll never get in the way of us again." I say, nodding.

"Good, just focus on moving forward together, not the past."

He goes to Mom first and hugs her, then moves to Dad. Dad says something in his ear that I can't hear, and he pats Casey on the back three times.

I stand when he moves over to me, and I reach up to hug him. He lifts me a little and then sets me down, but doesn't let go.

"Please keep an eye on him for me. I can't lose him again. I don't want him to go silent on me."

"I won't, I promise. You know he loves you more than anything. Let him work this out, and everything will be okay." He lets go of me and starts walking to the door. "I might not see you guys tomorrow before you leave, so if I don't, I'll call you when we get back to Walker. Love you guys."

We all respond with, "Love you," back to him, and when the door shuts, the tears fall.

My parents both come over to me and say all the things to make me think everything will be okay, and I really hope they're right.

CHAPTER
TWENTY-SEVEN

BECKHAM

TIME. It's supposed to heal all wounds.

Sometimes, it just serves as a Band-Aid until it's ripped off and you have to deal with reality.

My dad came to see me in my room the night of our win. He told me about my mom's release and explained that he hadn't wanted to tell me about the details until after the playoffs. I'd figured as much, but I would have preferred the heads-up at least. I don't do well with surprises. But I'm not upset with him.

Sure, there were times when I was little that I would cry or beg him to stay before he left so we weren't alone with our mom. And maybe I was a little angry too. But with all the years of counseling we've had individually and as a family, I understand how my mom's alcoholism affected us all. All three of us were victims of her abuse.

I've been checking in with him and Brooke every day. My mom can't leave the state, but I still want to make sure she hasn't tried to contact Brooke. I know my dad has a handle on it, but I was Brooke's protector from the time she was born basically. Mom has no parental rights to Brooke, but there's nothing that says she can't contact her. I'm a legal adult now, so she knows any contact with me would go unanswered. I just hope, for Brooke's sake, she stays away from her. My mom might have turned her life around, but I will never forgive her for what she did to us.

Carol has stepped in as a mom for Brooke, and I know they've gotten even closer since Casey and Charlie left home. I want Brooke to have a strong female in her life. I want her to learn how to be open to that kind of love and maybe not be so closed off to talking about her feelings, like I am.

When we got home from Pennsylvania, some of Charlie's things were gone. Did it hurt? One thousand percent yes. Did I blame her for going? Not one bit. I'd told her I wanted space, but I only meant that night. And, well, maybe a few days after, but I never wanted her to leave.

Casey and I talked about everything, and he encouraged me to let Archie and Pitz know what had happened to me and why Charlie was staying with Arbor.

Of course, when we sat down to talk about it, the first question Archie asked me was, "What the fuck did you do to mess it up this time?" He's never been one to beat around the bush.

I've texted Charlie every day and asked her to come over, but she tells me she wants me to focus on the upcoming game. While I appreciate that, I also need my girl. I don't like waking up in my bed without her.

I know I probably didn't handle the whole situation in the best way, but it's not every day you see your mom, who you thought was in prison, at your playoffs game.

I've been sitting in my room for the last thirty minutes, thinking about everything but the paper I should be writing about the different rock elements of Missouri. We're not even in Missouri. And also, why the fuck did I have to take Geography as an engineering major?

There's a knock on my door, and I holler over my shoulder, "Come in," not bothering to see who it is.

I know it's not Charlie or Casey because neither of them would knock. So, that leaves Liam or Arch.

"Hey, brother." It's Liam.

"What up?" I spin in my chair and face him.

He's looking down and rubbing the back of his neck, and he looks like he might be sick.

"You okay, man? What's going on?"

Pitz is usually a pretty happy guy. But I know this playoffs run hasn't been easy with Callaway basically taking over his spot.

"Yeah—I mean, no, but I hope it will be." He laughs a little and lets go of his neck. "I wanted to tell you guys first before the whole team finds out. I've decided to enter the transfer portal after the championship game. I have one year left of eligibility, and in order for me to get a decent call in the draft, I need to get more field time. Callaway's arm is a missile, and after this play-offs run, I know he'll be starting next year. I can't sit on the side-lines, man. My talents might be different from Bo's, but I'm a good fucking quarterback." He looks up at me for the first time since entering my room and has a smirk on his face.

"Dude, you are one of the best out there. As your friend and roomie, I hate to see you go. As your teammate, I totally get it. I would probably do the same if I were in your shoes."

I get up from the chair and walk over to him. We grab hands to shake, but I pull him into a hug. He pulls back, and I go sit on the edge of my bed.

"Thanks, Beck. It wasn't an easy decision to make. I've been here my whole college career. Walker was always my first choice, and I was hoping to end it with a ring here, but I might just have to get it somewhere else." He laughs and points at me.

I laugh, too, but it's never easy to see a friend like Pitz go. I meant what I said; he is a great quarterback and one of the best in college football. I have no doubt he'll find the right team.

"Okay, so now that that's out of the way, we have pizza. Come eat with us. You've been locked up in the room since

Charlie left. Snap out of it, man. It's cheat day, fucker. Let's eat some greasy goodness." He waves his arm for me to follow and steps out of my room.

When I get to the kitchen, it's just the four of us. Archie's head is down as he chomps on two piled slices. Casey and Liam are talking about some girl Pitz hooked up with last night. Which, of course, makes me miss Charlie even more.

When I sit down, Archie looks up at me and nods. "Sup, Linson? You done crying in your room?" he teases.

"Fuck you. I wasn't crying. I was working on a paper and trying to manage my fucking schedule with our practices. It's killing me, man. I'm exhausted."

I pull three pieces of pizza from the box. When I realize I just pulled three, it makes me think of Charlie. And how I want her to come back.

"Heard. There's a shit ton going on right now, but we're so close, baby. We work hard; we play harder. We own those Southeast fuckers," Archie says.

He shoves the last huge bite of pizza in his mouth. I'm surprised the dude doesn't choke.

"Yeah, speaking of a lot going on, where have you been lately, Arch? We know your class schedule, so where do you go when you aren't here, at class, or at practice?" Casey asks.

"In due time, my friends. In due time," Archie says while nodding.

"Well, that's cryptic as fuck. I just told you guys about one of the hardest decisions I've had to make, and you tell us in due time? I call bullshit." Liam slaps a hand on the table, laughing.

"Fellas, there are a lot of wheels in motion, and I can't wait to tell you about all of them. But for now, let's stay focused on winning the whole fucking thing." Archie reaches into the box and grabs two more pieces of pizza.

We shoot the shit for a little longer. Then Liam gets up to take a call, and Archie goes to his room. Casey and I are still at the table. He's typing something on his phone, and I'm watching him as I spin my water bottle around in circles on the table. He's either texting Noelle or Charlie. My bet is on Noelle, but then he looks up.

"You look like shit, you know?" He points at my face and the stubble that's gone too long without shaving.

I glance down at the table and rub my jaw. "I'm going for the mountain-man look."

"Really? Because I thought it was a hermit you were aiming for. Aside from practice, you've barely left your room."

"I have to keep my GPA up in order to keep my scholarship. You know that."

"Doesn't have anything to do with avoiding life," he says, and I look up at him. Casey tilts his head and doesn't flinch when he says, "Your mom is evil."

As much as I know it's true, I flinch at his words because I hate hearing about her just as much as I hate talking about her.

He must sense my unease because he pauses, as if choosing his words carefully. "Listen, Beck, we're not the kind of friends that share every detail of our lives. Mostly because you like to keep things to yourself and I respect that. That doesn't mean that I won't be here to listen if you ever want to talk."

"I don't," I say quickly because I'm already fidgeting in my seat at the notion that Casey is gonna want to have some sort of heart-to-heart moment where we dissect my past.

He laughs lightly. "I figured." His tone turns serious. "It also doesn't mean I haven't been listening all these years to things you don't say."

I furrow my brow in confusion.

He continues, "Yeah, you say a lot without even speaking. You said, *I love my little sister, Brooke,* every time you babysat her when your dad had to work late and never complained about it, even when everyone else was out at the movies or at a party or riding our bikes around town. You said, *I'm a good son,* when you asked my mom to teach you how to cook when we were only ten because you wanted to do something nice for your dad when he came home from a long day at work. You said, *I'm a fucking awesome friend*, when you didn't go on the eighth-grade class trip to Six Flags because I broke my leg and couldn't go and knew I was upset about it. You say, *I'm a great fucking person*, when you live every day as Beckham Linson—son, brother, friend, baller, and one of the best fuckers I've ever met—despite having a shit childhood. You don't have to talk about shit, but there's no one in this world who thinks about other people the way you do, man. Sure, you're anal as shit with your things, and you're a neat freak like I wouldn't believe. And only a good guy would find goddamn peonies in the winter to give to a girl. That's you, Beck. So, we don't have to talk about your past. That's cool. But don't you dare lock yourself away and start looking like some kind of mountain man because of it. It sucks, but it's who you are. My best friend. Who needs a shave."

Casey leans back in his chair, and we sit here for a while. It's a lot to process, his words. So, we just stare at the oak table for a bit with a weird kind of silence in the room.

I let out a deep sigh. "You been working on that speech for a while?" I ask.

"No. It was impromptu. How'd I do?"

"It was no Oscar-worthy monologue, but I think it could find its place in a Matt Damon, Ben Affleck screenplay."

"Fuck off."

"I love you, too, brother." I lift my water bottle to my mouth and take a sip.

Casey laughs and grabs his phone.

"Hey, Charlie forgot her favorite pink sweatshirt. She says it's in the closet next to your hoodies. Do you want to take it over to her?" He smirks. "You'd really be helping me out if you did. I have other shit to do."

"Oh, yeah? Like what?" I prod.

"If you must know, it's time for my daily jerk. Plus, Noelle just sent me a snap of her at that bar, The Font, in her overalls, and she just took a blow-job shot. Dude, there's a little bit of whipped cream on her upper lip. Hard as steel right now, and I need to go take care of it." He adjusts his junk and stands.

"Bro, I think you've been around Pitz and Archie too long. You're starting to sound just like them."

"Fuck you, Beck!" he says with a laugh.

As he walks away, Archie comes back into the room and heads for the door. "Later, boys."

"Where you going?"

"I'll see you all tomorrow." And then right before the door closes all the way, I think I hear him say, "Going to see my girl."

But that can't be right.

Even though it is cold as shit right now, I decide to walk the two blocks to the sorority house to take Charlie her favorite pink sweatshirt. I didn't text her before I left. I didn't want to give her the chance to say never mind.

As I round the corner, I pull out my phone and text her.

> Beck: Hey. I'm outside with your sweatshirt.

> Charlie: I told Casey to bring it to me. Sorry!

> Beck: Don't be sorry. I'm happy to do it.
> Come out.

> Charlie: Okay, give me a sec.

When she steps out the door, she's in tiny shorts and a long-sleeved shirt, which is so old that it's practically see-through.

And UGGs on her feet. At least she put shoes on. Charlie hates wearing shoes.

Her arms are crossed tightly around her body, and I can see her starting to shiver already. She takes the last step down and comes to stand in front of me.

"Hi," she says cautiously, and I hate it.

I want to reach for her so bad and just pick her up and carry her back to my house with me—and then of course fuck her all night. I miss her so damn much. It takes everything in my power not to kiss her too. Her lips are begging for me to kiss her. But I won't tonight, unless she reaches for me.

"Hey. You didn't answer my text this morning. Did you get the peonies?"

"Wait, what? I did reply. You didn't get it?" She pulls out her phone. "Ohmigod. I forgot to hit Send. I'm sorry. Yes, I did get them. Thank you, Beck. But you really didn't need to do that. You have a lot going on right now."

I nod. "I do, but you will always be my priority."

I'm looking at her, and I'm trying to will her to meet my eyes, but she turns her head to the side.

"Beck, I know I am, but you need to stay focused right now, okay? And I feel like there is a lot we still need to say to each other, and it's just not the right time to hash it out."

"Hash it out? What does that mean? We're not broken up, and we never will be again."

She interrupts me before I can say more, trying to get me to look at her, "No, wrong word choice. I just mean, we need to talk about some things, and those things can wait until after the championship game, Beck."

"Okay, Charlie. I hear you. I'll just head home then."

I hand her the sweatshirt and step back from her. I start to turn to leave, but she grabs my arm.

"Beck, it's killing me to stay away. You know that, right?"

Turning to face her, I can't keep myself from touching her. I bring my hands up to cup her face and look her in the eye. I need her to hear what I'm saying.

"Charlie, this time away from you has killed me too. I can't even come up with enough words to say I'm sorry. I understand why you've done it, and I know I deserve it after I blew up at you after seeing my mom. But don't for one second believe that I don't need you. I need you and want you every second of every day. You are and have always been my reason for moving forward, for trying to heal, for proving to myself that I *am* worthy of your love. I'll probably always be a work in progress, and I am back in regular counseling sessions, but I beg you to be patient with me. Because I promise you, everything I do is for you."

Tears are running down her face, and she reaches up to grasp my wrists. "Beck, I'm sorry for how I handled it too. I didn't know what to do or say. But one thing you never, ever, have to be unsure of is my love for you. You are a part of me, and I will never let you go again. And I'm so glad you're going back to counseling. I think that's amazing, and I'm so proud of you. Let's just get through this last game, okay. Stay focused. *Win.*"

I nod, then bring my forehead to hers. "Okay, baby. I'll give you, us, this time, but you better be ready for me. Once we win this game, you're mine."

She laughs. "Oh, I know I'm yours. Always have been."

Pulling back, she softly kisses me. "I better go inside before I freeze."

"We don't want that. Although...I'm happy to warm you up. Just say the word."

"Beck! Don't tempt me. You better go before I change my mind and follow you home." She lightly pushes me away.

"Okay, okay. I'll talk to you later." I turn and walk away from her. Again. But when I round the corner, I look back and see her still watching me so I stop and she blows me a kiss. I give her a wink and a smile in return.

When I get home, I pull out my phone to put it on the

charger. I just want to shower—and probably jerk off—then go to bed. When I plug in my phone, I see a missed text. It's the text she forgot to send earlier today, then another one right after.

> Charlie: I love you, Beck. Good night.

> Beck: I love you, Boss. Night.

I know I told her I needed some space, but I never meant for it to be more than one night. And maybe she's right. It's probably not the right time to talk about everything, but, fuck, I miss her.

CHAPTER
TWENTY-EIGHT

BECKHAM

THE LAST WEEK and a half has been brutal, and to be real, I haven't been playing my best. We were in the field house, running plays more than anything. Training for the championship game, eating, sleeping. The university even waived attendance in class due to our practices and travel schedule.

I've texted Charlie every day. Sometimes just to say I love her. Been talking to my dad and sister too.

We're playing this championship game in Miami, and I can't complain. We get some cold weather at Walker, but playing in warmer weather is top choice. And this time of year in Florida isn't as hot, so it's prime.

My family is on their way down here now. Their plane should land in the next hour or so. The Kings, including Charlie, are traveling with them. The hotels we stay in try to keep blocks of rooms reserved for family for games like this, so they were able to get rooms at our hotel again. Which is great because I love seeing her and my family before we get on the bus to head to the game.

This morning, after we got here, we watched film in one of

the conference rooms the hotel set up for us. Now, we're pulling into the players' entrance at the stadium parking lot. We have to do some press, and we'll be running some drills. Southeast had the field this morning since they hadn't had to travel as far as we did. So, aside from stadium staff, we—the trainers, coaches, and team—are the only ones here.

After dropping our gear in the locker room, we're escorted out to the field. We've played in bowl games like this before, but last year, we didn't make it to the semifinals. This hits different.

Casey is walking next to me, and I elbow him. He turns to me, and we smile at each other.

"Beck! Can you fucking believe this? Every-fucking-thing we've worked for is right here in our hands. All the blood, sweat, fucking two-a-days got us to this spot. I'm so pumped right now. I just want to get dressed and win this motherfucker!" Casey is practically bouncing on his feet.

It's not that I'm not excited. I am. I think I'm just trying to absorb it all. There's a confidence I feel in our team, and assuming we don't royally fuck up, I think we can win this. I want to win it for all of us because we've worked so hard this season, but I also want Liam to leave Walker with this win on his stats sheet.

Archie comes up behind us and gets us both in a headlock. "Hey, dickheads. Can you believe this? This is the tits. We're gonna blow those Southeast fuckers away—ya feel me? Oh shit, hold up. Where's Pitz?"

He lifts his arms off Casey and me and looks around for Liam. He's across the field with the quarterback coach and Bo, but that doesn't stop Archie from letting out a piercing whistle to get his attention. When the entire team looks at Archie, he puts a hand up.

"Pitz, get your ass over here for a minute."

The quarterback coach just shakes his head at Archie and shoves Liam toward us.

Pitz jogs over, then jumps on Archie's back. "You dick. I was going over a few new plays with the coach."

Archie flips Liam off his back, but before Liam lands on the ground, Arch grabs his arm. "Can't have you getting injured before your last game as a Stallion." Then he smacks Pitz on the ass.

"Ow, asshole. That hurt. I don't have pads on yet, you dick," he says as he shoves Archie.

Archie hardly moves and laughs at Liam's attempt. "Okay, fellas. Let's be real for a few minutes. This is my last college game. Last game Pitz will play as a Stallion. Linson, I didn't know when I met you—what, two years ago now?—that you would become one of my best friends. You're a hell of a player, but an even better friend. And, King, you level out Linson's moodiness, which is why we've kept you around."

We all laugh.

"I'm just playin'. You would do anything for any of us, and that's appreciated more than you know, King. We know you have our backs, no matter what, on and off the field.

"Now, Pitzy, we've been playing together for three seasons. You've been my QB, my wingman, and one of my best friends. I'm really going to miss seeing your ugly mug every day.

"Okay, enough sappy shit. Let's bring it in." He holds out his arms and waves us in. "Come on, fuckers. Let's do this."

The four of us stand in a circle, arms around each other's shoulders.

"Here's to the games we've won together and the one we're about to win. And here's to our brotherhood. We might not be related by blood, but I wouldn't want to do this without you guys. Now let's go get that fucking trophy!"

We all yell, "Hell yeah!"

"Hold up. Let me get a pic of the four of us on the field." I pull out my phone and put it in selfie mode.

Since Liam has the longest reach, I hand my phone to him. The four of us squeeze in the frame. We're all smiling, and

Archie is holding up his index finger next to his face. Liam takes a few in rapid succession, then hands my phone back to me.

I'm really missing Charlie today, and I feel like she should be here with us on this field. So, I send her one of the pics.

Beck: Go, Stallions!

Charlie: Oh my God, I love this! 😍

Beck: I love you.

Charlie: I love you too. See you soon!

I drop my phone into my pocket then turn and jog to meet Casey, Liam, and Archie.

Archie has an interview he needs to do, and the rest of us need to run drills. Then we will be watching film and shooting commercial shots.

After we leave the field for a break before the game, we'll eat as a team, run over a few more plays, then go to bed. Coach has set a curfew tonight—not that we need one. We all know what's at stake here. And we're not walking away from this game without the trophy.

We're standing in the tunnel, waiting to go out onto the field. We're all shifting on our feet, anxious to get out there. Coach is near the opening, leading the team. Casey, Archie, and I are near the front, but behind Bo and Liam. They are holding hands, standing calm and ready to take the field.

That's just another thing that makes Bo Callaway special. He is a team player and already a great leader, and he's respectful of his teammates. This show of solidarity is also a sign of respect to Pitz and the time he's played at Walker. Gotta admire that.

Archie is standing next to me, and Casey is on my other side.

Archie is hyping the team up, jumping around. "Let's fucking go! Who are we?"

"STALLIONS!" the team yells.

"What are we gonna do today?"

"WIN!"

Then he turns to me and smacks the top of my helmet and then Casey's. "Let's go, baby! Linson, I got you, man. I won't let anyone get by me today." He turns to Casey. "King, you get the ball, and you run like your life depends on it!"

"You know it, baby. Let's GO!"

They grab hands and pull each other in and bump chests.

We can hear our fight song playing, so that's one of our signals that we're about to run out onto the field. The fireworks on either side of our tunnel start to go off, and then we hear our cue.

"Please welcome the Walker University Stallions!"

We all run out as a team. Archie is bouncing up and down and waving his arms, trying to get the fans to cheer louder. Casey and I jog over to the sideline, find our spots, and place our helmets on the bench. When I look up, I see my dad and sister. Next to them are the Kings. And Charlie. I knew she would be here, of course, but we didn't get a chance to see our families before we left for the field this morning or talk to them before the game because we couldn't use our phones. Coach didn't want us to get distracted.

Charlie waves at me, and I get a glimpse of her jersey. My fucking number is on her chest. I nod and smile at her. We're not supposed to talk to anyone before we play, but fuck it.

I move around the bench and walk toward the stands.

"Dude, where are you going?" Casey yells over the noise of the crowd.

I tilt my head toward Charlie, and Casey just shakes his head and smiles.

When I get to the wall, I reach up and slap my dad's and sister's hands, then Carol's and Tim's. They all wish me luck, and I smile and nod, gaze still on Charlie. She's watching me and smiling.

"Come here, baby."

I reach up to the bar she's leaning on and pull myself up a little. She bends down to meet me.

"You're crazy! You know that, right? Coach could bench you for this!" She's laughing and shaking her head, her eyebrows raised.

"I don't care. Give me a kiss. You are my good-luck charm."

I tilt my head up and pull myself up a little more to reach her. She leans over as far as she can and puts her hands on either side of my face.

"Good luck, Beck. I love you so much. Keep yourself safe out there. And tell Archie he'd better protect my guy."

And then our lips meet. It's too short, but it's sweet.

I drop down and walk backward, still looking at Charlie. I put two fingers over the four-leaf clover tattoo over my heart, then kiss my fingertips and point them at her. She hasn't stopped smiling.

When I get back over to my teammates, Coach is standing there with a scowl on his face.

"Nice of you to join us, Linson. It's only the biggest game of your fucking life, but please, don't let us interrupt your time with your girl. Now get out on the field for warm-ups!"

I grab my helmet off the bench and follow the other guys on offense out to the field.

When we're doing our warm-ups, I take a minute to look around and soak it all in. This is it. The big show. I smile to myself, then look over at Casey next to me. We both smirk at each other.

We fucking did it.

About three hours later, we're in the fourth quarter. We are behind—twenty-eight to twenty-four—with twelve seconds left to play, no time-outs, after Bo called our last one while he was lying on the ground. The Southeast Bulls have no time-outs left either.

We are on the left hash mark, at the thirty-seven-yard line, on the Bulls side, with the wind in our faces. It is now the third down, after Bo got sacked by their blitz. My back is killing me from the last hit I took two plays ago.

Archie stands beside me and smacks my chest with the back of his hand. "Man, I'm so fucking sorry I missed that block. He got me on my blind side. I promise you, it won't happen again."

I pat his shoulder and nod.

All eleven guys in the huddle, including Archie and me, are tired, sweaty, and bloody, but as we look at each other, I know without a doubt that we won't accept anything but a win.

I follow Bo's glance to Coach Pettys on the sideline, who taps the top of his hat, telling Bo that he should call the play. Bo turns to look at me and nods his head, letting me know that he wants to hand me the ball. It is all on me now.

We practiced a swing pass that we called Elvis. Once Bo receives the ball from our center, he'll then toss the football to me as I move to the right. In order for this to work, Archie has to seal the outside of the D-end for the wide receivers and tight end to get solid downfield blocks to spring me to the end zone.

Bo looks at us. "Okay, boys, this is ours! Let's finish this now! We won't need a fourth down! All right, trips right, two swings, X left, shotgun, on one!" He claps once.

We break the huddle. The three receivers split to the wide side, with the X receiver, Casey, headed to the nearest sideline. I'm two yards in back of Bo, three yards to his left. Our center is over the ball, ready to hike. The guards and tackles get into their pass blocking stance, and the tight end is slightly outside our right tackle on the line of scrimmage, giving him leverage on his coming block. I look at the defense as they get set.

With this Elvis call, I know that if there are only four defenders in the box on the line of scrimmage, Bo will audible the call to red, meaning he will hand off the ball to me and I'll run sweep to the right side of the field and the blockers will know to go into run block action. Our left guard will pull to the right, and the other linemen will seal block to the run side.

If there are five defenders in the box, he'll call blue, so he will throw a Z-out pass to Casey, streaking down the field, with the play designed for him to throw the ball into the outside deep corner of the end zone and for Casey to catch it. Pass blocking will stay the same as Elvis, with me staying in to guard the left side if we have a corner blitz from Bo's blind side.

I look out over the defense and see the Bulls shift into a blitz with both linebackers ready to come on the snap. This is just what we wanted.

Bo yells, "Elvis," meaning we run the play we called in the huddle.

I take a deep breath as I watch the end zone clock ticking down.

Nine, eight, seven …

Bo calls, "SET," and the ball is tossed to him from the center.

I start to move, and our line goes into pass blocking, shifting to the right to zone block. The tight end chips the defensive end, knocking him off his feet, then heads downfield to block the weak side safety, following our play to the right.

It feels like time is moving in slow motion. Bo looks to his left, faking a pass to the left, temporarily holding the weak side safety and left-side defensive end, then quickly flings the ball to me. I catch it, then plant my right foot hard and head downfield. Our wide receivers all hit their blocks and hold them long enough for me to clear and get a wide-open field into the end zone.

Holy shit. We fucking won!

I turn toward my teammates on the field. I see Bo rushing to the end zone. The receivers and tight end run over to me. Archie reaches me and lifts me up, and all I can hear are my boys yelling and the crowd going crazy. Archie sets me down, and we're all jumping and hugging each other. Helmets are flung off, and the fans start pouring onto the field. It's pure insanity.

Casey runs up to me from the side, stopping and grabbing my shoulder pads. "We fucking did it, brother! You fucking did it!"

He pulls me in for a hug. I close my eyes for just a second. All the hard work, two-a-days, camps, blood, bruises—it was all worth it for this moment.

But now I want to go get my girl. This all means nothing without her by my side.

CHAPTER
TWENTY-NINE

CHARLIE

THERE ARE SO many people rushing the field, and I'm afraid I'll get trampled if I try to go down there right now.

My dad tugs at my arm and leans over to speak in my ear. "We need to wait a few minutes until they can clear some of these fans off the field. It's too crazy right now."

Ryan leans forward against the bar in front of us. The look of pride on his face is unforgettable. I can only imagine what he must be feeling right now. They've been through so much, and to see his son achieve an accomplishment of this magnitude has to feel incredible.

"The security guard is waiting for us at the end of the row. He's going to lead us down to the field. They're keeping the family in the tunnel until they get the stage set up and some of the fans cleared off."

My dad pulls me in front of him, putting me in between him and Mom. Brooke is in front of me with Ryan leading. I grab Brooke's hand, and she turns back to look at me and smiles.

"Can you believe this, Brooke? They did it!"

"I'm so excited for Beck and Casey! I just want to get down there and hug them!"

We reach the tunnel and see Archie's family, and it looks like some of his brothers are here too. They all look alike. Liam's parents are talking to Coach's wife near the front.

Ryan turns to say something, but we can't hear him over the noise of the crowd. Brooke shakes her head at him and points to her ear. He just laughs and turns back around.

The crowd on the field is starting to thin out a little, and we can now see the platform for the awards. There are two security guards in the front, and we see them raise their hands, signaling for us to head onto the field. I'm still holding Brooke's hand, but I start to jog and pull her with me to find Beck.

I see the guys standing in front of the stage. Beck isn't on the stage this time, but he's with Casey and Liam. Archie is, of course, on the stage. He's eating this up.

As we get closer, Beck turns and tilts his head up, searching the crowd. When he spots me and Brooke, she lets go of my hand, and I run to Beck. His arms are open, and I leap into his arms and wrap my legs around his waist. We're both laughing while we kiss.

I pull back from our kiss and search his face. He looks so happy and tired, and he's still dripping in sweat, but he's never looked more handsome.

"You did it, baby!" Tears prick my eyes, and I see his eyes turning glossy too.

He tucks his head into my neck, and I can feel his chest heaving against mine.

"I love you so much!" His head is still in my neck, and I can hear the tears in his voice.

"I love you so much, Beck. That was absolutely incredible. I'm so, so proud of you!"

He pulls back and kisses me again. This kiss is wet from both of our tears, and it's a moment I will never forget.

He sets me on my feet and wipes his eyes with his gloves. Brooke and Ryan come over, and he wraps his arms around them both. I want to give them this moment together, so I turn and look for my parents and Casey.

They're a little closer to the stage, so I make my way through the families and congratulate the guys as I pass them. Mom is still wrapped around Casey, and the tears are falling down her face. I look at Dad and see he's wiping his eyes with the palm of his hand. Casey looks up and spots me and smiles. He had a great game today and caught one pass for a touchdown.

"I'm so proud of you, little brother!"

I wrap my arms around him, laughing. He lifts me up, squeezes me, then puts me down.

"Char, can you fucking believe this? We did it!"

I hug him again, and then the announcer starts to speak. Beck and his family have moved in close to us, and Beck stands behind me and wraps his arms around my waist. I turn my head and look up at him, and he leans in for a kiss.

We stay like that as the announcer issues congratulations and awards for MVP of the game. Archie is still standing on the stage with some of the other guys and the coach. He sees us in the crowd and points at us and nods. Beck straightens one of his arms and points back at Archie.

I turn my head again and kiss his jaw. "I love you, Beck. Watching you out there today was amazing. You deserve all of this and more."

"We do, baby. We all do. I still can't believe it. Is this for real?"

He rests his chin on my head and wraps both arms around my chest. I grasp his arms with my hands and lightly squeeze.

The rest of the ceremony goes by in a blur, and then we are all being led off the field. When we reach the hallway to the locker room, we all hug each other again. The guys will be a while—between the coach's speech, showers, and interviews—so we decided to head back to the hotel to wait for them there.

As I turn to walk away, Beck grabs my arm to stop me. "I need you tonight. After we're done with the family, you're coming to my room." He kisses me and turns to walk away.

My face flushes with heat as I think about being with him again. It's been weeks since we've had sex. I need him just as much as he needs me.

———

There are tables set up in one of the conference rooms at the hotel. There have been more toasts and speeches than I can count, and all I can think about is getting upstairs with Beck. His hands haven't left me since he got here, and while he's never been shy about giving me attention, he's definitely not caring at all about anyone seeing him rub up on me. I should feel a little embarrassed, considering our parents are with us, but I don't.

And I can't lie—all the touches and kisses have me seriously turned on. I'll be ready to explode by the time we get to the room. I know Beck is feeling the same because I let my hand travel up his thigh, and I can feel the tip of his erection. I look at him and smirk, but pull my hand away. He doesn't say anything, just leans toward me and kisses my neck.

My mom and dad stand from our table to leave, giving us all hugs.

My mom leans down and whispers in my ear, "I assume you'll be staying with Beck tonight?"

Again, I should be embarrassed, but I'm not. "Uh, yeah. Sorry if this is awkward for you," I say with a laugh.

She just shrugs. "If you think I don't know you've been having sex since you were sixteen, you don't give me enough credit." Her lips touch the top of my head. "Good night, sweet girl."

I tilt my head up to look at my parents. "Night. Night, Dad. See you guys in the morning. I'll be back in the room by six to leave for the airport."

Dad looks at my mom, then me, then back at Mom. I guess he hasn't caught on that I'm not staying with them tonight. Awkward.

Mom ushers him away, and she turns and waves. Ryan and Brooke are saying their goodbyes to Beck, then hug me too.

When they walk away, Beck grabs my hands. "Can we leave now?"

He's got a heated look in his eyes that tells me my answer had better be yes.

When I nod, he lets go of one of my hands, and we head to the elevators.

"Wait, don't we need to tell Casey? I don't want him trying to get in the room tonight."

Beck looks at me. "Boss, if you thought I didn't have a plan in place, you don't know me at all. Casey is going to stay with some guys in another room. It's all good."

He's all but dragging me to the elevator. He nods and waves at people we pass, all of whom congratulate him. And when we reach the elevator, he notices it closing and holds a foot out to stop the doors.

He pulls me into the elevator and into his chest. He reaches behind me to push the button to our floor. I can't help the bubble of laughter that comes out. I've seen him anxious to get me naked before, but this is a whole new level.

My laughter stops when he leans his head down to mine and kisses me. It's the kind of kiss that I feel from my lips to my toes. It's desperate and wet. His tongue invades my mouth, and I meet it with mine. His hands move to the bottom of my jersey, and he lifts it up until he can touch the skin on my back. It tickles and has me squirming just a little. But he doesn't stop. His hands travel up to my bra, and he unhooks it.

"Babe, we're in the elevator."

"Uh-huh." Then he covers my mouth again.

The elevator stops at our floor, and as the doors open, he releases my mouth and pulls his hands from under my jersey.

Taking my hand, he steps out, and we practically race down the hallway. I'm grateful we don't see anyone. With the way we're rushing, there's no mistaking what we're going to do.

Beck taps his key to the door lock and opens it. I'm barely inside before he's got me up against the door and reaching for my jersey to pull it off. He dives back in and kisses me, a little slower this time. This kiss is teasing. His mouth opens, and he touches his tongue to the center of my upper lip.

"Have I ever told you that I love your mouth? You have the most perfect lips. The way you kiss me. The way they wrap around my cock and suck me in. Your mouth was made for me, baby." He pulls away and walks backward toward one of the beds.

Before he sits, he pulls his shirt off and slides his pants and boxers down his solid thighs. He kicks them off to the side. "Come here, baby." He holds his hand out to me, and as I reach him, he pulls me between his legs.

He unbuttons and unzips my shorts and slides them, along with my panties, down my legs in one swoop. Leaving me completely bare to him. Beck leans forward and licks me from my center to my lower belly. His eyes are watching mine as he licks, nips, and sucks his way back and forth.

His hands are moving up and down the back of my thighs and up to my ass. Then he brings them to the front and smooths them over my breasts, waist, and finally down to the front of my thighs. He pulls my legs apart. "Open for me. I need to taste your sweetness. It's been too fucking long, and I want dessert."

I widen my stance as his hands travel to my center, spreading me open with his thumbs. He leans in, eyes on mine, and with a flat tongue, he licks me from my opening to my clit. I moan and reach out to run my hands through his hair. I start guiding his movements and thrust my center into his face.

"Beck, oh God. Don't stop."

In response, he grabs my right leg and sets my foot on the bed. He rubs his hand back up my leg to my ass and squeezes as he pulls me into his face. His other hand moves to my opening, and he slips in one finger as his tongue twirls around my clit.

When he groans against my clit, the vibration from it shoots right through me, and I feel the first pulse of an orgasm. I'm so close.

"You taste so fucking good. I'll never get enough of this." He adds another finger and sucks on my clit.

My hips are rocking against his face, and I pull his head into me even more, like I can't get him close enough. "Keep doing that. Right there. Don't stop." I feel like I'm starting to lose control, and for all I know, the whole hallway can hear me panting.

White-hot heat spreads through me as I start to pulse around his fingers. He doesn't stop sucking until I pull on his hair to push him away. My orgasm is still rippling through me as he brings his fingers out, and he starts kissing the inside of my thigh.

"Beck, that was ..." I don't think I can form words yet. But I do know that I need to taste him as much as he needed to taste me.

I drop my leg from the bed and bring my hands to cup his jaw. I lift his face to mine and kiss him. I slip my tongue into his mouth, and I can taste myself. I deepen the kiss and suck on his tongue, making him groan. His mouth opens as I pull back, my lips still wrapped around his tongue, sucking. I release his tongue with a pop. I straighten my body and look down at him. He's watching me, but also telling me so much in the heat of his stare.

This man loves me. I don't know how I could have ever questioned that.

His hands smooth up my body to my breasts. He palms them and squeezes. Then he leans forward and takes one of my nipples into his mouth and sucks. When he pulls away, he scrapes his teeth and bites the tip. It makes another ripple roll through my body.

When he releases my nipple, I pull back slightly and go to my knees in front of him. He moves his hands from my body, bracing his arms with his hands at his sides. I look up at his face as I slide my hand up and down his erection. As I reach the head of his cock, I twist my fist slightly and pull. Beck's eyes close, and his head drops back between his shoulders.

He looks back down at me as I bring my tongue to his tip, licking the pre-cum.

"You look so good on your knees for me, baby. Open that pretty little mouth and take what you want." His right hand comes to my face, and he traces his thumb from my cheekbone to my lips.

Leaning into him, I open my mouth and take him all the way in until I gag. He loves it when I gag, so I don't feel self-conscious about it.

"Beautiful, baby. You're so fucking beautiful."

I pull my mouth back to the tip and wrap my hand around him. I slide my hand up and down in sync with my pulls on the head of his cock. His hand drifts from my face into my hair, and he tugs on it lightly. I move my hand to the base of his cock as I slide my mouth all the way down. He starts to thrust into me when my mouth reaches my hand, and it makes me gag again. When I pull back up, saliva is dripping from my mouth, and my eyes are watering. But I don't stop.

When I reach between his legs and grab his balls, Beck thrusts up into my mouth. He pulls on my hair again in warning. "Baby, I'm about to come."

I don't stop.

"Baby, please. I need to be inside of you. I'll let you suck my cock again later if you're a good girl," he says with a smirk.

Then he puts his hands under my arms and starts to lift me up. His cock falls out of my mouth with a pop, and I stand.

Beck scoots back to the headboard, and I crawl onto the bed in between his spread legs. Stopping at his erection, I flatten my tongue and give him one more long lick and then kiss the top of his cock.

I spread my legs to straddle him, but I don't put him inside me yet. I lean forward, hands running up his chest, over his tattoos, stopping on the four-leaf clover.

"Beck, I have missed you so much. I hope you know that me staying at Arbor's wasn't to punish you. It killed me to do it, but you'd asked for some time, and I guess after I got over the hurt of thinking you meant you wanted a break from me, I realized that you did need some time. You needed time to focus and prepare for what you did out on that field today. And I'm so glad I did it. Because you won the motherfucking national championship, baby!"

I lean in and kiss him. He deepens the kiss, and we just sit there, kissing for what seems like hours. When he pulls back from the kiss, his gaze travels down my body to where his cock rests in my crease. I start to slide back and forth on his erection, making him groan.

"You have about two seconds to put my dick inside of that pussy before I flip you over and take what I want."

I lean forward and kiss him as I lift my hips and grab his erection, positioning the head at my entrance. Placing my hands on his chest, I ease my body down his cock. We both moan at the feeling of coming together. When I look up at his face, he's watching his cock slide into me.

"Don't move, baby. Give me a minute to catch my breath, or I might come with you just sitting on me like this." He closes his eyes for a second and squeezes my thighs with his hands.

I start to move because I have to. He's still sitting with his eyes closed, but his hands are rubbing up and down my thighs now. I lean forward and kiss him while I rock back and forth. He tells me he loves me each time our lips part.

Sitting up again, I continue to move up and down on him. He grabs my hips and starts driving his cock in as deep as he can.

"Baby, you need to get there. I can't hold this much longer. FUCK! Baby, come!" Beck demands.

I place my hands behind me and grab his thighs. It makes my chest push out, and Beck runs his hands up and down my body. I feel sexy and loved and worshipped. When he grasps one breast with one hand and brings his other to my center and starts circling my clit, I lose control. He thrusts up into me, and I let him take over while I chase my orgasm.

The pulsing starts at the base of my spine and shoots through me, right to my clit. I can't hold it back, and I can't wait for him to meet me. I look at his face to see him watching where we're coming together. But I know he feels my eyes on him, and he looks up. Our eyes lock, and I feel the first jump of his cock inside me as my orgasm cascades through my body. Beck's mouth drops open a little as he continues to release into me. I stop moving altogether, coming down from the high. Beck moves his hands to my hips, and he squeezes me playfully as his breathing also starts to return to normal.

I lean down and kiss him again, whispering, "I love you," across his lips.

Then I pull back up to a sitting position and sit by his side. He scoots down on the bed so his head now rests on a pillow. And I lie down next to him. He lays his arm out, and I rest my head on his shoulder.

Between Beck's muscles and his tattoos, his body is truly a work of art. I bring one hand to his chest and trace the planes of his abs and chest. Then I trace each of his tattoos on his chest. Goose bumps pop as I do it, but he doesn't stop me. We lie there like that for a few minutes, lost in our afterglow.

"Do you know that I've fallen in love with you three times?"

I look at his face. "What do you mean?"

"The first time I fell for you was when you came hopping over to my house the day we moved to Troy. You were so happy, and I was so sad at the time. Not because we'd moved, but because I was still dealing with so much. I saw how happy you were, and I wanted to soak it up. When you walked away, I watched you until you went inside your house. Of course, I didn't really know what falling in love felt like at that age, but that was what I felt. I loved you already."

"Beck …"

"The second time I fell in love with you was the day you almost beat me at the tree. I watched your braids flying behind you, and I couldn't help but smile. You were so focused and so determined to beat me. And when we reached the tree, I knew I had to kiss you. By then, I had an idea what love was, and I knew when I was with you, I could feel you, soul deep."

Tears are forming in my eyes. It's not like this is the first time he's told me he loves me, but he's telling me how he felt while falling in love with me. I'm not taking this time for granted with my words, so I sit and listen.

"And the third time? I know you might laugh at this, but it was when I walked out my front door and saw you standing near Casey's truck when we moved you to Walker." He laughs. "The look on your face was priceless. Of course, I knew it was my fault. I put that look on your face, but I was also going to be the one to take it off. I'd had plans to win you back, even before you decided to come to Walker, but when you figured out you couldn't live without me either, well, that just played right into my plan."

"I did not decide to come to Walker for you, Beckham Linson, I assure you."

"Oh, baby, but you did. You can't stay away from me, just like I can't stay away from you. And when I got in the truck after you and looked at you in the mirror … our eyes met, and I knew I hadn't lost you. That's when I fell in love with you again."

"So, you're saying you stopped loving me between those times?"

He sighs. "Charlene, don't ruin it. I've heard that there are three loves of your life. I don't know all the reasons for it, but I know that you're all three of mine. You were always meant to be mine. And, baby, this is it. We're forever."

I'm watching his face while he speaks, and I feel a tear run down my face. This gorgeous man, inside and out ... is mine. And he always has been. The first time I saw his blue-gray eyes, I knew he was the one meant for me. And I get what he's saying about falling in love with me three times because we never stopped loving each other, but there were key moments that made that love deeper.

CHAPTER
THIRTY

BECKHAM

WE'VE BEEN BACK on campus now for two weeks. It was chaos when we returned with a university parade, interviews, and parties. It didn't seem like things were ever going to go back to normal. And maybe they won't. All of us on this team have accomplished something so few ever will in their lifetime. I won't ever forget that or take it for granted.

Playing football for the NFL is my dream, and if I have a good season in the fall, I'm hoping to enter the draft next spring. But it can all go away in the blink of an eye. One pull, tear, or broken bone can end a career.

And watching Liam pack up his things and clear out his locker two days ago was tough. He accepted a transfer to Michigan, of all places. Poor guy. But there, he'll be starting again, and he'll have a real shot to make it in the draft when he goes next year. I'm going to miss him. He's been a good friend to me and a great leader on the field.

So, things have gotten quiet around here.

Casey seems to be hanging out with Noelle more and more. I can't tell what the deal is with those two, and every time I ask him, he blows me off. He did tell me she got back together with Trey, but he's in season now, so she doesn't get to see him as much. But I don't want Casey to be used by her as a fallback boy. He's the best of the best, and he deserves a girl who will love him the way he loves.

Charlie's room finally became available at the sorority house, but she decided to stay with me because it didn't make sense to move her so close to the end of the year. There's also a chance I might have begged her not to go. Her terms in order for her to stay here were for me to allow her to redecorate our room.

So, we returned the cot, which she'd only used for a month or so really. Then we pulled everything out of the room and painted it. Pink.

We're permitted to paint the walls during our lease period, which we renewed for another year, as long as we paint it back to the color it was when we moved in. Fair enough. So, now my girl has her pink palace on the prairie.

Along the whole wall where her cot sat, she put a large group of peonies, like a wallpaper or sticker thing. I mean ... it's covered. Above my desk, which we now share, she framed new and old pictures of us. Some just the two of us, some with Casey in them too.

My Star Wars comforter has been replaced with a pink one, but she did let me keep my pillowcase with the Millennium Falcon on it. And there's a huge picture above the bed; it's an arial photo of the championship game that she had blown up to a canvas print. It's awesome—I'm not gonna lie. Even though she had it tinted ... pink.

If I thought she had all her stuff in the bathroom before, I was wrong. I don't even remember seeing half of this stuff in the boxes in the closet before she completely unpacked. But it was all in there. We have glass canisters that hold some of her things and some that hold Q-tips and cotton balls and a fake plant. In the bathroom. Oh, and a picture hanging over the toilet that says, *If you sprinkle when you tinkle, please be neat and wipe the seat.*

For the record, I don't sprinkle when I take a piss. But she thought it was funny, so up it went.

She made some additions to the house as a whole, but thankfully didn't go the pink route. But she did reorganize the kitchen, and we now have containers holding cereal, pasta, and oatmeal. Everything that should be in boxes is now in containers. Same with the fridge—God forbid someone sets the milk in the wrong place. Where she had hidden this creature before she officially moved in, we can't figure it out. And, yes, she did all of this since we'd come home from Miami.

Surprisingly, her parents and my dad weren't shocked that Charlie had decided to stay in our house. Tim knows I love his daughter, but I'm sure it was a little weird for him to know she'd be sharing my bed. I think it makes him feel better in some way, knowing Casey is here. And that maybe we aren't banging on every surface of the house.

Spoiler alert: We are.

Speaking of my girl, where the fuck is she? She should have been home forty minutes ago.

I haven't seen her since this morning. Between classes and the gym, our schedules don't mesh well.

I hear the front door open, and I peek around the wall from where I'm sitting at the kitchen table with my afternoon mac 'n' cheese. Now that we're not in season, I'm a little more liberal with what I eat. At least until spring ball starts.

Archie comes through the door with a huge bag in his hand. It doesn't look like his gym bag, but maybe he got a new one for his training gear.

He's leaving for the combine in Indiana soon. NFL coaches, scouts, managers, and team owners attend. Players are tested on not only their physical abilities, but their mental abilities as well. It's an intense four days. I wish I could go with him, but we'll be able to catch some, if not all, of it on TV.

"Yo," he says, dropping his bag and walking into the kitchen.

"Sup, man?" I nod to his bag. "You just coming in from training?"

"Uh, yeah. And then I had to go pick something up for a friend of mine. I'm just stopping here for a few before I need to head out again."

"Dude, you've hardly been here at all lately. I know you're not out partying, and you aren't training all night. So ... where are you spending all your time?"

He looks at me for a minute, and I can't read his face. Like he kind of wants to tell me something, but he's not really sure if he should.

"I've just been spending some time with a friend, is all."

"Aha! A girlfriend?"

He huffs, "She's a girl, and she's my friend. I'd like her to be more, but she's not there yet. And with me about to get drafted, well, it complicates things a little bit."

I'm too in shock to reply. Archie has a girl. One girl. Who he likes.

Seriously, what has been happening here lately?

His phone starts ringing; it plays our fight song, and every time it goes off, it makes me jump. Not because I don't like it, but because it's loud as shit. He pulls it out of his pants pocket. He doesn't answer it, so I assume it's not a call, but a text. Fucker has that song set for both.

"I gotta run, but I'll see you later, my man. Don't do anything I wouldn't do." He pats my shoulder as he walks out.

"Which leaves a whole lot of trouble."

He picks up the bag and goes to his room. He must toss it in there because, seconds later, he's walking back out the door with a wave.

Twenty minutes later, Charlie finally walks in the door. "I'm so sorry I'm late! I stopped by the house after class and found Lily crying in her room. I couldn't just leave her. Arbor wasn't back from class yet. So, I stayed with her and got to hear all about the drama she's having with this guy at the Lambda Xi house. I mean, that should have been her first clue, but what do I know?"

She walks over to me, and I scoot my chair back slightly to give her room to sit on my lap.

She wraps her arms around my shoulders when she sits and leans in for a kiss. "Hi."

"Hey, you."

"I missed you today. Did you have a good day?"

"Uh, yeah. Just class, and then I went to the gym. Finally saw Archie. He stopped in for a hot second. When I asked him where he'd been lately, he kind of acted weird, then told me about a girl."

"SHUT UP! Archie has a girlfriend? No freaking way." Her mouth is hanging open.

"Well, not really, I guess, but he wants her to be. He bolted out of here within a few minutes of getting a text, so I assume it was her. He's gotta leave soon for the combine and then the draft, so I guess that might be causing a problem or something."

"It's funny that you bring that up. What are we going to do if you enter the draft next year? I'll have one more year of school left. And once you get drafted, you'll pretty much leave right away, right?"

She bites down on her lower lip. I want to pull it out and kiss it.

"I don't know. I guess I've never really thought about it. I mean, I know we're always going to be together, so I just assumed you'd go with me or come as soon as you could. Either way, it has to be your decision. You know I want you with me all the time."

She scrunches up her face. It's both adorable and disturbing. So, I reach out and brush my thumb along her nose and cheek, across the freckles that are lightly scattered there.

"Oh! Speaking of the draft, I thought we could have a draft day party. I was thinking I could invite Arbor and Lily so I had someone to talk to while you guys watched."

"You don't want to watch?"

"Of course I will, duh. But I mean, you guys start talking about plays and all kinds of stuff that I don't know about."

"What are you talking about? You know more about football than any girl I know and even some guys."

"You're cute for saying that, but that's not true." She shakes her head a little. "Okay, maybe I do know more than the average girl, but I still want friends here too."

"Fair."

"Okay, yay! So, I think it would be fun if we watched—"

"*Draft Day.*"

"Yes! Like we always did. And I'll make some snacks, we'll get some beer or whatever you guys want, and we'll watch some of our friends have their dreams come true." She smiles and kisses me. "Sound good?"

"Whatever you want, babe. I'll see if Casey wants to invite anyone over, but I'll probably invite Callaway and a few other guys."

"Perfect." She kisses me. "So, tell me, what was the best part of your day?"

I stand with her in my arms. "How about I show you instead?"

As soon as we get to our room, I drop her onto the bed, where I do, in fact, show her what the best part of my day is. Her coming. On my tongue.

CHAPTER
THIRTY-ONE

CHARLIE

IT'S NOW APRIL, and it has been a few weeks since the combine. We've seen Archie very little since he's been back, but when he is here, he's either eating or sleeping. We did get to say goodbye to him before he went back to Texas to be with his family for the draft. He opted to be at home instead of going to the draft ceremony. But we'll still get to see him on TV.

He's FaceTiming with Beck and Casey right now. He's in the kitchen at his parents' home. From what I can see, there is a ton of food there. A whole crowd of people circling it, laughing, patting Archie as they walk by.

And Archie is the same ol' Arch. He's calm and smiling.

"I'm pumped, man. I just want it to start already."

"Do you know where you're going yet? Or can you not say?" Beck asks him.

Archie winks at him in response.

"Okay, so you know or no? Come on, brother. You're killing me!"

Archie laughs. "How about this? You'll find out in about thirty minutes or so. Along with the rest of the country."

"Dude! You suck. That's so mean. I thought we were your friends. Pssht."

Casey pops in. "That is cold, Arch. You could give us a little hint. Not like we're gonna tell anyone."

"Oh, yeah, right. Just the dozen or so sitting with you in the house. Ha!"

I take the phone from Beck. "Don't listen to them, Arch. We'll be watching the whole time. We're so excited for you! I can't wait to see where you're going. But tell me, for reals, are you happy?"

"You know, Chuck, I am. I really, really am." He winks at me.

"Good enough for me. Have fun! We'll call you later so you can give us the details." I blow him a kiss and hang up the phone.

"Babe, why did you hang up? I wanted to ask him one more question."

I put my hands on Beck's face. "Beckham, this time next year, when you're in the same spot he is, the last thing you'll want to be doing is talking on the phone, avoiding spoilers with your buddies. And don't even act like that's not true."

"Well, no, because I will have you, Case, my family, and yours with me. That's all I need." He lifts me up and kisses me.

He starts to deepen the kiss, but I pull back.

"Uh-uh. Later. We have to watch the draft!"

He sets me down and smacks my butt as I walk away into the family room. A few of the guys are here from the team, including Bo Callaway. He's been super sweet and polite. Arbor is sitting next to him on the couch, but she's deep in conversation with Lily. Bo looks at me as I come to sit next to Lily and smirks and nods to the girls. He must hear their conversation. He's likely getting some juicy bits.

The guy Lily was upset about back in February begged her for another chance, and they've been together since then. She was a virgin before they started dating. Now … she is not. And she wants to tell us about every little detail of her sex life.

"And then he slipped his finger—"

"Lil!" I stop her. "There are other people in the room with us. Who can hear you." I nod toward Bo.

He doesn't look at us, but he does smirk. He totally heard the whole thing.

"Ohmigod," she whisper-yells. "Do you think he heard me?"

"Uh, yeah, I think he did."

Then the three of us start laughing.

Beck comes into the room with a beer in hand. He doesn't drink much, and when he does, it's usually only a few beers. I always wondered why he never got carried away like some of the guys do, but now it all makes sense.

He sits down next to me, then lifts me up and sets me on his lap.

"Was that necessary?"

He kisses the tip of my nose. "Yep."

I kiss him back. On the lips.

We hear the commissioner come on the TV, and I turn to watch. He says a few things about congratulating all the players and then dives right in.

The first two picks are called. The first is from Ohio, and the next one is from Southeast, who we beat in the championship game.

The guys are still talking about the skills of the guy from Southeast when the commissioner comes back on. He introduces a man who's representing Dallas.

The guys stop talking, and we all watch. I see Bo's left leg bouncing up and down.

"You anxious there, Callaway?" I ask.

He looks at me and nods once. "I'm good. I'm just hoping to see Archie come up here in the next few rounds."

As soon as he says that, we hear it.

"With the third pick of the 2025 NFL Draft, the Dallas Cowboys select Archie Griffith, tackle from Walker University."

The camera cuts to Archie in his family home. He's sitting on the couch, next to his mom, who I recognize. On his other side is a girl with sandy-blonde hair. He hangs up the call he's on, puts a Cowboys hat on his head, then stands. He hugs and kisses his mom on the cheek. Then he hugs his dad, and some of his brothers pile in and slap him on the back. Then he walks over to the girl who was next to him on the couch.

He takes her by the hand and pulls her up gently. He kisses her on the lips and hugs her. His body is covering her, so we can't really see a close-up of her face yet. But when the camera zooms in as Archie takes a seat, we see it.

Casey jumps up from his seat in the chair, hands flying on top of his head. He looks at Beck. "What the actual fuck? Did you know about this?"

I look over my shoulder at Beck, who is shaking his head. He looks just as surprised as Casey.

"Holy shit. I know her." Bo points at the TV.

Casey pulls out his phone. "Okay, we're about to get some answers up in here. What the fuck?!"

Archie is on TV, talking, but we're all too stunned and speaking over one another that we don't hear anything that he says, and then it cuts to a commercial break.

I look over my shoulder at Beck. "Don't get any ideas."

He just smiles at me and kisses my lips. "Not yet, Boss."

EPILOGUE

CHARLIE

ONE YEAR LATER

IT'S DRAFT DAY AGAIN. But this time, we're at Beck's house. It doesn't actually start for another hour, so we're all just hanging around right now, eating and watching highlights of Beck, which the media team made for the players at the university. We didn't win the championship game this year, but we did make another playoffs run. Still, Beck had a great season.

Casey is staying at Walker one more year, and depending on how they do next season, he may or may not enter the draft. He hasn't decided if the NFL is the right move for him yet.

I'm sitting on the couch next to Beck, and my mom leans over the back of the couch and whispers in my ear, "Honey, I need you to run home and get that gift I got for Beck. I put it on the desk in your bedroom."

"Why would you put it in my room?"

"Because I've been using your desk, and, well, you don't live there anymore, so I've been storing some things in your closet."

"Mom! That's kinda harsh."

Dad, who's behind me, leans over and squeezes my shoulder. "You always have a room at home, Char."

"Thank you, Dad. Glad one of you still wants me around." I turn back to my mom, "Seriously, Mom, why do you hate me?"

Mom huffs and rolls her eyes. "Just go."

Dad looks at me with a pointed look, so I relent and stand.

Beck, who apparently missed this exchange, grabs the waistband of my jeans and tugs. "Where are you going?"

"I have to run home and get something for my mom. I'll be right back."

I lean down to kiss him and stand back up. He nods, then turns to his dad.

I walk out the door and cross the street. We live in a safe area, so the door is unlocked. I climb up the stairs, then walk down the hall to my room. The door is open, and I look at the desk and see a smallish box sitting on the top. I grab it, then turn to leave when something catches my eye on the bed.

I suck in a breath when I see three pink peonies sitting on the comforter and a handwritten note next to it.

> *Charlie,*
> *I promised you that, someday, I would make you mine for real. Meet me at our racing tree.*
> *Yours always,*
> *Beck*

I drop the box and the note on the bed and run down the stairs. The elementary school we went to is at the end of our street. The tree we would race to sits in front of the school. I'm walking quickly, but my curiosity makes me anxious, and I start to jog, but I really don't want to get too sweaty, considering I'll be on national TV in less than an hour.

As I get closer, I see him. He's standing in front of the tree.

His hands are in his front jean pockets. He has a smile on his face.

When I reach the tree, I'm slightly out of breath. "Hi."

"Hey, Boss."

Beckham

My hands are in my pockets to keep them from shaking. It's not from nerves though. It's because I'm trying to slow down. I'm anxious. I want to walk back down the street, hand in hand with her, and go celebrate.

When she's standing in front of me, I pull my hands from my pockets and reach for her hands.

"Charlie, do you remember when I told you that when I made it to the NFL someday, I would get you tickets to my games?"

She nods.

"You'll be at every one. Then I told you I wanted to kiss you and that you were mine."

She nods again.

"I still don't have the best way to say what you mean to me. You know I'm not great at sharing my feelings, but one thing I know for sure is that you have always felt like mine." I pull her hands up to my lips and kiss her knuckles.

When I look at her face, tears are streaming down her cheeks. I let go of one of her hands and wipe them away with my thumb. Then I lean in and kiss her. The kiss is salty from her tears.

"Beck ..."

Before she can finish, I get down on one knee. I reach into my pocket and pull the ring out.

Her hands cover her mouth. "Beck, ohmigod!"

"When you ask me what the best part of my day is, it's always you. Always has been. You are everything to me, and I want to call you my *wife* too. So, Charlene May King, will you do me the honor of becoming legally mine forever?"

She laughs through her tears and nods. "Yes! Yes! A thousand times yes!"

I stand up and slide the ring onto her finger. Once it's on, she adjusts it slightly, but it's the perfect fit.

She puts her hands on my face and pulls me in for a kiss. "Beck, I love you so much. I can't believe I'm going to be your wife!" she squeals.

Laughing, I pick her up and spin her. When I put her down, we hear cheering from down the street. Our families and a few friends are standing there, watching us.

"You know what this means, right?"

"What does it mean, Beck?"

"It means you're mine for real reals, and I get to kiss you whenever I want." I kiss her again because I can. "Come on. Let's go wait for that call so we can finally tell everyone where we're moving to." I turn my back to her and lean down a little. "Jump on, baby. We're running out of time."

Charlie jumps on, putting her arms around my neck, and I take off down the street.

WANT MORE CHARLIE & BECK?

Read Charlie and Beck's next chapter here!
https://BookHip.com/KSLBVLK

ZONE PROTECTION SNEAK PEEK

Archie's book is next! Here's a sneak peek.

ZONE PROTECTION

Emma

The last place I want to be tonight is at a party in some football player's house. My next paper for my Organic Chemistry class is due on Tuesday and isn't going to write itself. But my roommates, who are also my teammates on the Walker University Women's Golf team, have dragged me out thinking I need to let off some steam and have a little fun.

Our first tournament in California wasn't my finest performance, and the pressure I feel from my course load this semester is enough to drive an average person crazy. I'll compartmentalize it, as I usually do, and keep moving, but my friends might be right. I'm a perfectionist to a fault, and admittedly take on more than I should from time to time. Okay, all the time, but I can't help it. So maybe I should just let myself have some fun tonight.

Problem is, this house is filled with ego-driven fuck boys. Don't get me wrong, I've played around with my fair share, but I'm just not in the mood tonight. The music is too loud, the sorority girls are decked out in their short skirts while I'm in jeans and a cropped t-shirt, and it smells like a distillery in here. I feel like one drop of a match and this place would go up in flames just because of the amount of alcohol in here alone. Which surprises me a little bit, to be honest. The football team won today, so they deserve to celebrate, but most athletes don't drink too heavily during the season. Or at least the ones who plan to take their career past college.

I have no intention of playing golf beyond my college years. My track has been clear to me since my sister died when I was only nine years old. I need to finish my four years here at Walker near the top of my class in order to get into the best med schools. Right now, my top choices are NYU, Case Western Reserve, and Duke. They have the best pediatric cardiology programs, which is what my specialty will be.

"Emma, did you hear me?" my friend, Olivia Lewis, aka Livi, asks.

"I can barely hear anything in here. What did you say?" I lean in closer to her to hear her more clearly.

"You need to get out of your head. Your paper will still be there tomorrow. This place is swimming with endless possibilities. I feel like you need to get laid. Like not only let loose and have a few drinks, but you need to get some D, my friend." She wraps her arm around my shoulders and laughs.

Just as she does, a loud boom of a voice comes from the doorway. Now, I'm standing next to the speaker, but I can still hear Archie Griffith's voice over the sound.

"Ladies and dicks, the party can begin. I have arrived! Let's get fucked up, motherfuckers! Cowboy up!" he yells. Then he gallops—yes, gallops—into the room and straight for my other two friends, Peyton Adams and Mia Wallace, who are dancing on the makeshift dance floor in what is probably the dining room.

"Holy shit, that man is a snack!" Livi laughs.

I mean, she's not wrong. He's tall with blond hair that's long enough that he can pull it back, and he's covered in tattoos. Not at all my usual type. But he's fucking fine. I can only imagine what he looks like under that t-shirt and jeans that fit like a glove. He's gotta have one of those Adonis belts, the holy grail for thirsty women everywhere.

"I'm going over there. You should definitely come too! Come on, Em." She tugs on my arm, but I pull it back.

"A shot is calling my name. I'll be right back."

She nods and heads out to the dance floor.

I walk into the kitchen, which is the room next to where I've been standing. There's a bar set up on the island in the center of the kitchen. Bar is a loose term. Really, it's just a bunch of liquor bottles, although they are lined up neatly.

"Can I get you something? I'm the rookie on bar duty tonight. Whatcha thinkin'? Wait, don't I know you from somewhere? Emma, right? Golf?" he asks then holds out his hand for me to shake. "Leo Morris. I'm the new kicker for the football team. I saw you at the Fellowship of Athletes meeting a few weeks ago."

I take his hand and shake it. "Oh cool, nice to meet you, Leo. Congrats on the win today."

"Thank you. It was—" He's cut off by Dan Smith, who I've known for a few years now. I actually hooked up with him once, and it wasn't memorable enough for a repeat.

"Sup, Emma. Looking good. Want to come out back and get a beer?" He loops his arm around Leo's shoulders and basically puts him in a headlock. "It's time for this guy to pay his dues."

"I thought I was paying my dues by manning the bar!" He coughs out a laugh.

"I'm gonna pass, but you guys have fun. Nice to meet you, Leo." I wave.

Dan gives me a wink and turns with Leo still in his hold toward the back porch. I'll admit, he is hot and a possible contender for the D, but I don't really do repeats. That gets messy, and I don't have time for messy. Or feelings. Easy hookups are all I can manage right now, so one-night stands work for me.

I peruse the options on the bar and settle on a shot of Fireball. I have no intention of getting fucked up tonight, but maybe a shot will make being here less ... annoying. So, I grab one of the red Solo shot glasses and fill it to the top. At least my breath won't smell as horrible with the cinnamon aftertaste.

Wasting no time, because I don't want to stand around with a shot in my hand like a weirdo as people wander in and out of the kitchen, I knock it back in one go. It burns like a mother-fucker and I wince but also try to seem unaffected.

I grab a bottle of water from the fridge on my way back to the dance floor. One shot was enough for me tonight, though I'm never a big drinker anyway.

Finding my spot by the speaker again, I see my friends still dancing with Archie. Well, dancing isn't really the term I would use. They're grinding up against each other. Peyton is in the front, and Mia is behind him. Livi is dancing near them, but she's with some guy I don't recognize.

Honestly, there isn't a guy in here who isn't hot, but there is something about Archie Griffith that draws you in. I don't know him personally, but watching him on the field and in interviews, he's got that southern boy charm that apparently makes the guys envious and the girls lose their panties. Literally.

His arms are draped over Peyton's shoulders, but he's not touching her with his hands. He leans in to hear something she's saying, and when he looks up, our eyes meet.

I'm not sure if it's the Fireball making its way through my body or if it's him, but heat rises from my toes to my cheeks—

with a little extra heat making a pit stop at my lady business. I can't say a guy has ever had this effect on me before.

I break my gaze first, so I don't look like some stalker. But I can't help but look back, and when I do, he's still looking at me and now has the sexiest little smirk on his face.

He leans in to say something to Peyton and moves his hands to Mia's wrists that are wrapped around his waist, removing them from his body. His eyes never leaving mine.

Jesus, this man is sex on a stick and is now walking toward me. *Wait! He's walking toward me. Do not act like a nerd, Emma.*

"Hey. You having fun tonight?" he asks me, crossing his arms across his chest, making his biceps look enormous. Standing this close to me, I can see just how big he is. And I'm not short by any means. I'm 5'8" and he is still towering over me.

"Huh? I can't hear you over the base, what did you say?" *Way to play it cool, Em.*

He takes hold of my elbow and drifts us a little further away from the speaker.

"I asked if you were having fun." He gives me a sexy smile.

Leaning in a little closer to him, I reply, "Yeah, I guess so. These parties aren't really my thing, but it's been a stressful week, so my friends insisted on getting me out tonight. How about you—are you having fun?"

"Sweetness, I'm always having fun. Even better now that I'm talking with you," he says a little too smoothly.

"Ha! Look, I know who you are. Everyone on campus knows who you are. If you're looking for an easy hookup, I'm not your girl." I turn my head toward where my friends are dancing.

What am I doing? I'm not one to flirt or play games with any guy. When I want a hookup, I'm pretty clear about it, so I don't know why I'm acting flustered and kind of bitchy. I don't mean to be. And I'm also a big fat liar. I absolutely wouldn't mind hooking up with him.

Lifting his hand up, he reaches for my face and cups my cheek while his other hand takes hold of my waist. "Hey,

Darlin'." He guides my face to look at him then drags his fingers to my chin and tilts it up. When I finally look at him, that heat … it's back.

His smirk falls and he sucks in a breath. "Goddamn, Darlin'. You are fucking beautiful."

I huff out a laugh. "Yeah, okay, player." But I don't move away.

He moves his hand back up to my cheek. "I'm dead serious. I don't think I've ever seen anyone so pretty."

We're locked in a staredown when a slower song comes on.

"Dance with me, Darlin'." He moves his hand from my face to my waist and pulls me into him. Instead of pulling away, I wrap my arms around his shoulders.

We're moving together, and neither one of us has taken our eyes off each other. I'm not sure what it is about him, but I like the way it feels to be in his arms.

I can't help but brush my hands over his shoulder muscles and to his back, wrapping my arms around his neck. My breasts are brushing against his chest, and I can feel his warmth through his shirt and mine.

Moving his hands from my waist to my lower back, he continues drifting a little lower. I'm not gonna stop him, so he keeps sliding his hands down until they're cupping my ass.

He pulls me in a little closer, and our noses practically touch. "You wanna have some fun with me, Darlin'?"

My tongue peeks out and touches my top lip, then I look over to my friends. Mia gives me a nod and a wide smile, while Peyton gives me two thumbs up and smiles. Livi … she's sucking face with the guy she was dancing with. I roll my eyes at them but smile.

"So you know who I am, but I don't know your name. Are you gonna tell me?" he asks.

When I meet his eyes again, butterflies flutter around my belly like they're having a party that only Archie is invited to. He smiles at me, like a real smile, not a "let me get in your panties" smile, and I'm done. I surrender all the panties to this man.

"Emma. My name is Emma." My hands move from his neck to the sides of his face. "So, Archie Griffith, are you gonna keep giving me lines, or are we gonna have some fun?"

He leans in a little closer to my face, close enough to kiss me. "That's up to you. I'm more than ready to have some fun with you, *Emma*."

No guy has ever made me feel like this. Regardless, this can only be one night. "Here's the deal. My friends dragged me out, because like I said, it's been a shit week. But what the hell, maybe my friends are right, and I just need a good lay. Do you think you're up for that, Archie? No catching feelings." I'm so close to him now, I can feel his breath on my lips.

"Oh, I'm up for it. You gonna let me kiss you? I really want to taste those lips."

Instead of answering him, I lean in and kiss him. If I thought his eyes and smile did me in, nothing could have prepared me for this kiss. It's electric.

Our tongues tangle almost immediately, and there's no way in hell he doesn't feel this too.

His hands grab onto my ass, and he pulls me in even closer. I can feel his hard-on through his jeans, and I think … he might not be wearing boxers. Just that thought alone makes me moan into his mouth, and it makes me feral. I'm completely lost in him and practically forget where we are when he pulls back.

"Do you want to go upstairs?" I ask him.

He tilts his head and smirks.

"Yeah, Darlin', I do. But you know, I live right down the street. We could have a little more privacy and more time for me to do everything I want to do with you. This ain't gonna be a fast fuck. I wanna take my time."

"If we leave to go to your house, there's a chance I might change my mind. So, while the thought of having sex in this house makes me question my sanity, it's now or never, Archie."

He nods and slides his hands from my butt to my waist. Leaning in, he kisses me. "Come with me. I know where we can go." He lets go of my waist and grabs my hands.

I nod and release one of his hands. "Show me the way."

————

When we get upstairs, he knocks on a door, and when no one answers, he opens it.

As soon as I get through the doorway, he turns to face me and closes the door behind me with one hand and turns the lock.

Neither of us says anything, but I can see the heat in his eyes.

"Are you sure about this, Darlin'," he asks.

I appreciate that he's asking for my consent, but I really just need him to take my clothes off. Like, now.

"Oh, yeah. I'm sure." I reach up and wrap my hands around the back of his neck and lean in and kiss him, slipping my tongue inside of his mouth. The kiss goes to an inferno level immediately.

I slide my hands from his neck down to the hem of his shirt and lift it up as he raises his arms. Wrapping his now bare arms around my waist, he lifts me and carries me over to the bed and sets me down at the edge.

He kisses me again, then pulls back and kneels in front of me, dragging his hands down my chest and pulling the neck of my shirt down a little. I lean back on my elbows and watch him. When he gets to my waist, he pops open the button of my jeans and pulls the zipper down. He doesn't say anything, but he looks up at me as I lift my hips as he pulls my jeans from my legs.

Moving his hands from my calves to my hips, he dips his head and starts kissing up my thigh and to my center. "You smell so good, Darlin'. I can't wait to taste you."

Annnd why does that sound so fucking hot? But also, I'm

glad I didn't wear my comfy panties tonight. Archie Griffith should not see my comfy panties.

He pushes my thighs apart and swipes his tongue over the lace from my clit to my opening. Then, sliding his hands under the waistband in the front, he grabs my underwear and pulls them off, and continues to lick me.

"Archie, you really don't have to do that. I mean, it feels so good, but I don't usually get off from oral." I'm almost embarrassed to admit it while his face is literally in my vagina, but I'm kinda anxious to get to the good part.

Instead of replying, he presses his hand on my stomach gently to get me to lie down. He continues to flick my clit with his tongue and slips his index finger into me. It feels so good, I start to rock my hips to move his mouth back and forth.

"I'm gonna make you come, Emma. You're gonna be a good girl and come all over my tongue. Then I'm gonna fuck you so hard you'll feel me all week." He dips his head back between my legs. "You taste so fucking good, I could do this all night."

Yes, please. Sign me up for the all-nighter!

His hands are wrapped around my thighs and he's using one hand to keep me open as he licks and sucks my clit, while his other hand continues to pump in and out of me.

It feels so good, and I'm on the verge of coming. I move my hands from my sides, which are gripping the comforter, and move them to his head and slide my fingers through his hair. I hear him moan when I pull on his hair slightly, which only turns me on more.

My head falls back onto the bed, and I'm gripping his hair so tightly as I start to come. "Oh my God, Archie, don't stop. I'm so close." I move my hips in sync with his mouth moving back and forth over my clit. I'm just about to explode when he adds another finger and presses on my G-spot. I swear I black out for a minute until I feel him kissing his way up my stomach.

"Holy shit," I pant out. "I've literally never come like that before."

"I'm just getting started, Darlin'." Then he leans in and kisses me. I can taste myself on his tongue, and I don't hate it like I thought I would.

"Do you have a condom?" I ask him.

He lifts his head and nods, looking into my eyes. "I do." Then he stands and pulls his wallet from his pocket and grabs a condom. He tosses the wallet on the table beside the bed.

I scoot back toward the headboard and watch him unbutton his jeans. Just like I thought, he's not wearing any boxers. And what's hanging between those gorgeous thighs is impressive. In fact, I'm slightly nervous about it. "Umm ... do you think we need lube or something?"

Archie smirks but shakes his head. "Don't you worry, Darlin'. I'll make it fit."

And now I definitely don't need lube.

He tears open the wrapper and starts to roll it onto his cock. My eyes devour his body. This man is a work of art. Muscles for days, and the tattoos, he's got quite a few. Including what looks like a deck of cards, all aces and one joker, resting on his heart.

"You a poker player?" I nod to his chest.

With both hands, he pulls my legs apart again and crawls up the bed. Crawls. To. Me. Could this man get any sexier?

"Texas Hold 'Em is my specialty," he says with a laugh. "But let's talk about my tattoos later, yeah?"

Leaning over me now, he dips his head for a kiss. His body is pressed against mine, and I can feel his covered cock at my entrance. As we kiss, our bodies begin to rock in sync. Archie deepens the kiss as he pushes into me.

I gasp with the sensation as he continues kissing me. He's moving slowly, letting me adjust to his size. He stops for a second and asks, "You okay?"

"More than okay. You feel so good, Archie." I take hold of the back of his neck and bring his lips back to mine. I slip my tongue inside his mouth and twirl it around his.

His hips start to roll into mine, and his pelvis hits my clit in just the right spot. I'm not sure I've ever felt so in sync with someone during sex. It's like our bodies instinctively know how to move together.

"You gonna come again for me, beautiful? I want to feel you choke my cock." His breathing is getting heavier, and his thrusts are getting faster.

I nod because I don't think I can speak right now.

Leaning in to kiss me again, I pull in his bottom lip with my teeth and suck, making him moan.

The moan triggers me, my orgasm hitting me hard, and my whole body feels like it's shaking.

"Fuck!" he yells as he comes.

Our bodies still connected, he gives me a soft kiss, once, twice, then pulls his head back. "I think it's safe to say you rocked my fuckin' world, Darlin'. Give me a minute and we can go again. I need more of that."

I start to laugh and he groans. "Sorry, did I hurt you?"

"No, but your pussy just squeezed my cock when you laughed and think I might just be ready to go again. I think you have a unicorn pussy, Emma." He's smiling, but his hips are already moving in and out again.

It feels so good, I almost forget to remind him to get another condom. "Archie, wait. You need a new condom."

"Give me one more minute." He pushes in to the hilt and pauses. "I want you to ride me this time."

He doesn't need to ask me twice. "Yes, let's do the riding." I nod and he laughs.

Reaching between us, he grabs the base of the condom and pulls out, and then he gets off the bed. He takes off the condom and ties it, wraps it in tissue sitting on the bedside table, and then tosses it in the garbage.

"Do you have another one?" I ask as he looks through his wallet.

"Fuck. I don't. Let me see if Schuster has some in this drawer." He pulls the drawer open and rustles through it. "Got it!"

I sit up and scoot over to give him room on the bed. He lies next to me and pulls me to him, setting the unopened condom on his stomach. "Come here."

Everything that comes out of this man's mouth sounds sexy. He's got this husky deep voice, with a southern accent. No wonder girls fall at his feet all around campus.

My head is resting on his chest and I tilt my head up and kiss his jaw first, before propping myself onto my elbow to lean over him. "What do you say, cowboy? You up"—I pause and look down at his dick—"for a ride?"

He barks out a laugh and pulls me in for a kiss. "Giddy up, Darlin'."

ALSO BY AVA SUTTON

ACKNOWLEDGMENTS

To my family, thank you for your patience and confidence in me. Everything I do is for you, and I couldn't have done this without you. I love you all, eternally.

Compass Press, thank you for believing in me and taking a chance on this debut author. I can't wait to see what we can accomplish together and I wouldn't want to be on this journey without you.

Jovanna Shirley, when Autumn told me to turn this over to you, I didn't hesitate. Thank you for your guidance and patience. Cheers to many more books together!

Jeannine Colette, this couldn't have happened without you. Thank you for helping me make my book baby shine! Can't wait to work with you on the rest of the series.

Sarah Sentz, my covers for this series are *chefs kiss* and exactly what I wanted. Thank you for all of your hard work on my series. I can't wait to work with you on the next one!

Tina Otero, thank you for catching all the boo boos. Your eye for detail is impeccable. I can't wait to work with you on the rest of the series!

Sam, thank you so much for your invaluable feedback and encouragement! Also, thank you for giving me a chance. You're one of my favorites to follow and I'm honored you agreed to read my first book baby. Autumn was right, you are a ray of sunshine in this community.

To all the readers, thank you for giving me a chance! Your reviews, edits, and simply the fact that you are reading my book is surreal. Thank you!

Wordsmith Publicity, Autumn and Roxie, thank you for helping me reach readers and your guidance and support!

And finally, to my sisters, ITB.

ABOUT THE AUTHOR

Ava Sutton is a sports enthusiast and author of spicy college and professional sports romance.

When she's not writing, you can find her nose in a book, scrolling social media or planning dream vacations she someday hopes to take. She lives in Dallas, Texas with her two dogs.

Connect with her on Facebook, Instagram, and TikTok. @avasuttonbooks, www.avasuttonbooks.com